Beautifully Damaged

by

Laura Pavlov

Shine Design Series, Book 1

Beautifully Damaged

Cover Art by *Kim Mendoza*

The Wild Rose Press, Inc.
PO Box 708
Adams Basin, NY 14410-0708
Visit us at www.thewildrosepress.com

Publishing History
First Champagne Rose Edition, 2019
Print ISBN 978-1-5092-2653-5
Digital ISBN 978-1-5092-2654-2

Shine Design Series, Book 1
Published in the United States of America

"How long have you been dating the *want-to-be* mayor?"

Her eyes widened. "You can't say things like that, Jackson."

"I believe I just did. Why are you avoiding the question?"

"I'm not. We've been dating for six months. He's a great guy."

He slipped off his jacket and set it over the back of the chair beside them. His muscles pressed against the crisp fabric of his white dress shirt, and she couldn't look away.

He tilted his head. "Are you happy?"

"What's with all the loaded questions? I don't know. I guess I'm pretty happy."

"Interesting answer."

"Forgive me if I'm not answering to your desire." She lifted her hands in dramatic surrender.

"Trust me. My *desire* isn't the problem."

With a frustrated sigh, she pulled her bottom lip between her teeth. His appearance shook the ground beneath her feet. Did he want to hurt her? Again? Had he come back to turn her life upside down?

"I'm teasing you, Peanut. Your answers are fine. This is going to be good. Us working together," he said. A playful grin spread across his face.

Her breath quickened at the flirtatious tone. "You think so, huh?"

"I wouldn't have hired you if I didn't."

"*Why* exactly did you request me in particular?"

"You're extremely talented. No doubt about it. I want the best person designing my restaurant."

He was all man. Strong and powerful.

Praise for BEAUTIFULLY DAMAGED

"*BEAUTIFULLY DAMAGED* is purely beautiful. This second chance romance had me feeling emotionally invested from the very beginning. From the first pages the dynamic between Jackson and Peyton is pure FIRE. Jackson is confidence, charisma and so much heart. This story is passion and angst and everything that makes it impossible to put the book down. An added bonus, Peyton and her two best friends from Shine Design are #squadgoals! This is a beautifully told story. FIVE STARS!"

~Anonymous

Dedication

greg~
thanks for making me believe in fairy tales
and happily ever after…
love you.
xoxo

Acknowledgements

Greg, Chase, and Hannah—
thank you for your endless support.
Love you so much!
To the two best betas around—Pathi and Natalie!
I would be lost without you!
Eric & Abi—love you guys
and appreciate your feedback so much!
Sissy, thank you for the awesome book swag.
You complete me!
Thank you to the best dad around.
I'm so happy you taught me to never give up and
to work hard for the things that are important to me.
Semper Fi!
Mom and Sandy, thank you for always believing in me.
Caroline Tolley, thank you for your wisdom
and guidance and setting me on the right path
to achieve a long-time goal.
Judi Mobley, you have the patience of a saint.
Thank you for your help and support.
I appreciate you so much.
To everyone at The Wild Rose Press,
thank you for taking a chance on me!!
A special thanks to Nicole, Annette, Thompson, Sue,
Steph, Marge, Bell, Leigh Anne,
Julie, Jen, and Jim
for listening and encouraging me
when I needed it most.
xoxo ~ Laura

Chapter One

Present

Camera flashes lit up the night sky. Sebastian took her hand as they exited the stretch limo. They were currently San Francisco's "*It*" couple, and the paparazzi took every opportunity to get in their faces, swarming and crowding as often as possible.

"Smile for the camera, beautiful."

"How does this *not* get old to you?" she whispered, plastering a fake smile on her face.

"It comes with the territory," he said, leading her to the door. "Once I'm in office, things will settle down. Trust me."

"Why are they even here?"

"You know how Wolf is. He never misses an opportunity for them to capture us together." He shook his head and held the door for her.

Sebastian's campaign manager, Kenny Wolf, used ruthless tactics. A very fitting last name, and why most people called him Wolf. He needed constant play-by-plays of their whereabouts. It was invasive and unnecessary. Relief filled her once they entered the corporate cocktail party and left the pack of obnoxious photographers behind. Sebastian was the current front-runner in the race for mayor of San Francisco. They were constantly hounded by the unwavering and relentless press

Sebastian strode over to the bar. She took a seat at a high-top table and scanned the room. Ah...San Francisco's elite never disappointed, showing off the latest fashions. The designer labels impossible to miss. How many Louis Vuitton, Chanel, and Birkin bags could fit in one banquet room? Two women tossed one another air kisses. Their outlandish diamond rings glittered in the light from the chandeliers above. Nothing beat people watching at these events.

"Would you like a bacon-wrapped shrimp, Miss?" A waiter approached with a fragrant fishy appetizer. Ewww. She and seafood—were not one.

"No, thank you, I'm okay." She scrunched her nose, and he walked away.

She smiled at the loud group of men sitting one table over, each clad in a fancier designer suit than the next. One guy laughed so hard he swiped the tears streaming down his face, and she chuckled. Sebastian returned with two glasses of Chardonnay.

"Thank you. I need this after the day I've had," she said with a sigh.

"Ah, the life of an interior designer."

"Trust me, running for mayor is definitely more stressful, but I still have my fair share of crazy days," she conceded.

"Of course, you do. While I try to win the people of San Francisco over, you need to make sure they're living in style."

"Good point. I win." Tonight's event, hosted by a few local interior design firms, bustled with past, present, and future clients. The room practically vibrated with loud conversations, chatter, and boisterous laughter.

He chuckled. "Yes, you do. Where are the girls tonight?"

"Elle's working late at the hotel. It's a large project, and she's trying to make her deadline. Dani went to a charity dinner with her clients for the Mathews Foundation. I'm the lucky one because I wrapped up with the winery yesterday. Camille said she has something new for me, so maybe she'll fill me in tonight." Rubbing her hands together, she flashed Sebastian a mischievous smile.

"Before you know it, people will line up to work with the famed Peyton Kroft."

"Hmm, could you be a tad bit biased?"

"It's possible. I am sleeping with you."

"Yes. Good point." She smiled, the insinuation generous at best. Sex with Sebastian proved to be vanilla and unimaginative. They made up for it, though, in other ways. They both shared a strong work ethic, supported one another at professional events, and they were compatible on an intellectual level. Would she call it a match made in heaven? No. Was she content with what they had? Yes.

The rich smells of caviar, scotch, and fresh-cut peonies filled the air. Her boss, Camille Chadwick, came her way.

"Have I got a surprise for you, darling." Camille displayed an eternal intensity when it came to the company she'd built from the ground up, Shine Design. Draped in a tailored-to-perfection gray pantsuit with her shiny white hair styled in a clean A-line bob. Not a strand out of place.

"Oh, do you?" She let her enthusiasm show. As

Camille's go-to designer for the past three years, she loved everything about her job. On the list to make partner meant any opportunity her boss wanted to throw her way left her eager to impress.

"Yes. There's a new client opening what will be *the* restaurant to go to in San Francisco, and he wants Shine to design it. Permits and licensing are in place. This is a big-money project, Peyton. They plan to open three restaurants over the next eighteen months. He did his research on designers and requested *you*. I invited him here this evening. When he arrives, I'll introduce you. Bring your A-game, kiddo." Camille winked and scurried off to greet yet another client. Polished, experienced, and an expert when it came to interior design, Camille Chadwick never stopped working a room.

Peyton stood and smoothed the wrinkles on her black, fitted cocktail dress. This introduction might prove the professional turning point she'd been waiting for. She pushed the butterflies away and combed her fingers through her long dark hair, a habit to give it a little boost. Her mind raced over this new project, unable to focus on Sebastian, busy texting his over-the-top campaign manager.

"This room is full of potential voters, yet I can't take my eyes off you." Sebastian set his phone down, and his flirtatious tone returned her to the moment.

"You need to schmooze, and I need to meet my new client," she teased, straightening his already straight tie.

"How long are we staying?"

"A few hours. I promised Camille."

"Only for you." He pecked her cheek before

picking up his phone when it vibrated once again.

She admired the exquisite pink and peach floral arrangements scattered around the banquet hall before taking a sip of wine. Camille greeted a man across the room and gave him a considerable amount of attention. *Hmmm—this guy must be important.* Unable to see his face, she did, however, get a fantastic view of his backside. Her cheeks heated with curiosity, studying the yummy-looking man, who hadn't turned around yet. Broad shoulders and defined muscles filled out his black, fitted jacket. Tall and lean with tailored slim-cut black slacks showing off his masculine shape. He ran his hand through his dark hair as he spoke to Camille, who looked thoroughly enthralled with the well-built man standing in front of her.

He must be the new client.

Time to take the bull by the horns. Why wait for him to come to her? She set her glass on the table before tapping Sebastian on the shoulder and silently mouthing the words, *I'll be right back.* Her boyfriend, still on the phone with his nutjob of a campaign manager. He nodded and kissed her cheek. Dabbing a bit of color to her lips before dropping her favorite pink lip gloss back in her purse, she pivoted on her sky-high Louboutin's and crashed right into a muscled chest.

Startled, she jumped back. "Oh, excuse me."

"Peyton, there's someone I'd like to introduce you to." Camille chuckled, standing beside the hard body Peyton just collided with.

Her gaze locked with unforgettable emerald-green eyes. Words escaped her. Her heart pounded in her chest.

"This is Jackson Vance. He's opening the new

restaurant, which I'm sure will be *the best thing* San Francisco has seen in a long while. And you'll be the lead on this account."

"Hey, Peanut." His deep and sensual voice sent a ripple of awareness through her.

All the air left her lungs, and the room started to spin. She never thought she would see him again. How was this happening?

"Jackson?" The word came out just above a whisper.

He tilted his head and smiled. A flush of adrenaline tingled through her body. He pulled her close, wrapping her in a hug. She inhaled his scent—cedar and mint and all man.

Warmth flooded her. Her arms remained stiff against her side, unable to move. Though she enjoyed the feel of him pressed against her, she pulled away. He had no business touching her. Not now. Not ever. Warning bells sounded in her head. He'd torn her heart in two. She didn't know what to feel. Love or contempt?

"You know one another?" Camille gasped.

"Um, yes. Jackson and I were friends when we were kids. I haven't seen you in, what, nine years?" She forced herself to look up at him. Her voice strained and breathless.

Jesus. Jackson Vance. A familiar pain settled in her chest.

"Yep, it's been about nine years," he confirmed. His big, strong hand grazed his jaw as he spoke.

"Did you just call her Peanut?" Sebastian's tone held a sharp edge. He squared his shoulders and directed his question to Jackson.

"Yes," he said, his stare hard, assessing her boyfriend.

"Oh. I'm sorry. Jackson, this is Sebastian Worthington. You already know Camille."

Her cheeks heated as she remembered the way she'd eyed him just moments before. No wonder her boss was enthralled with the man. She, too, found it difficult to look away. A flash of her last memory with him raced through her mind. He'd cut her off with no warning and getting over him was the hardest thing she'd ever done. But she was different now, more cautious about who she trusted. And she most definitely did not trust Jackson Vance.

Jackson extended an arm. He and her boyfriend briefly shook hands. Sebastian wrapped a possessive arm around her waist and stood as close to her as possible without stepping on her feet. He'd never been a jealous man, yet his tight hold made it difficult to breathe.

"I bet you're thrilled to learn one of the most sought-after designers in the city is none other than your childhood friend," Camille said.

"She's always been talented. No surprise there."

"You two lost touch over the years?" Sebastian's voice remained clipped.

Talk about a loaded question.

She stammered, noting Jackson's calm, cool demeanor remained unruffled. "Yes, you know how it goes. Went our separate ways when we left for college."

Jackson's heated gaze met hers. Her nerve endings tingled. The familiarity in those green eyes threatened to knock her on her ass. An encounter with her first love was not on tonight's agenda.

"So Peanut is a nickname, then? Cute."

Sebastian's need to push this ridiculous topic irritated her. Why he decided to make it an issue left her baffled.

"Kids give one another nicknames when they're ten." It came out with more bite than she intended.

"Did you have one for him?" He shot her a curious look.

"Good question. What did you call me, Peanut?" Jackson teased. His deep, masculine voice oozed confidence.

"Well, I wanted to call him Stubborn Ass, but I was ten, so it wasn't an option."

"Did you find an alternative name?" Camille inquired, dazzled with the conversation and the connection to their new client.

"Peanut here refused to give me a name because I wouldn't change hers." His gaze never wavered from hers. Memories flashed through her mind, causing a sharp pain in her chest. They'd been the best of friends back then. A friendship which bloomed into so much more.

So. Much. More.

"I suppose it works to my favor. I wouldn't want you calling our client Stubborn Ass." Camille's head tipped back with an amused chuckle.

A man walked over and introduced himself to Sebastian, insisting *the future mayor* join the rest of his party at their table as they were huge fans. After mumbling something about *duty calling*, Sebastian excused himself and sauntered away with his new friend. Not an uncommon occurrence these days with the election nearing, but she admired her boyfriend's ambition.

"Okay, I'm going to let you two catch up. This project begins tomorrow, and we need to get you both on a plane to New York in the next two weeks. Jackson wants to design the bar area after a well-known restaurant in Manhattan. We'll meet in the morning at the office. Does nine work for you?" Camille directed her attention to him.

"Absolutely. I'll be there."

She walked off, waving her hand in the air. They stood alone for the first time. The space suddenly more intimate. Earlier chatter quieted, as guests made their way out. The air in the room shifted. Her belly fluttered at his nearness. Jackson's hungry gaze slid over her, and her heart pounded so hard she was certain he could hear it. His mouth curved, and she took in his defined shoulders and chest. Her fingers itched to touch him, but she would never allow herself to act on the attraction.

"How have you been, Peanut?"

Being alone with him left her—anxious. How could he be so familiar after all this time? *So freaking familiar.* "Fine. I mean, it's sort of a loaded question. It's been nine years since you've spoken to me," she said, her arms crossed in front of her chest.

"Fair enough." His potent green stare never leaving hers.

"Fair? There isn't anything *fair* about it," she hissed.

He ran his hand over the shadow of stubble on his strong, square jaw. The move so sexy it made her squirm, shifting on her feet. Her lady parts tingled, and she bit down hard on her lip.

"I meant you were correct calling my question unfair. But make no mistake, we're in agreement—nothing about what happened was fair."

She sucked in a strained breath; memories flooded her. This man had been such a large part of her life for so many years. He'd taken a piece of her heart with him when he left. Maybe all of it, if she were honest with herself. The lump in her throat made it difficult to swallow. She nodded. "Agreed. How have you been?"

"I've been good. Missed you, Peanut."

Pleasure rushed through her like some sort of sick masochist willing to walk right back toward the fire. "I'm surprised to hear you say that."

"You shouldn't be." His intense stare left her legs trembling. Her control slowly slipped away.

She squared her shoulders and reminded herself why they were here. He needed a designer and hired her to do a job. Nothing more. "So you're opening a restaurant here in the city."

"Yep. That's the plan."

"Always was."

His tongue darted out to moisten his lips, and she remembered the soft feel of them against hers. She patted her sweaty palms against her thighs, hoping he wouldn't notice.

His slow smile built. "And the plan was for you to design it, right?"

"Right."

"How long have you been dating the *want-to-be* mayor?"

Her eyes widened. "You can't say things like that, Jackson."

"I believe I just did. Why are you avoiding the question?"

"I'm not. We've been dating for six months. He's a great guy."

He slipped off his jacket and set it over the back of the chair beside them. His muscles pressed against the crisp fabric of his white dress shirt, and she couldn't look away.

He tilted his head. "Are you happy?"

"What's with all the loaded questions? I don't know. I guess I'm pretty happy."

"Interesting answer."

"Forgive me if I'm not answering to your desire." She lifted her hands in dramatic surrender.

"Trust me. My *desire* isn't the problem."

With a frustrated sigh, she pulled her bottom lip between her teeth. His appearance shook the ground beneath her feet. Did he want to hurt her? Again? Had he come back to turn her life upside down?

"I'm teasing you, Peanut. Your answers are fine. This is going to be good. Us working together," he said. A playful grin spread across his face.

Her breath quickened at his flirtatious tone. "You think so, huh?"

"I wouldn't have hired you if I didn't."

"*Why* exactly did you request me in particular?"

"You're extremely talented. No doubt about it. I want the best person designing my restaurant."

He was all man. Strong and powerful. "Thank you," she said; however, she didn't trust him or his compliments.

"You're beautiful."

Her cheeks heated, and she reached for her glass of

Laura Pavlov

wine, taking a long, slow sip.

"We were dealt a shit hand." His words stole the very air from the room.

"Understatement of the year."

"Is this where you want to talk about it? In a hotel ballroom with your mayoral boyfriend twenty feet away?" His voice remained smooth and controlled.

She sucked in a shaky breath. "No. Not here. Not now."

"Agreed."

A soft melody played in the background. The night sky peered through the windows, darkening the room, and the tiny lights from the crystal chandeliers danced on the walls beside them. She looked away for a moment, feeling exposed. The unmistakable familiarity zipped around them like a bolt of lightning.

All consuming.

"When did you move to San Francisco?" she asked, treading with caution.

"A few weeks ago."

With her hands on her hips, she cocked her head to the side. "Are you married?"

"No."

"Kids?"

He chuckled. "No. You?"

"No. Well, not really. I mean, there is Mr. Whiskers. He is sort of like having a child."

"What the hell is Mr. Whiskers?" He frowned.

"He's a maltipoo. A mix between a Maltese and a poodle."

"Why did you give your dog a salutation?"

"The name fits him. Trust me."

"Does he have some kind of kick-ass whiskers?"

She searched her phone and held up a picture of her pup. Jackson's fingers brushed against hers, and the slight touch sent shivers down her spine.

His eyes narrowed. "*Fucking ridiculous.* He hardly has any whiskers at all. Mr. Whiskers is the best you could come up with?"

His deep masculine chuckle surrounded them. My God, he even managed to make laughing sexy, just like the man behind it. Fighting her desire-filled haze, she kept her tone light. "Says the man who calls me Peanut. At least Mr. Whiskers' name isn't listed on every warning label found in the grocery store."

He tipped his head back with an amused smile. "Touché."

"Can I ask you something?"

"Anything." He leaned in closer.

"When you decided to move here…" Pausing, she studied every facet of his face.

"Yes?"

"Did you know *I* would be here?"

"Yes."

Her skin tingled. "Oh."

His green gaze darkened, and she stepped back. His nearness made her senses spin.

Sebastian startled her when he wrapped his arms around her waist and rested his chin on her shoulder. "How are we doing over here?"

"We're doing well. Finalizing the time to meet tomorrow." She tucked her hair behind her ear and hoped no one noticed her trembling hand.

"I venture you'll be seeing more of her than I will over the next couple weeks," Sebastian said, inserting himself between them, linking his hand with hers.

Jackson countered, his voice unwavering, "I'll try not to take more time than necessary. I'll see you in the morning."

"Yes. Nine?"

"Sounds good."

He turned his back, and for some reason, even after all these years, watching him walk away hurt all over again. Or maybe it never stopped.

"Are you ready to get out of here?"

"Yes, let's go," she said, reaching for her purse.

They said good-night to Camille and a few others before leaving the event. Sebastian slipped into the limo beside her and brushed the hair back from her shoulder. "Shall I stay at your place tonight?"

Her body tensed, her mind still racing about seeing Jackson after all these years. The good, the bad, and the ugly. She wanted to take a hot bath and call Dani and Elle and fill them in on her eventful evening.

"I'm exhausted. Do you mind if we sleep at our own places tonight?"

"Of course not. I have an early morning meeting tomorrow anyway. You okay?" Sebastian turned to face her, clasping her hand in his.

"Yes. I'm fine."

"You sure?"

"I promise." She forced a smile and kissed his cheek.

As Sebastian stepped out of the car to walk her to her door, she sensed him stewing. "Is it strange to see your old friend after such a long time?"

"A little bit," she said, unsure how much to share. Even now, still protective when it came to Jackson. Shielding their relationship.

She unlocked her door, and he leaned down to kiss her good-night. His lips were cold against hers.

"Get some sleep. I'll call you in the morning," he said before jogging down the steps.

"Thanks for coming with me tonight."

He paused and turned to face her. "Sure. Can I ask you something?"

"Of course." She scooped up her eager pup and leaned against the doorframe.

"Was it more than a friendship between you two? I couldn't help but notice the way he looks at you."

Jackson Vance had been the love of her life, her best friend, and the center of her universe for many years. She didn't like to think about it, let alone talk about.

"We dated for a little bit. We were young."

"You broke up when you left for college?"

The moment of truth. "Yes, something like that."

Or not.

The moment of truth would have to come later. She locked the door behind her and dropped down on the couch, slipping off her heels. And, for the first time in a long time, she allowed herself to remember the day her life had changed forever.

Chapter Two

Seventeen years ago

She sat on the window seat in her bedroom, staring out at the pretty blue water. Her fingers absently ran along the pink velvet fabric covering the cushion beneath her. The large trees leading down to the lake swayed in the breeze, and the branches looked like brown and green feathers dancing in rhythm. So different from her home in San Francisco. Her dad had bought the new vacation home at the lake, a surprise for her and Jayden, her older sister. They'd never been to Lake Tahoe before, and now they would spend the entire summer here. Ugh. Why would she want to be somewhere she didn't have any friends? She preferred home. It was so quiet here. She heard herself breathing. Her dad had insisted this would be a fresh start for everyone. Who wanted a fresh start? She wanted things to go back to the way they used to be.

Resting her forehead against the glass, she covered her mouth to muffle the cry she couldn't hold back. Tears blurred her view, causing the colors on the other side of the window to run together, resembling a painting hanging in her father's office. Her mom had left over a month ago, without saying a word to Peyton. No note. No phone call. Her dad and Jayden were angry, and Peyton's sadness only frustrated them more.

She couldn't talk to her friends about it, because they wouldn't understand.

Her father sat her and Jayden down and told them their mom was in love with another man. A famous country singer named Brad Boone. She didn't know him, beyond her mom referring to him as her old high school boyfriend. Now she didn't have a mom. And she hated Brad Boone. Her stomach hurt all the time.

She stood and kicked a pillow across the room, wanting to kick something even harder. Punch something with enough force to smash it. Scream at the top of her lungs. But she tried all those things and none of them made her feel better.

She looked around the bedroom taking in the pale-pink walls, and the cozy gray comforter with tons of throw pillows covering the bed. Her dad had tried so hard to make things better. He'd hired a decorator to come in and have the house set up for them before they arrived. She should be thrilled. But she didn't want a beautiful room. She wanted a normal family, and no matter how many decorators her dad hired, he couldn't give it to her. She stormed out of the bedroom and down the stairs.

"Where are you going?" Jayden called from her room. Her sister's phone permanently attached to her ear.

"Away from here," she shouted, slamming the front door with enough force to make a statement. She hated this house. Hated Lake Tahoe. And hated her dad for bringing her here.

"Where are you off to, sweetie?" Her father stopped her when she made her way around the driveway. For a moment, she wanted to break down and cry. Tell him how sad she was. Holding her tears at bay, she traded her sadness for anger. It would end the conversation faster.

"I don't want to be here. I want to go home. Mom doesn't even know where we are." She still hoped her mom would rush back and realize she made a huge mistake. Her dad reached for her hand, but she pulled away. Allowing him to hug her would only make her cry.

He cursed under his breath. "Mom isn't coming back, Peyton. This isn't the life she wants anymore. I'm not sure it ever was. I'm sorry I can't fix this for you. I would if I could."

"You could go find her and bring her back, but you won't."

"You can't find someone who doesn't want to be found. She's with someone else."

"So you won't even try?"

Her dad ran his hand through his hair, his face stern. "What exactly do you miss, sweetheart?"

"What do you mean? I miss Mom."

"You miss Mom or the idea of Mom? Because from what I remember, Mom hasn't been around much these past few years. She never took you to or from school, sleeping every chance she got, and rarely joined us for dinner. The nanny took you and Jayden shopping when you needed things. Your mother spent no time with you or your sister. So what, exactly, do you miss?"

She gasped. How dare he say these things? Of course, he'd act like this, which was why she didn't want to talk to him about it. He didn't understand. No one did.

"You don't care that she's gone. I hate you." She

turned and ran toward the back of the house. There was nothing more to say. She hurried down the grassy area toward the lake, looking around at the enormous property for the first time since they arrived this morning. Her dad had built up this big surprise, and Peyton hoped it would have something to do with her mother. Instead he'd brought them to this big, stupid house on the lake.

She peeked around the large pine trees surrounding the yard and spotted the beach area down by the water. Her dad had told her and Jayden they had their own private beach at the house. She loved the water, but right now, she didn't want to be there. Didn't feel happy anywhere and may never be happy again.

She noticed a path in the trees and walked along the dirt trail. Pine flooded her senses and soothed her. She ducked under a few branches forming a canopy overhead. The sun struggled to shine through, shading areas along the path as she moved. A large log blocked the way, so she climbed up onto the rough wood. The bark chipped against her shoes. She pulled her legs close to her chest and wrapped her arms around to hold them close. So quiet and peaceful. Birds chirped, and she buried her face in her knees. She sat there for a long time, letting go of the hurt and frustration. Safe from anyone hearing her or forcing her to talk, she cried for her mom. Cried for her dad and Jayden and the way she'd treated them when they were only trying to help. But most of all, she cried for herself. For what she didn't have anymore and maybe never really had at all. The tears kept coming.

"Are you okay?" a voice called out, startling her from her sobs.

What the heck?

Hundreds of miles from home. In the middle of the woods of Lake Tahoe. Could a girl not have a meltdown alone? She sniffled a few times before wiping her face with the back of her hand. She met his gaze when he knelt in front of her. Friendly green eyes and dark shaggy hair framed his face. He looked to be her age, or maybe older, because he appeared tall, even huddled down near the ground.

"I'm fine."

He cocked his head to the side. "I don't think you're fine. Do you want me to go get someone?"

"No. I came out here to be alone," she croaked.

"Why?"

"Because I don't want to talk to anyone." She swiped angrily, though the tears continued to fall.

He sat down beside her on the log. His scruffy shoes were tattered and dirty, and he had a large scrape across one knee. "What's your name?"

"Peyton."

"I'm Jackson."

"What are you doing out here?" she asked, realizing these woods were on her property.

"I do yard work, and the man who owns this house just hired me to pick up pinecones."

It didn't surprise her. Her dad was the nicest person she knew. They were very close, but these past few weeks, they'd been fighting constantly. Guilt hit her hard, thinking of the things she said to him.

"He's my dad. How old are you? You don't look old enough to have a job."

"I'm ten. I'm old enough to work. How old are you?"

"I'm ten, too. Are you going into sixth grade?"

"Yep. So you just moved here?"

"Yes. We live in San Francisco. My dad bought this place so we could spend our summers here."

"Are you crying because you didn't want to leave San Francisco for the summer?"

"No. I'm not a brat."

He laughed, and the sound echoed under the tall trees.

"Okaaaaay. I thought maybe you didn't have any friends here, and you're upset about it."

"I *don't* have any friends here. Well, you're ten, so I guess you're my first friend. But I wouldn't be crying over not having friends."

"If we're friends, then tell me what's wrong."

"I don't think you can help with this."

"Try me. You'd be surprised. I've seen it all." He laughed.

She rolled her eyes and gave him a questioning look. "You're ten. How could you have seen it all? Do you live in Lake Tahoe year round?"

"Yes, we live here. In a trailer behind my friend Joseph's cabin. Trust me. I've seen a lot for my age. My mom's got problems."

She sensed his discomfort. "What kind of problems? Is Joseph your mom's boyfriend?"

"No. He's sort of like a grandpa to my sister, Chloe, and me. My mom has drug problems. We lived in the trailer park Joseph owns down in Reno for a few years. He helped Chloe and me all the time and convinced my mom to move us up here. He thought if he got her away from the people she hung out with in Reno, it might help."

"Has it?"

"Not so much."

She knew how tough it was when family disappointed you. For the first time since her mom left, she didn't feel like the odd man out.

"I'm sorry. Joseph sounds nice though. So do you work to help your mom?"

"Yeah, he's great. I'm saving up for a new bike. Your turn now."

She kicked a rock, smudging the toe of her white sparkly tennis shoe. "My mom left us a couple weeks ago."

"Where'd she go?"

"I don't know. She ran away with her high school boyfriend. Some country singer. Packed one small bag and left. My dad has only heard from her once." It was nice talking to someone who didn't know her family. He didn't act surprised or shocked by what she shared, the way most of her friends back home would be.

"She sounds kinda selfish. My mom is selfish, too. It sucks, huh?"

Tears streamed down her face once again. He didn't say a word. They just sat this way for a few minutes while she cried, and he stayed quiet beside her.

"Hey, you want to help me pick up pinecones?" he said, breaking up the quiet, which caused her to laugh.

"Why would I want to pick up pinecones?" she asked, pulling herself up and using the butt of her hand to wipe the tears away.

"You got something better to do?"

"I guess not. Thanks," she said. The kid did just sit there while she cried it out. He seemed nice.

He held his arms out beside him in question. "Hey,

what are friends for?"

"I think you just *might* be my new best friend."

"You clearly have good taste in friends."

She nudged him with her shoulder. "I agree."

"Come on. Let's go before it gets dark."

"Hey, what do you think of nicknames? My sister says it's a sign of true besties," she said with a laugh. Jayden, being four years older and very popular in school, considered herself an expert in social skills.

When they jumped down from the log, he stood much taller than her. He looked like he played football or something sporty. He moved fast down the trail, and she didn't ask him to slow down, determined to keep up.

"Nicknames, huh? Let's see. I could call you P for Peyton, but it's kind of lame. Hmm…how about Peanut? It starts with the letter P, and you are small, so it works."

"What?" She gasped, fumbling along the path. "No. Not Peanut. First off, being small does not make me a nut. It's a well-known fact the best things in life come in small packages. Second, six kids in my class are allergic to peanuts, so they are somewhat offensive to many people. Third, nothing about it describes me."

"You see? You're salty, too. I'm definitely feeling Peanut."

"No. I don't like it," she insisted, picking up the pace almost to a jog and surging past him.

He taunted, "Are you racing me, Peanut? Let's see what you've got."

She ran out into the open grass with him right beside her, bending over and resting her hands on her knees to catch her breath. "You won't tell anyone what

I told you, will you?"

"Never. Your secret's safe with me. Why don't you want to talk to your family about it? Your dad seems nice."

She pulled her lip between her teeth. "My dad's the best. But every time we talk about my mom, we end up in a fight. He and my sister, Jayden, think my mom checked out a long time ago. They weren't surprised she left. They don't want to fix it. They just want me to accept it, and I don't want to."

"So you ran into the woods to be by yourself."

"Yeah, I don't want them to know I'm upset. I usually just yell and pretend I'm fine after. If they knew I was out here crying, they'd both worry. It probably sounds dumb, huh? I'd rather fight with them than say I'm sad."

"Nah, not dumb at all. Joseph told me about this thing we have. It's called like a fight or flight or something."

"What does it mean?"

"Well, Chloe and I get upset about my mom a lot. It has something to do with how you handle it. I guess you either fight it, or you run from it. Fight or flight."

"Which one do you do?"

"I'm a fighter." He smiled. His white teeth stood out against his tanned face. He had a boy-band look, and all the girls in his class probably had a crush on him.

"This is why we're a great match to be besties. You fight—and I flight," she said with a giggle.

"You're a runner, Peanut."

She chucked a pinecone at him, and he somehow managed to catch it in one hand. The sun shone on the crystal blue water. She squinted up at the sky, watching the clouds move in slow motion.

"Am not, I don't even like exercise." She laughed again, picking up another pinecone and hurling it his way.

"Whether you like it or not, you are. And every runner needs a friend who's a fighter. Keeps things balanced." He smirked. She sat on a large rock holding the trash bag while he deposited the cones inside.

"How about Warrior Princess, Dynamite P, or Super Peyt?" she suggested.

"Nope, none are as good as Peanut," he insisted. Boys could be so annoying sometimes.

"I won't give you a nickname if you don't change mine," she challenged. He made a goofy face and went back to work.

"Suit yourself, Peanut," he teased.

She liked him. He made her laugh. For the first time in over a month.

She giggled. A lot.

Chapter Three

Present

Camille greeted him when the elevator doors opened onto the twentieth floor of the swanky downtown office building. "Good morning, Jackson. I spoke to Peyton, and she already has a ton of ideas to run by you. I'll confer with you both later today to see how things are going. She will devote her full attention to this project for the next eight weeks."

She guided him down the hallway. He couldn't ask for anything more. Not for his restaurant nor for himself. Two women huddled around Peyton's desk, both attractive, in their late twenties, and dressed in stylish business attire.

"Ah, what a surprise to find the three of you gathered in here. Jackson, this is what I like to refer to as my 'Dream Team.' Dani, Elle, this is Jackson Vance. Now, ladies, please scurry back to your offices so Peyton can get to work. Our timeline is tight, so the sooner we get started the better," Camille said, shooing them toward the door.

The women gave Peyton a knowing look, eyebrows raised, as if they spoke their own language. Making it obvious they were close. It pleased him to see she had good friends, though he'd been unimpressed with her boyfriend. He'd seen several pictures of them together in the press over the last few weeks and watched Sebastian as the political guest on a local TV station. He could sum the guy up with one word.

Douchebag.

"Nice to meet you, ladies." He shook their hands, and Dani gave him a slow nod, while Elle studied him with complete focus. Neither attempted to hide their blatant head-to-toe perusal.

"Nice to meet you," they called on their way out the door, Camille waving her hands forward with impatience.

As Peyton walked around her desk, he tried to control his reaction to her. She brought something out of him no one else ever did. His desire for her so damn strong, even after all this time. Yes, he'd come to San Francisco to open a restaurant. Chosen the city she resided in for a reason. He wanted to see her. Owed her an apology, but he had no intention of interfering with her life. He wasn't staying. The goal was to open this restaurant and move on to the next in a few short months. If he could make amends with her in the process, it would be the icing on the cake.

She greeted him with a smile, wearing a fitted cream dress showing off her slim, feminine figure and hugging her curves in all the right places. Elegant and sexy as hell. Still, he towered over her, even with her wearing sky-high heels. A long, dark ponytail trailed down her back. A memory of wrapping her ponytail around his hand and pulling her back for a kiss flashed through his mind. Lips so goddamned soft nothing had ever compared. He scanned her gorgeous face, dark brown eyes large and full of emotion.

Intoxicating.

Fucking perfect.

He tried not to think about the way things had ended. So much left unspoken. So many mistakes. *A darkness that swallowed him whole.* The undeniable familiarity still lived between them. Their connection just as strong. He hadn't lied. He'd missed her. She'd never been far from his thoughts. He'd stayed away because it was in her best interest. Forgetting Peyton had proved impossible.

"Good morning, Jackson," she said curtly.

"Good morning."

Camille chuckled. "Still can't get over the coincidence of it all. Childhood friends. Who would have guessed? So let's discuss New York. Do you have a few days you can get away, Jackson?"

"Yes, I think a week from Thursday will work. It'll give us some time to get things going here before we fly out to look at the design at Lago's," he confirmed while Peyton fumbled with some files on her desk.

"Yes. Of course. It will help me to grasp your vision, so I'm looking forward to going to New York. I want to meet with the contractor this week and get some of the larger orders placed for the kitchen and dining area. Next Thursday will give me enough time to get things moving on this end, and then we can focus on the design for the bar."

"Let me get Grace, our office manager, on it right away. I gave her the name of the hotel you prefer to stay at, Jackson. The company will pick up all expenses for the travel. I appreciate you going with Peyton. It's important for her to know what you like and don't like." Camille glanced down at her phone when it vibrated.

"Not a problem. Thank you for the offer to cover expenses, but it's not necessary. I'd prefer to pay for my own."

"Sounds good. Let's touch base later today. Go over and see the site, have Peyton meet the contractor, and let's get things moving."

"We'll get started right away." Peyton guided him to the white leather chairs across from her desk. She sat in one, her posture so stiff he could bounce a tennis ball off her back. He dropped down in the chair beside her. Camille left, closing the door on her way out.

Last night he'd caught her off guard. Today—she'd come prepared, and her walls were up. He couldn't blame her. He'd left her. Been cruel. He'd seen her through good times and bad. She had the etiquette of a royal princess, the perfect manners of a debutante, but the girl could fight like a caged pit bull when she wanted something.

"I think it's best we keep things professional. I take my job very serious, and I don't want any complications. Let's start fresh as work associates." Her voice as distant as her eyes.

"Ah. So this is how we're going to play it," he said with a chuckle.

"Excuse me? I'm not quite sure how to act around you, Jackson. You show up here out of nowhere, and you're judging my behavior?"

"Since when do you have to *act* a certain way?"

"What? I don't. You're taking things out of context. I've never had a client who happened to be an ex-boyfriend. This is a first for me."

"I've never had a problem being your first." Yep, it

would get a reaction. They needed to get past the awkward bullshit and hash it out. Forcing her to engage would be his best bet.

She clenched her jaw. "I see you're still an asshole."

"Ahhh—there she is."

"Meaning?"

"Meaning, you need to stop putting on *airs*." Using his index and middle fingers on each hand and bending twice, he fought back a smile.

"Are you seriously using air quotes on me? How ridiculous are you?" She jumped up and stormed over to her desk.

"I'd say I'm pretty fucking ridiculous." His fingers intertwined behind his head, he leaned back to enjoy the show.

Goddamn, this woman only got sexier when she was pissed. He remembered how feisty she could be, but she appeared more controlled and refined now. He didn't miss the way she struggled to rein in her emotions, jamming things into her desk drawer now.

First, a stapler. A pencil. A couple of files.

She picked up her water bottle and tipped her head back, taking a long, slow sip. His heart pounded in his chest. He yearned to taste her soft lips. Maybe it would get him through the next decade. No woman ever made him so greedy for more. But he wasn't here to take anything from her. He'd taken enough.

"Peanut."

"What? And stop calling me that," she demanded, returning to sit beside him.

"I'm sorry."

"What are you sorry for?"

"I'm sorry for *everything*. I'm sorry for leaving you—for hurting you."

She studied him, lips pursed. "Is this really your apology?"

"What do you want me to say? I went fucking crazy. I wasn't equipped to handle what happened. It wasn't anyone's fault."

"No. Oh, no." She pointed her finger at him. "You thought it was *my* fault. You blamed me. Isn't that why you left?" She blinked, her gaze glossy.

Shit.

"Christ, Peyton. I never thought it was your fault. How could I blame you? I didn't handle it well. It took a long time for me to realize the mistakes I made. Pushing you away wasn't fair. But *fuck,* there's not a right or wrong way to grieve. We were young. I'm here to tell you I'm sorry for the way I left. I'm sorry it took me this goddamn long to reach out to you. All I can do now is move forward."

She swiped away falling tears. The sadness in her eyes engulfed him. Before he could stop, he moved to his feet and pulled her into his arms. He held her close. His chin settled on top of her head, and he breathed in the drifting scent of orange blossoms and vanilla. Her shoulders quaked, and soft sobs escaped her. Her arms came around his waist, and she clung to him as if he were her lifeline. Maybe he'd fucked up coming here. It was selfish. But she knew what he'd been like before the darkness consumed him. He needed to remember that time in his life. A time when things were good. He'd be gone soon enough, and they could both close the door on this chapter of their lives, once and for all.

"I'm sorry, Pea," he whispered repeatedly into her

Laura Pavlov

hair. Yes, he had a nickname for her nickname. That's what happened when you met the other half of your soul when you're ten years old. She'd been everything that was good in his life for such a long time.

Until it all went to shit.

Her sobs subsided, and he loosened his grip, not ready to let go of her yet. This would be more challenging than anticipated. He wanted to make peace with her, not get close to her. Not an option. With a bit of space between them, she met his gaze, and with trembling fingers, she swiped her falling tears. His thumbs gently rubbed away the last bit of moisture on her tear-streaked cheeks.

"You weren't just my boyfriend, Jackson. You were my best friend. Do you have any idea what your leaving did to me?" She pressed a hand to her heart.

"I do. It tore me apart more than you know," he said honestly.

"I wanted to be there for you."

"I know. But sometimes obstacles run too deep."

"It doesn't help you being a stubborn ass, either." She smiled, her gaze heavy and swollen.

That was his girl—smiling even in the darkest of storms.

"It shouldn't have taken me this long to apologize."

They'd dealt with some life-changing shit, and he hadn't been the same after. Forever damaged. Didn't mean he loved her any less, although he wished it were true. She deserved to be with someone who could give her what she wanted, and it sure as shit wasn't him. Though he'd thought about finding her a million times, he'd stayed away for her sake. It had taken him a long time to realize they both deserved some form of closure. After all they'd shared, he owed it to her. Hell, he owed it to himself, too. Shit happened, and he couldn't change it. But he could alter the way they left things. He didn't want her to hate him, as he suspected she did. Hell, maybe they could even become friends again, just the way they'd begun. And yeah, he wanted her. Heat streaked through his veins being near her again. Hadn't expected the pull to be so strong, but acting on it wasn't an option. That ship had sailed long ago.

"I wish it hadn't. I can't believe what a mess I am." She laughed and stepped away to grab some tissue from her desk. Relief spread through him as the hard conversation had begun. He owed her a hell of a lot more, but it was enough for today. They sat down and faced each other.

"You okay?" His voice was gruff. Hated to see her cry. Always had.

"Yes. I think it's good we cleared the air a bit."

"Yep."

She dabbed her face one last time. "Are you ready to get to work?"

"Yes. Camille insists you'll be giving me your full attention," he teased.

"Well, don't get cocky. All my clients get my full attention."

"I can be as cocky as I want, and you still have to put up with me, right?"

"Good point." She collected a pile of folders and magazines from her desk and set them on the small white table between their chairs. She handed him a bottle of water and sat back down beside him. "So what's the name of this restaurant?"

33

"You know the name." She'd fight him, but he wouldn't waver. He'd chosen the name as a kid, and it became a part of the vision he had for his restaurant. Made it clear to his partners he wouldn't bend when it came to the name.

Her head tilted to the side, "No, I don't believe Camille shared it with me."

"It's still PBV Bistro. Nothing's changed."

She sucked in a jagged breath. "Everything's changed, Jackson. Why would you use that name?"

Walking over to the window, he gazed out at the city high-rises surrounding the building and the mass of people moving below.

"I assume you heard Joseph died last year?" Joseph Langford, the closest thing to a father Jackson had ever had, stepped up for him and Chloe from the day they'd met him. Their drug-addict mother wasn't much of a parent, but Joseph, for no reason at all, took them both under his wing and became more of a parent than either of their biological parents were. Peyton had spent a lot of time with Joseph over the years. They were close.

"Yes, I heard. I'm sorry. I inquired about a service, but the nursing home said there wouldn't be one."

"He didn't want a funeral. He asked for his ashes to be spread across Lake Tahoe, which I did. He was crazy about you, you know."

"I adored him. A piece of my heart broke when I found out he passed away."

Pulling a napkin from his wallet, he stared at the tattered white tissue. It held a rough drawing of the restaurant he'd dreamed of opening one day. Peyton had sketched it while sitting in Langford's, the restaurant Joseph owned more than ten years ago.

Listening to his vision and drawing it as if she could read his mind. Pulling the image right from his head. He remembered showing it to Joseph, and the way his eyes danced with excitement when it came to Jackson's dreams.

"When I met with his attorney, he gave this to me. He left a letter as well."

She took the napkin from him. Her mouth fell open. "I can't believe he saved it after all these years. I remember drawing this."

She handed him the napkin, her face bright with nostalgia. Jackson folded it and tucked it back in his wallet. "Joseph told me about the flowers you sent him every month."

A chuckle escaped her. "He did? I asked him not to tell you. I cared about him. It couldn't have been easy for him to live in a nursing home. So I hoped the arrangements brought a little bit of the outdoors to his room once in a while."

"It meant a lot to him. He told me you stopped coming to Tahoe once you started college, though. Said you sent him letters. Did your dad sell his place there?"

"Nope. My dad and his girlfriend, Lael, spend a lot of time there in the summer. My sister and her family use it often, too. I didn't want to be there after you left. How about you? Do you still visit?"

"Not much. Joseph came to see me at school a couple times a year. Once he went into the nursing home, I flew back twice a year to see him. But Tahoe never seemed the same after everything happened."

"He sure loved you. You were the son he never had. I'm glad you found each other."

"Me, too. He saved my life."

He often thought about how different his life would've been if Joseph hadn't looked out for him.

"I think you saved each other."

"I hope so. I fucking loved the guy," he said before taking a long drink from his water bottle.

She reached for the book on top of the pile she brought over. "So PBV Bistro, huh?"

"It's what the napkin says, so…"

Peyton Blake Vance. When they were teenagers, he'd made a promise to marry her someday, open a restaurant, and name it after her. Her first and middle initial, along with the initial of his last name. Although it represented a promise long broken—the name would not change. It fit. Joseph treasured the sketch, as if it were something of value. All these years later, he understood Joseph wanted him to pursue his dreams.

"I guess no one else will know what it stands for, right?"

"Not unless you tell them," he teased.

"Let's go through a few look-books so I can get a feel for your design style. We can head over and see the location after."

"Sounds like a plan."

Grown-up Peyton was even more impressive than teenage Peyton, and she'd been pretty fucking impressive back then. Her determination prevalent in all she did. She appeared more confident now, yet, at the same time, more guarded.

They worked for a while in her office, moving over to the couch in the sitting area for more space to look at her design ideas. She sketched mock drawings, exceeding his expectations. A brick wall or two to bring in some old-world charm, rustic elements such as dark wood beams on the ceiling. Windows opened up to bring in additional natural light. She studied the architect's floor plan and added a ton of ideas on the layout of the interior.

"Do you see this doorway here?" She kicked off her heels and dropped to the shaggy white rug beneath the coffee table. The architect's plans sprawled across the surface. She highlighted and added sticky notes.

He leaned forward on the couch, erasing the distance between them. His chin hovered just above her shoulder, and the side of his face rested beside hers. Her hair teased his cheek; her hand moved with precision on the scratch paper. With her chest rising and falling, and her breathing labored, the space around them went deathly silent. He no longer heard the horns from cars outside or the background noise from the busy office. Neither moved or said a word, and after a long pause, she resumed drawing.

The fucking irony—the one woman he wanted more than he'd thought possible would be the one woman he couldn't have. Time to pull his head out of his ass and get himself in check.

"What if we opened up this wall? It will bring in natural light from these windows," she suggested, her voice shaky.

"I like it."

She pushed to her feet, putting distance between them, and slipped into her shoes. "Shall we go take a look at the space?"

"Yes. It's about a five-minute drive from here. We can take my car," he said, holding the door open for her.

"Sounds good."

When they stepped outside, a homeless guy taking a piss in the bushes beside the building asked him for a smoke. The fuck? Well, the dude probably didn't know it was the middle of the day, seeing it was gloomy as shit outside. Typical San Francisco weather this time of year. Two men holding cameras hurried toward them, turning their lenses in Peyton's direction. Unphased, she looked straight ahead and didn't acknowledge their presence.

"You do see those men taking pictures of you, right?" He tried to block their view of her, leaning down to speak close to her ear.

"Ignore them. They're relentless. They have no shame when it comes to personal space and boundaries."

She tilted her chin up, shoulders back, and continued her brisk pace. He saw past the phony, confident bullshit she portrayed. They made her uncomfortable. He knew it the minute she stiffened beside him. A small dog wearing a ridiculous hooded sweater sauntered past, more prepared for the North Pole than September in San Francisco. Jackson's charcoal Jeep Wrangler pulled up in front of the Shine office building, and the valet left it running. He slipped the older man a tip and opened her door as she climbed in.

She concentrated on her phone. "Sorry, I need to respond to this email."

"Not a problem."

He buckled up and waited for her to do the same. She looked down at her phone and continued to type, and he reached over and grabbed her seatbelt. She startled and slapped his hand away. He ignored her, yanked the strap across her body, and once it clicked, he put the car in drive.

He pulled from the curb, and she looked over at him. "You do realize I can buckle myself?"

"I would have hoped so. Maybe next time you'll prove it."

She laughed, dropped her phone in her purse, and looked around the inside of the car. "I couldn't have chosen a more fitting vehicle for you if I tried."

"You must know me well."

"I did. But I don't know anything about you anymore."

With one hand on the steering wheel, he took a swig of water with the other. "Ask away."

"Hmm, open book?"

"Absolutely."

"Did you end up staying at the Naval Academy? Did you take the wrestling scholarship?"

"Yep. Wrestled all four years and graduated with a degree in business. Served my time after in the navy. And here I am."

"Your dream never wavered about opening a restaurant?" She traced the stitching on the black leather armrest with her finger.

"Not really. Some of the instructors at the academy encouraged me to pursue a career as a SEAL, which I thought about for a brief time. But *this* is what I'm meant to do."

She nodded and turned to look out the window, as if deep in thought. An accident up ahead caused traffic to back up.

"Do you miss wrestling? It was a big part of your life for a long time."

"Not anymore. I started MMA training after I graduated." He'd keep this part of his life light. The truth—fighting was an outlet for him, a way to deal with his anger and grief.

"MMA?"

"Mixed martial arts."

"Like UFC fighting?"

"UFC fighting is for pros. I only do amateur fights. But yes, it's similar."

"Do you want to become a professional fighter?"

"Nope. I want to say who and when I fight, so I won't go pro." He liked the control fighting amateur offered. Fight as often as he liked, and nobody owned him.

"Oh. Okay. Good. Obviously, it's not my business, but I wouldn't want to see you get hurt."

"Pea, you're not going soft on me, are you?" he said She chuckled and fiddled with the straps of her purse.

"How's your mom? Is she still in Tahoe?" she asked, her voice just above a whisper.

Unease rolled through him. "She's in Reno now. I haven't seen her in years. I send her money when she needs it. Not much of a relationship there. How's your sister? Did she and Zach end up together?"

"Yes. Jayden's great. She and Zach are both attorneys now. Jayden works at my dad's firm and Zach made partner at a law office in the city. They've been married for almost five years and have the most beautiful boy on the planet, Harrison. He's three years old."

"Not surprised to hear they ended up together. They were inseparable in college. I'm happy for them.

How's your dad?"

Her face lit up when she spoke of her father. "He's great. You know he's going to want to see you. I got home too late last night to call, so I haven't told him you're in San Francisco yet. But I'll fill him in later."

"You tell me when and where. I'd love to see him."

She let out a slow, hesitant breath. "Maybe we can all have dinner and catch up."

"Sounds great. So what's the deal with the photographers waiting for you?"

"It comes with the territory. My boyfriend is running for mayor. They're very persistent, but it'll settle down once the election is over."

"And Sebastian is fine with them stalking you?"

It annoyed the hell out of him seeing her face splashed all over the press, as the want-to-be mayor promoted their relationship in the media. The *Chronicle* made a point of saying his well-liked girlfriend cleaned up his playboy image and should be thanked for his increased popularity. It appeared Sebastian benefitted by being photographed with her every chance he got. Not his business, but just because he couldn't be with her didn't mean he wanted some piece of shit dating her, either. He cared about her. Always would.

"It's not a problem." She twisted her purse straps around her hand.

"If you say so. How about your mom? Do you see her at all?"

Her shoulders stiffened, and a long silence followed. "No. She called when she found out Sebastian and I were dating, and she wanted to get together, though I haven't seen her in years. She's suddenly very interested in politics. Brad has a new

41

album releasing in December, and you know *Mrs. Boone* works every angle she can."

When they were young, he and Peyton's connection intensified when it came to their mothers. They were from two different worlds, yet they were similar in more ways than most thought. Though a single addiction did not own Monica Kroft—now Monica Boone—her ability to put herself first rivaled his mother. She'd traded her old life for a new one in the spotlight with her current husband, country singer Brad Boone. Monica had made endless promises to attend important milestones for Peyton throughout the years he'd dated her, and she never followed through on a single one. Her husband and his career were her priority.

He pulled in front of the restaurant and put the car in park. His next words came out harsher than intended. "Monica always did like attention."

"Nothing's changed."

He came around the car and opened her door. "This is it."

"Wow. You can't beat this location. Right in the heart of downtown, next to the best shopping and bars in the city. Prime space." She scanned the exterior brick building, his hand on the small of her back, guiding her toward the door.

He stepped inside the restaurant and held the door open for Peyton, watching for her reaction. A little gasp escaped her. Her gaze gleamed, taking in the large room as if it were one of the Seven Wonders of the World. Windows lined the entire front wall, and the ceiling stretched at least twenty feet in height, still raw and unfinished. Concrete floors covered the interior, and the walls were in desperate need of repair with holes and dings throughout the space. Natural light came through the large wall of windows and brightened the shabbiness of the restaurant's present condition.

"Walk with me," she said, her voice eager.

She set her purse on a table and moved to the far wall. "Picture this. Cover these two walls in distressed natural brick similar to the picture I showed you. Red brick instead of white since seeing the space. The red hues would be gorgeous in the sunlight streaming through the windows," she said, as she crossed the room. He couldn't look away. His gaze locked on her every movement. "Take down this wall. It opens up the whole place. I envision large rustic wood beams on the ceiling giving the room a natural vibe. Stain this concrete floor and keep everything very urban, or we can go with a dark plank wood and give it an earthy feel. Both options work."

She continued to move, her brow creased in concentration, studying the area. Mesmerized, he watched her hips sway against the fitted fabric of her dress. So fucking sexy. Was her skin still as soft? Would she still make those sweet sounds of pleasure if he touched her again?

She pointed toward the ceiling. "The lighting we choose must make a statement. I have some pieces in mind to bring in an industrial element. Metals, antique brass, and cool wood accents will keep our lines clean and simple. We can head back to my office and start narrowing things down. With the tight timeline, I need to get orders placed right away."

"Okay, boss. Sounds like you've got it covered." He reached for his ever-present water and made a conscious effort to get his shit together.

Her narrowed gaze met his. "You see it, though, right?"

"I'm starting to. But I know you see it, which is what matters most."

"I see it," she said; a wide grin spread across her face.

Fucking adorable. How had he ever walked away from this woman? Remarkable how one tragedy damaged so many lives. He scrubbed a hand over his face, questioning his decision to come here. A knot formed in his stomach. Watching her walk to the other side of the room, he remembered the ten-year-old girl so wounded and lost. An instant connection from the moment they met. The best of friends. Hell, they were only kids. But it'd bloomed into the kind of love you only read about in fairy tales. He hadn't even believed in that shit. But they'd been the real deal. He'd have bet his life nothing could come between them. She used to thank him for pulling her out of the dark and lonely place he'd found her in when they met, but the truth was, she'd saved him. The girl like a ray of light in a world that did everything it could to tear him down.

They walked down the hall off the dining room to look at the space where the restrooms were going to be. Her gaze scanned the area with intent.

"We've got a lot of work ahead of us," she said, leaning back against the wall in the darkened hallway. The space was narrow, and the air around them grew thick.

"Are you up for it?"

"I'm up for a challenge," she replied, her voice just above a whisper.

He wanted to move in. Pin her to the wall. Crush his mouth over hers. Feel every soft curve of her body. Wanting. Needing. Everything he despised. What the fuck was he thinking? He cursed under his breath with frustration, and she looked away. Maybe she understood the war going on in his head. He didn't know. He needed to get out of the confined space as soon as possible.

"You ready to head back to the office?"

"Yes." Her irritation impossible to miss in her clipped tone. Storming out the door ahead of him. Did she want him to kiss her? Touch her? Or had she read his thoughts and been disgusted by them? Regret and remorse surrounded him. He wanted her. With every part of his being. However, feeding his need would mean hurting her. He had nothing to offer her aside from a roll in the sheets—which no doubt would be mind-blowing. But without question—it would be a mistake. And he'd made enough of those for a lifetime.

Chapter Four

Present

Peyton hurried to the office to meet Elle and Dani for a quick powwow before heading to the restaurant for the day. She grabbed a few files to take to PBV and slipped them in her briefcase.

Dani stepped in with two coffees in hand, her light brown wavy hair spilling over her shoulders. Black slacks accentuated her long, lean frame, and her silk blouse matched her sapphire eyes. Elle rushed in behind Dani, donned in a cute pink shift dress with her floral Kate Spade bag strapped over her shoulder. She shut the door and her two best friends sat down on the sofa in her office. She dropped to the floor on the white furry rug beneath the coffee table to face them.

Nothing beat a good surge of caffeine. "Mmm, thank you. Just what I needed this morning."

"Do not make me slap you to sleep. This is a gossip session. There's no time for small talk," Elle drawled, kicking off her heels and joining Peyton on the carpet. She could be the poster child for charming southern belles, with her witty little sayings and sassy attitude. Her shoulder-length golden hair bounced, and her elbows rested on the glass coffee table. She beamed with excitement, and they chuckled at her dramatics.

"You worked late again last night with Jackson,

right? It's been almost two weeks now. How's it going?" Dani asked before sipping from her steaming cup.

"It's complicated. A part of me loves having him back in my life. Which is ridiculous considering he broke my heart. But seeing him every day—I don't know. I like it. I shouldn't because it can't go anywhere, but I like being around him."

Elle rubbed her hands together as if this were the best news. "Y'all, the man is one masculine masterpiece. He could charm the dew right off the honeysuckle. I don't blame you one bit for wanting to be around him. You thought he was going to kiss you the other day. Have there been any more close calls?"

"Thankfully, no. But I'd be lying if I didn't admit a tiny part of me was disappointed when he stopped it. Which is sick and twisted considering I have a boyfriend." She paused, took a sip of her drink, savoring the hint of spice when it hit her system. "But no. We've been keeping it professional since. It's not like he's a normal client. No matter how hard I try, I can't help it. I try to form clear boundaries, but he's so damn familiar. I'm drawn to him in a way I can't explain. So most of the time, I'm short and snippy, distant for my own well-being."

"Maybe you *shouldn't* keep him at arm's length," Dani said, shrugging her shoulders.

"Are you crazy? He's like a bad wet dream. He's driving me nuts. When he looks at me, I break out in a sweat. I feel so guilty I can't even put it into words. And now I have to go to New York with him tomorrow."

"What would the harm be in seeing where it goes?

47

You have a history with him. He's your first love." Elle raised her eyebrows in inquiry.

"Umm, have you both forgotten about Sebastian? I can't drop everything for the man who left me. Also, *he* keeps his distance from me, too. He's mentioned several times that he'd like to be *friends*. I can't risk a fling with a guy it took me forever to get over the first time. Been there, done that. And it proved to be enough heartache for a lifetime."

"How are things going with Sebastian? Has he inquired more about your connection with Jackson?" Dani asked, fiddling with the cozy wrapped around her cup.

"He doesn't know the extent of it. Telling him about our relationship would mean sharing how it ended. It's not my story to tell. I don't feel right about it."

"You've been with him for six months, and you don't feel comfortable telling him the truth? You told us the whole story. Do you not trust him?" Dani asked, her tone skeptical. She wished her friends knew Sebastian better; however, the campaign kept him very busy. They both thought he pressured her to move the relationship forward, which was true. He'd told her he loved her recently, but she didn't say it back because it didn't feel right. Not yet at least. He promised he'd make more of an effort to get to know her friends and family after the election was over. She would make sure it happened.

"No. I trust him. You know it takes me a long time to open up. And out of loyalty to Jackson, I don't feel right divulging something so personal."

Yes, she worried about the man who ripped her

heart out. Even after all these years.

"Is the attraction just physical? Or is it more?" Elle leaned in, her topaz gaze danced with curiosity.

"We always had a strong physical connection, and that hasn't changed. But we also shared a strong emotional connection, too. He was my first—everything."

It bothered her, the strong attraction still there between her and Jackson. Stronger than ever. She woke up last night amid the sexiest dream of her life. "I have to tell you guys something." Heat spread across her cheeks with embarrassment.

"What? Did something happen?" Dani questioned.

Guilt consumed her. "No. I—I don't know. I had a crazy, um, *inappropriate* dream last night. And it wasn't with Sebastian."

Her two best friends howled with laughter. It took every ounce of strength to hide her own smile. "Thank you for not laughing."

"Well, butter my butt and call me a biscuit. You had yourself a dirty dream about Jackson, didn't you?" Elle blurted, and Peyton could no longer avoid the humor of the situation.

She nodded in agreement. "It's bad, right?"

Dani wiped the tears escaping her eyes. "It's normal. You're too hard on yourself. Of course, these feelings are coming up. He's the love of your life. And now he's here." She held her hand up before Peyton interrupted. "I know, I know, you're with Sebastian. But you've been with him for six months, and it's not like you guys spend a ton of time together. We hardly know the man. You attend events and go to dinner. It's not deep. You have a history with Jackson. Things didn't end because you fell out of love. You never had any closure, so it's still very raw for you."

Elle clapped her hands. "Girl, you could give Dr. Phil a run for his money. Peyton, I think you had the dream because you *want* him. You want him so bad your subconscious is making it happen for you. There's a fire inside our girl, and it's dying to get out," she sang.

No longer able to keep it in, she burst out in a case of uncontrollable giggles along with Elle and Dani.

"You literally have *no* filter, do you?" Peyton asked. Elle, ever the straight shooter, always spoke her mind. Peyton loved her for it, even when she didn't want to hear it.

"I speak the truth. Yes, you have a nice boyfriend, and he comes in a pretty little package. But this is your—*person*. You've told us nothing has ever come close to what you shared with Jackson. So maybe you shouldn't fight it so much. And this isn't easy for me to say, especially when you could become the *first lady of San Francisco* if you were to marry Sebastian. You know it's my dream to be a first lady of anything, or maybe a duchess?" Elle teased, sidetracked by the conversation.

"No filter at all," Dani said, rolling her eyes.

"Yeah—and marriage is far from my mind right now, so let's not go there. Fantasizing about another man should be enough of a red flag. But Sebastian's not the only reason I can't be with Jackson." She stalled to sip her coffee before saying aloud what she knew to be the real reason. "I could never survive him leaving me again. Mind you, we don't know if he has a girlfriend or is even attracted to me anymore. Why are we even talking about this?"

"Are you kidding? This is the most exciting thing to happen to the three of us in years," Dani said, pulling her phone from her purse to check the time.

"I think he came back for a reason—and I think *you* are the reason," Elle chimed in. "Call me old-fashioned, but I believe if something is meant to be, it will find its way back to you."

She shook her head at her friend but couldn't help but ponder if there were some truth there. Elle grew up in Georgia. She was, in her own words, heavy on the twang when referring to her hometown, "Savannah born and bred." A hopeless romantic who wanted the fairy tale. Dani and Peyton were far more cautious when it came to matters of the heart.

"Sometimes, I actually think you might be insane." Dani balled up her napkin and chucked it at Elle. Dani and her boyfriend, Cam, had been dating for just over two years. Elle and Peyton adored him, but Dani seemed to be just one foot out the door. Cam loved her like crazy, but Peyton didn't think her best friend reciprocated those strong feelings.

"Hey, how did dinner go last night? You went out with some of Cam's work friends, right?" Peyton purposely changed the subject.

Dani rolled her eyes. "Cam's friend Jay brought a date he'd just met the night before. They didn't even know one another and were not meshing well at all. Jay acted like such an asshole."

"Well, I've told you many times, Jay is so stuck-up he could drown in a rainstorm," Elle blurted.

Again, the office rang out with laughter. Chuckling over Elle's witty banter, which was completely on point. Jay had hit on Elle numerous times over the past two years but proved he couldn't go more than forty-five seconds without talking about himself. No kidding. Elle had actually timed him on two separate occasions with her phone. And no one was more accurate than Elle Fiore when it came to the manners of her male suitors. Currently single, she dated more than most people went to the gym. No one had swept her off her feet yet, but she remained hopeful. Convinced her Prince Charming was out there somewhere. A knock at the door startled Peyton from her thoughts.

"It's open," she called out.

Surprise slammed her when Jackson opened the door. Striding in all manly and commanding in dark jeans and a gray T-shirt. Sexy and handsome. He made it look effortless.

Jesus.

"Good morning, ladies." He smiled, his gaze landing on her.

"What are you doing here?" she asked, hurrying to slip into her heels.

"Camille asked me to stop by to sign some papers. She said you were here, so I thought I'd see if you wanted to drive to PBV together."

"I would, but I need to have my car at the restaurant. I have an event tonight with Sebastian, so I'll go home from work to change. But I'll follow you over now."

"Sounds like a plan. No hurry if you want to finish things up here," he offered.

"No, I'm ready."

"So, Jackson, may I ask you something?" Elle's expression so full of mischief, she dreaded what her friend might ask.

"Anything."

"Ah, good answer. So Peyton, Dani, and I make it a point to eat lunch together as often as possible no matter how busy we are. But this one here"—she jerked her thumb in Peyton's direction—"she's like a dog with a bone. She'll never leave a project for lunch unless we insist on it."

She wanted to beg her to stop speaking, while Dani appeared thoroughly entertained by the conversation. "This is a bit unprofessional, don't you think?" she shot at Elle with raised eyebrows.

"I don't think so. I'm all about lunch." Jackson winked at her two best friends.

"Well, bless your heart. I agree with Jackson." Elle's grin spread clear across her face.

Peyton rolled her eyes at the camaraderie already forming. She glared at her friends and spoke through clenched teeth, "I said I'd make it work."

Jackson's laugh bellowed through the office as he watched her with amusement. "Listen, Peyton's free to leave whenever she wants, and you are both welcome to come to the restaurant and eat lunch as often as you'd like. The space is still pretty raw, but I can have a card table and chairs set up for you to use. Fair?"

"I'd say it's more than fair." Dani smiled, shooting her a knowing look, as if he were too good to be true.

"I think we're going to get along just fine, Jackson," Elle purred. Peyton shook her head in disbelief. The three of them had known each other all of what—five minutes? And they were already thick as thieves.

"Okay. Glad we have the important stuff out of the

way. Some of us need to get to work," Peyton said, leading Jackson out the door.

"Can't wait to come for lunch next week," Elle shouted down the hallway.

"Looking forward to it," he called back.

She tried not to laugh as he chuckled beside her and they stepped onto the elevator. She stood against the opposite wall from Jackson. The way he watched her left her legs shaky. The confined space magnified her need to move closer to him.

He destroyed you once. He'll do it again. You have a wonderful, loving boyfriend. She chanted this silent mantra in her head while the elevator moved down to the lobby.

"Your friends are great," he said.

"Yes, but they're pushy when they want something." She huffed but couldn't hide her smile.

Her phone vibrated, and she looked down to see a text from Wolf. For the love of God—the man needed to get a life. With the election nearing, Sebastian's campaign manager continued to breathe down her neck. He wanted her to walk the red carpet at a turtle's pace tonight.

Let them get lots of photos this evening. With each step you take, pause and smile. PDA is welcome. Don't hold back.

She didn't respond. The endless texts and calls annoyed her. She'd shared her irritation with Sebastian, and it proved pointless. She agreed to follow Jackson over to the restaurant, grateful for the few minutes alone in her car to pull it together. The chat with her friends left her questioning why he'd come back, and if they were destined to cross paths again.

She and Jackson arrived at PBV and spent the next few hours with Bob, the contractor, going over the details so he and his men could get started once they left for New York the following day. Jackson went off to work in his office when they finished up with Bob, and she set her computer up at the bar to place orders. After ignoring a dozen more texts from Wolf, she sent Sebastian a screen shot of the relentless requests. She was on the phone with the flooring rep when Jackson came up behind her. She somehow sensed him before she saw him. Always had. Never understood it. She ended the call, and his hand wrapped around her shoulder, causing her to suck in a jagged breath and turn around to face him.

He cleared his throat before taking the stool beside her at the bar. "You hungry? I'm going to order some lunch. How does a sandwich sound?"

"Great. I'm starving. What time is it?"

"It's one thirty. Still the same?"

"Still the same?"

"Turkey and cheddar on rye, light mayo?" he asked, typing the order into his phone, until he realized she didn't respond.

He cocked his head to the side, his eyebrows pinched together with confusion. "What did I miss?"

"I can't believe you remember my favorite sandwich. Yes, it's still the same."

"What can I say? I'm in the restaurant business. I pay attention to people's orders," he said, making light of it.

"Thanks for ordering. Let me grab some cash." She reached for her purse, and he placed his fingers around her forearm.

Damn it. He needed to stop touching her. She pulled away quickly and fell from the stool. Jackson's reflexes were fast. He caught her by the arm and steadied her. Why the hell was she such a bumbling mess around him? The physical draw was so strong she couldn't seem to control her own body. She despised being weak and vulnerable.

"Don't offend me. It's my treat," he said, his voice gruff.

"Thank you."

"Not a problem." He grabbed two bottles of water from behind the bar.

In desperate need of space, she excused herself before their lunch arrived. Leaning against the bathroom door like some sort of hormonal teenage girl who couldn't control her sexual desires. After splashing some water on her face, she took a long look in the mirror and shook her head in disbelief. Falling apart in the presence of an attractive man was not an option. Channeling her inner strength, she gave herself a silent pep talk before heading out. Sandwiches arrived before she returned. Her phone vibrated with a text from Sebastian.

Hey, beautiful. Wolf promised to leave you alone for the rest of the day. Pick you up at seven?

Yes. I can't wait.

"This looks so good," she said, biting into the delicious sandwich.

"Yeah, it's from a great little place I found around the corner. What time do you need to leave today?"

"Around six fifteen unless you need me to stay later? I could meet Sebastian at the event."

"Don't be silly, it's not a problem. Why don't I

pick you up in the morning for the airport? No sense in taking two cars."

"Oh, sure. Sounds good."

"Perfect." He snatched her phone off the table and typed something into it.

"What are you doing?" She reached for her phone, but he held it out of reach with a playful grin.

"Do you have something on here you don't want me to see?"

"No. Give it back," she hissed, jumping up to get it. He looked down at her with a cocky smile, his face inches from hers. She steadied herself, placing her hands on his chest. Hell, she'd been dying to feel his muscles ripple beneath her fingers for days. The contact burned in the most delicious way. So much for her plan to keep her distance. The *new and improved* Peyton would need a little more time before turning her ridiculous self around. He studied her before handing over the phone.

"Someone's touchy about her phone, huh?" he teased.

She snatched it from his grip. "You really know how to annoy me."

He spoke between bites. "I texted myself from your phone so I'd have your number. I just sent you a text with my info. Send me your address."

Her cheeks heated at her overreaction to him taking her phone. He'd just needed her address, yet she reacted like a cat in heat. "Oh. Okay."

****

At six fifteen, she contemplated knocking on his office door to say good-bye. It was time to get home and changed for the event. Should she just leave him a note and give herself some space? Or send a text now since they exchanged numbers?

The main door swung open, startling her. The water bottle slipped from her fingers, and the liquid spilled down the front of her blouse. A gorgeous woman strode in, rocking a sexy black bandage-style dress, more of her on display than covered. Her breasts spilled from the narrow strap covering them, yet gravity appeared to be on her side. The sky-high red heels and platinum-blonde hair made her even more alluring. The woman was the epitome of a bombshell.

"Sorry, I didn't mean to startle you. Is Jackson around?" the woman asked in a silky voice.

Jackson walked up behind her. His tone didn't hide his surprise seeing the woman here. "Hey, I thought I was meeting you at Giordelli's?"

Is this his girlfriend? Her mind spun at a mile a minute, and her mouth went dry.

"I decided to Uber here and surprise you." The words rolled off her tongue.

He looked between the women. "Peyton, this is Lana. Lana, Peyton."

"Nice to meet you," she lied to the sex-on-a-stick woman standing before her.

"It's a pleasure. Jackson tells me you're the best designer in all of San Francisco." Her sultry voice was like a swift kick in the gut.

Peyton smiled, her stare following the woman embracing Jackson, running her hand up the back of his neck and into his hair. Who the hell did she think she was? Fury nearly choked Peyton. She swallowed hard, trying not to reveal her anger. *What right did she have to be angry?* Sebastian made her happy. Didn't stop her from wanting to throat punch the sex goddess. All logic left Peyton the day Jackson Vance sauntered back into her life.

He pulled away from Lana. His gaze landed on the front of Peyton's blouse, still wet from the spill. Looking away, she didn't want his pity. This was like a bad episode of *The Bachelor*—where the hot girl rode off into the sunset with a rose and the dowdy girl stood there like a fool, with a stain on the front of her blouse. No, thanks.

Ever so casually, she hoisted her briefcase strap over her shoulder. "You guys have a great night. See you tomorrow."

"Here, let me help you with your bag," Jackson said, coming up behind her and grabbing the strap of her briefcase.

"I've got it." She kept a tight hold, not wanting his help, but he slipped it from her fingers with ease.

Stepping outside, she walked beside the couple like a pathetic third wheel. Her breaths came faster, and it took all her strength not to run for her car. Lana wrapped her hand around his bicep, and they strode along the sidewalk like a picture-perfect couple. Peyton bit down hard on her lower lip and fought the urge to demand Lana remove her hand from his body. He paused at his car, parked right in front of the restaurant, and unlocked the door for Lana. His date. They were going on a freaking date. Nausea rose in her throat.

"I can take my bag. I'm parked right over there," Peyton snarled and grabbed at the strap with impatience.

Lana stepped into the car, and he shut the door, his voice calm and controlled. "Stop it. I'm walking you to your car."

She marched ahead of him, unable to stop the onset of a full-blown meltdown. She unlocked the passenger door and held her other hand out for her bag, avoiding his gaze.

"Bag, please," she hissed.

"You're mad." He chuckled, the man obviously pleased with himself.

"Don't flatter yourself."

"Okay, Pea. See you tomorrow."

He continued to stand there when she walked around to the driver's side.

She was irked by his cool, aloof manner. "Your date is waiting for you."

"And I'm waiting for you to get your ass in the car." His emerald-green stare drilled into her.

With a dramatic eye roll, she hurried into the car and slammed the door. She needed to rein it in, always prided herself on her ability to stay in control. Keep her cool. She looked in the rearview mirror. Jackson and his *seductive bombshell* waited for her to pull away. Of course, even in the midst of her toddler tantrum, he remained a gentleman. The way she'd just behaved was so out of character. The sight of him with another woman had her all spun up. But why? They'd been apart for nine years. Of course, he'd been with other women. Yet seeing it—made her sick to her stomach.

****

Sebastian knocked on the door, and relief flooded her. A date with her boyfriend was just what she needed to take her mind off Jackson and his little blonde vixen. She never acted out around *this* man. She saw him through the large window of her front door and blew her sweet dog a kiss good-bye. She held up the bottom of her floor-length black slip dress to keep from dragging on the ground, and grasped his arm for support.

"Wow. You look beautiful."

"Thank you. You look very handsome as well. You know I'm a sucker for a man in a tux."

"Good to know," he teased.

Miguel, his black-hatted chauffeur, waited at the curb with the back door open for them to slip in. The man in his mid-fifties was so sweet. He'd driven her and Sebastian to more events than she could count. Did he choose to wear the hat and the full chauffer outfit, or did they require him to? He'd worked for the Worthington's for over twenty years, first for Sebastian's father and now driving Sebastian full time.

Peyton leaned back against the black leather seat and straightened the hem of her dress to adjust the slit running along the side, exposing her leg. The last few days had been emotionally taxing, putting in long hours at the restaurant with Jackson. Working with him proved—frustrating. Irritating. And amazing all at the same time.

Between her embarrassing jealous tantrum and the erotic dream playing on repeat night after night, his presence left her on edge. She needed an exorcism from him, and hopefully an evening with Sebastian would cleanse her. Memories of Jackson had haunted her over the years, but having him here in the flesh proved far more torturous. He stirred emotions she'd worked so hard to put away. When he was near, everything else around her evaporated. His presence eclipsed everything. The way she'd reacted when she saw him with Lana was even more of a reminder to be careful about getting too close to him again. This man had ripped her heart out once before, and he wouldn't hesitate to do it again.

"Tired, gorgeous?" Sebastian inquired. He handed her a glass of wine, his fingers brushing against hers before letting go.

"A little bit. I had a full day."

"The restaurant is a big project, huh?"

"Yes. There's so much to order and take care of."

"You leave for New York tomorrow, right?"

"Yes. We'll be home Saturday."

"How's it been going with Jackson? Is it awkward, or is there still a friendship there?"

"There's still a friendship there. But it's been a long time."

"I'm sure there's a lot to catch up on." He leaned forward, his hand caressing her knee.

No warm-fuzzy feelings. No butterflies. No tingle of desire shooting up her spine. Damn it. Not a good sign.

"How about you? What's the latest with the election? Only a few more weeks to go."

"Yes. We're getting down to the wire. Cane is still breathing down my neck, so I need to keep pushing."

"Photos of him with another woman went viral. He looks so guilty. I can't imagine people are okay with him cheating on his wife of twenty-five years with a starlet. It's so scandalous."

"Yeah, well, Dereck Cane has the luxury of being the beloved incumbent mayor. People have a way of turning a blind eye. Yet I can't catch a break."

"Yes, I can tell the pressure is on. Wolf is out of

control with his texts. The man actually tried to tell me what to wear tonight." The guy gave *creepy* a new name, whether Sebastian wanted to admit it or not.

"Yes. The race is neck and neck right now. He thinks you're my golden ticket."

His words rubbed her wrong, as if he agreed with Wolf. Sebastian campaigned the entire time they'd been dating. Would things be different when he didn't need her at his side in public the way he did now?

"I think all your plans for the city are your golden ticket. Moreover, his texts and calls are excessive. He's not my stylist. I can dress myself. I have been for many years." She didn't even attempt to hide her annoyance.

"I'm sorry, beautiful. I'll speak to him again. The most important thing for me is that I have you by my side." His gaze locked with hers.

"Of course. Nowhere else I'd rather be," she said, trying to sound convincing.

"When the election is over, I want to focus on our relationship more. Take things to the next level." He reached for her hand, and a grin spread across his handsome face.

"Sounds good."

"You make me want things I've never thought about before." He pulled her close to him. Her body tense, she leaned into him, desperate to get lost in the moment.

"Such as?"

"Everything, Peyton. Whatever you're willing to give me. Moving in together, marriage, kids, the whole package." He turned to meet her gaze.

Wait. What? She hoped the panic making its way through every single part of her body didn't show. He'd never talked like this before. Marriage and kids? What the hell was happening? Her universe continued to spiral.

"I think we should get through the election and then see where things lead. One day at a time."

He kissed the top of her head. "I love my ever-cautious girlfriend. I don't mean to push you or scare you off. But I love you, and I want a future with you, whatever way I can have it."

She placed her hand on his cheek, didn't want him to feel rejected by her answer. "I want a future with you, too. I just don't want to rush things."

"I'm not in a hurry. I can wait as long as you need me to."

On paper, Sebastian was her perfect match. You didn't get much safer than someone willing to wait as long as you needed him to. It was a hell of a lot better than wondering how long they'd stick around. She'd been so distracted by the blast from the past who'd turned her world upside down, and almost forgot how wonderful the man beside her was. They spent a beautiful evening together, and when he gave his speech, she watched with pride. Sebastian shared his big plans for the city they both resided in, and he wanted to see them come to fruition with her by his side. Hard to ask for anything more.

They arrived home late, and he asked to spend the night at her place. She fell into bed, and tried with everything she could muster to want to be there, with him.

However, when Sebastian pulled her close to kiss her, he was not the man who consumed her thoughts.

He flipped her on her back, climbed above her, and

whispered, "I've missed you. It's been almost two weeks since we've spent the night together. We've both been so busy."

She was more than aware. Hadn't spent the night with him since the day Jackson Vance strode back into her life. She found a way to buy time and try to sort out her feelings. His kiss turned needier. She squeezed her eyes closed and feigned desire. He pawed at her with a hungry need. The sound of a car alarm came from the street in front of her house. She focused on the sound and not on the lingering taste of whiskey on his lips.

She pushed him off and bolted upright. "I've missed you, too. I'm sorry. I just need a minute."

He moved beside her and placed a hand on her back. "Hey, what's going on? Are you okay?"

Pulling her knees up, she rested her forehead against them. "Yes. I've had this nagging headache all day, and it won't go away."

Guilt rushed through her—but lying seemed kinder than the alternative.

"There's no pressure here. Let's get some sleep." He didn't hide his disappointment.

"Thanks. I'm sorry."

"Don't say another word about it," he said, wrapping his arms around her, enveloping her from behind.

She closed her eyes on a silent prayer and hoped everything would go back to normal soon. A night of sleep without fantasizing about another man. Most importantly, she didn't want to be consumed by Jackson Vance.

"Sleep well. I love you," Sebastian said, holding her close.

With her eyes closed, she pretended to be asleep, because her reality had become her own private hell.

Chapter Five

Present

The tall, narrow, yellow Victorian on the quiet, tree-lined street fit Peyton to a tee. Traditional yet stylish—like the woman who resided there. No question, the architecture drew her to this place. The white molding displayed elegant detail, and the asymmetrical design oozed charm and character. Jackson walked up steep steps to the red doors with glass panels, as birds chirped. The sun not yet up, neighborhood residents slept soundly. The door flew open, and Sebastian walked out with a Cheshire cat grin spread across his face.

Douchebag.

"Jackson, hello. Thanks for getting my girl to the airport. I appreciate it." He offered an outstretched hand, and Jackson gave a reluctant shake.

"Not a problem." His jaw ticked, and anger simmered beneath his calm demeanor. The douche had obviously spent the night with her, which should come as no surprise. They were dating after all. Didn't mean he had to like it. A black car pulled up to the curb, and a man stepped out to open the door for Sebastian. *Christ.* He wore a traditional chauffeur outfit. Why? It looked ridiculous. The guy couldn't drive his own car? Did he not know about Uber? This was, most likely, going to be the next mayor of San Francisco.

The sound of a shrill, high-pitched bark was startling. Peyton appeared in the doorway with a smile.

"Oh, hey. Come in." She waved good-bye to the douchebag, and the car pulled away from the curb. Each time he saw her, he experienced both pleasure and pain. The awareness of how much he'd hurt her proved difficult to process. Yet the woman still managed to set his world on fire. The restraint it took not to act on it— more challenging than expected.

"Thanks for picking me up. I'm almost ready," she said, scooping up her pup.

"No worries. This must be the infamous Mr. Whiskers."

"The one and only."

"You do know it's because no one else would ever choose the absurd name, right?" He tentatively reached out to touch the mutt.

She huffed, "Maybe I should have named him Peanut. Or Pea. Because those are *so much better*."

"At least I didn't name you *Miss* Peanut."

Her grin was playful. "Here. Hold him for a minute while I grab my bag. He needs some love before we go. Try not to insult him if you can manage it."

He laughed when the ball of fur fell into his arms. He glanced around the living room at the white silk window panels puddled on the floor. Dark wood floors extended as far as he could see, and an oversized white couch covered in throw pillows filled the space. He never understood why people covered their couch with pillows they eventually tossed on the floor. Why go to all the effort to take them on and off? A large crystal chandelier hung from the center of the room, fighting the distressed vintage fireplace for best feature. Obviously a woman's domain. A dude wasn't going to kick up his feet and eat chili nachos while he watched football in here. He noted a framed picture of her and the douchebag on the mantel. They looked stiff and posed.

"Beautiful house. I'm guessing you chose the girly chandelier?"

"Thank you. Yes, you're correct. I love me a good chandelier." She laughed, wheeling her rolling suitcase behind her. The cream sleeveless blouse and matching fitted dress slacks stood out against her golden tanned skin. Hair pulled into some sort of complicated-looking bun at the nape of her neck. *Fucking gorgeous.*

"So what happens with the fluff ball?" he inquired while the frisky little guy tried to lick his face. Holding his head out of range while Mr. Whiskers attempted again and again to make contact. He was cute in an unusual way, with an awkward underbite and a wild mane of hair.

"Seriously, you can't call him by his name?" She rolled her eyes.

"I can't do it." He laughed.

She snatched the pup back and hugged him good-bye as if he were a child. An absurd display of affection, yet he watched her with amusement.

"Ready?"

"Yep."

She locked the door behind them, and they slipped into his car. When he pulled away from the curb, he dropped his phone in the center console.

"So the fluff ball stays alone for two days?"

"Don't be ludicrous. He's a dog. He can't feed

himself. My dad's coming by to get him in an hour or so." She leaned into him to set her purse on the back seat. Orange blossoms and vanilla surrounded him. He swallowed hard. He'd hoped his evening with Lana last night would've curbed his lust for this woman. It didn't seem to be the case.

"There is no way your father calls him by the ridiculous name."

She hesitated before admitting the truth, "He drops the salutation and calls him Whiskers."

Peyton's father was one of the most respected attorneys in the city. It would be tough to picture him coddling a lapdog, yet he adored his daughters in a way Jackson admired. His success never superseded his role as a parent.

"How did your dinner go last night?" she asked, staring out the window at the sidewalk bustling with people heading to work.

"We had a good time."

Jealousy bit her. She didn't hide it when she'd thrown a tantrum worthy of any headstrong five-year-old not getting their way.

She turned to face him. "Late night?"

"Nope. We got back to *my place* by ten." He knew this would get a reaction. It wasn't something he should mess around with, but he couldn't resist. He enjoyed seeing her all spun up.

"Where did you meet her?"

"We were set up a few weeks ago. A friend-of-a-friend type of thing."

"Interesting," she quipped, fiddling with her water bottle.

"Not really. Why all the questions?"

"I haven't asked a lot of questions." Her irritation was.impossible to miss. "You hadn't mentioned a girlfriend, so I'm getting brought up to speed."

Sure, she was. "If memory serves, you never asked if I had a girlfriend. You asked if I was married. I have no secrets. You can ask whatever you want. For the record, Lana isn't my girlfriend."

"It's not a big deal. It makes no difference to me. I didn't know what the situation was."

"Since we're getting brought *up to speed,* why does your boyfriend use a chauffeur? He needs a personal driver because he's *so* important? He can't drive his own car or call an Uber like everyone else?"

"He's an important man. He comes from an affluent family, and he has a driver. What's the big deal?" Her haughty-ass attitude rubbed him wrong.

"Ah, yes. Anyone running for public office, who wants to serve the people, should spend copious amounts of money on themselves. It's such an admirable attribute."

She didn't miss the sarcasm. "What is your problem? You don't even know him."

"Everyone knows him. He can't keep himself out of the spotlight for ten seconds. I've never seen a more media-hungry candidate in my life. I'd just never guessed you for someone who would be okay with being used as eye candy for the press."

Yeah, he was being an asshole. However, he'd never strayed from speaking his mind.

"Well, since you left nine years ago without a call or a note to check in, you don't get to judge who I am now. I believe you told me to move on with my life, which is exactly what I've done. And it appears you have your hands full with your sex goddess, so maybe you should focus on her and keep your opinions about my life to yourself." Anger radiated from her body.

Christ, she got under his skin. He stepped out of the car and grabbed both suitcases before opening her door. She tried to reach for her suitcase from him, but he held on to it. They walked in silence until reaching the line at security.

"You're right, you know, Pea?" he admitted just above a whisper.

"I usually am, but what *in particular* are you referring to?" She didn't meet his gaze, stared straight ahead.

"I have no business judging you. I left, and you moved on with your life."

Her face was smug. "Finally, the first wise thing you've said today."

He chuckled, couldn't help himself. "And as far as the *sex goddess*, you're correct. I do have my hands full with her. She keeps me plenty busy."

He followed her through the scanner at security, reaching for their bags while she slipped back into her heels. Her movements erratic. She dropped her bracelets three times while trying to pull herself together. His statement about Lana obviously left her flustered, and though he shouldn't be enjoying this—he couldn't help himself.

"If this is how you choose to spend your time, Jackson, go right ahead. You two seem like a match made in heaven, the way you paw all over one another."

He leaned close to her as she pulled her purse strap over her shoulder in a huff. "Is someone jealous?"

She clutched her chest in dramatic fashion. Her

reaction was worthy of an award-winning Broadway performance. Making all sorts of breathy noises, sure he understood how appalled she was. He rolled his eyes as they walked toward their gate.

"I'm not the slightest bit jealous of your *voluptuous vixen*."

"Sure, you aren't," he said with a chuckle.

This type of banter needed to stop. Starting something with Peyton wasn't an option. He'd come here to make amends, not fan the flames. She seemed happy, and he needed to let her be. But he was so drawn to her, like a powerful current he couldn't swim against. Always provoking and stirring and challenging him.

"You're so full of yourself. I'm in an amazing relationship with a wonderful man. He's about to be the *freaking mayor of San Francisco* for God's sake. I'm hardly jealous. I happen to care about you because you're my friend, and I don't want to see you get hurt."

"You're worried about me, huh?"

"Did I stutter?"

His laugh echoed, and they continued walking. The masses of people moving through the airport were on a mission to get wherever it was they were going.

"Let me get this straight. You're worried the *voluptuous vixen* is going to hurt me? Physically? I sure hope you're right." His night with Lana was a bust, mainly because he couldn't get the jealous pain in the ass walking beside him off his mind.

"You're disgusting. Forget it."

She wrestled her bag from his hand and walked ahead, her suitcase thumping behind her. Fucking adorable. Angry and feisty. He played with fire, teasing her like this. Choosing to argue about ridiculous

Laura Pavlov

bullshit instead of pressing her up against the wall and covering her mouth with his like he wanted. He didn't know how *not* to want her. Nor did he know if it were even possible.

They boarded the plane, and she attempted to stop him when he reached for her carry-on and placed it in the overhead bin. This particular battle she wouldn't win. He lifted both bags before taking his seat. They didn't speak until after the plane took off.

"Peanut."

She let out an exaggerated breath. "Will you stop calling me that, please? Especially when we're on a work trip."

He looked around at the other passengers and shook his head. "Because you work for all of these people?"

"What is it you want to say?"

Closing the magazine in his hands, he turned to face her. "I'm sorry for calling you jealous, and I'm sorry for accusing Sebastian of being a pompous ass."

He wasn't sorry. She *was* jealous, and Sebastian *was* a pompous ass. But he'd be the bigger person, because this back-and-forth shit wasn't a good idea. The truth—he seethed over the thought of her and Sebastian together. And not just because he couldn't stand the guy but because he couldn't stand the thought of her being with anyone.

"Well, thank you."

He smiled and nodded. "Sure."

"Let's discuss what we'll be doing in New York."

He would introduce her to his friends, she'd stay in the room next door to his at the hotel, and they'd be spending long days together. He'd share pieces of the last nine years with her by bringing her here, and maybe it would be part of the closure they both needed.

"We'll eat dinner at Lago's tonight. Roberto, the owner, is a close friend. I want to design the bar area at PBV similar to the layout at Lago's. It's unique."

"Roberto's one of the partners in the PBV you're opening in San Francisco?"

"This first bistro will be solely owned by me. Roberto and two other close friends whom you'll meet in New York, Davis and Nelson, have been involved in this venture with me. We came up with the idea of making it a chain on a national level. But financially I can't swing opening more than one, certainly not the first year in business. Roberto was looking for an investment, and Nelson and Davis were interested as well. So we pooled our money and decided to open two more this year. It'll be a lot of work, but I hope it's worth it in the end."

She listened intently before speaking. "It's an impressive plan. Very ambitious."

Christ. He didn't expect her to be nice. He should tell her he'd be leaving shortly after the restaurant opened. This would be the time to get it all out there. But she'd pull away and cut him off so fast his head would spin.

The partnership agreement entailed Jackson opening each location, spending three to four months getting them up and running before moving on to the next city. Exactly how he liked it. No long-term attachments. Build something new every few months. Permanent roots weren't his thing, so this business plan presented the perfect arrangement for him. The other three men were silent financial partners, while he held a larger stake in the company by investing financially and building each location. He'd tell her once they were back to work. Give himself a few more days to reconnect and then drop the bomb. No doubt she'd go cold on him, which would work in his favor, as keeping his distance proved more challenging than expected.

"Thank you." Her approval meant more than it should.

"So I talked to my dad last night. He wants to have you over for dinner. Jayden and Zach want to come, of course, too. Everyone's dying to see you."

"Does it bother you? Do you want me to keep my distance?"

"What? No. It's fine. I just need to run it by Sebastian."

"You need his permission to have dinner with your family?"

She fiddled with her laptop and met his gaze. "No. I don't want him to feel excluded. I haven't shared the extent of our relationship with him. If we all go to my dad's for dinner, it'll be obvious things ran a bit deeper than I've shared."

"I'm fine if you want to leave him at home," he teased.

She punched him in the arm. "You're unbelievable."

"He doesn't like me calling you Peanut. He made it very clear."

"I think he suspects we were more than friends. The ridiculous nickname is a bit of a red flag."

"So why not tell him the truth?"

"It would mean telling him everything. It's no one's business."

"You don't trust him?"

"Of course, I trust him. I just don't think it's necessary to share every detail of our past with him."

"I could bring Lana to dinner. She'd be a good distraction," he teased.

"No, thanks," she snarled.

"So did you bring some workout clothes and tennis shoes?"

Her puzzled dark stare met his. "Yes. Why?"

"Tomorrow morning you're working out with me. I have a course I run near the hotel. You'll love it," he insisted.

"I don't run."

"I do remember your lack of athletic ability. I'd hoped you'd improved since our last race, almost a decade ago," he taunted, before continuing. "I had to work double time to get us the gold at the Fourth of July obstacle course if memory serves."

Her head fell back in laughter. "Yeah, because there was *no gold* to go for. You turned an innocent family barbecue into the freaking Olympic trials."

"Oh, Peanut. There's always a gold when there's a competition. Once you taste it, silver just won't do."

"We were competing against five-year-olds and ninety-year-olds," she reminded him.

"*And we were losing.* You got passed by an eighty-five-year-old man in a walker." He'd never laughed so hard in his life. Tried to coach her from the sidelines during her relay leg, but the girl was hopeless. He'd given her an extensive lead, and she couldn't for the life of her jump in a potato sack without falling over. He'd teased her for hours after. Ended up being the last summer they spent together. He remembered watching

77

her with pride and knowing she was *his*. The sexiest girl he'd ever seen, even as she fell over again and again. So fucking beautiful and full of life. The memory stabbed him in the chest and threatened to slice him in two.

She took a sip of water and chuckled. "Mr. McCulky happened to be *eighty-three* years old, not *eighty-five*. And I swear his walker had some sort of motor on it because he blew past me hopping in the sack, like nobody's business."

"This is your story? The old man cheated?"

Goddamn, they'd shared so many good times. He'd forgotten so much, but seeing her brought it all back. They'd been really happy together. Nothing had ever come close to comparing to what he had with her. Though, he hadn't looked for it, nor did he want it again.

"I speak the truth. So I'll power walk your course. You can run. It's called compromise."

"We'll see."

She faced him, one cheek resting against the seat, her dark eyes wet with emotion from their journey down memory lane. He wanted to cover her mouth with his. Her gaze locked on his, and without thought, he grazed his knuckles, slow and gentle, down her cheek. Needed to touch her. Some sort of contact. As if he'd die without it. She startled a bit but didn't pull away, tugged her bottom lip between her teeth, a habit she'd had for as long as he could remember. Her stare never left his. The air around them sparked, and the slight touch heated every inch of his body. What the fuck was he doing?

The flight attendant approached to ask what they

wanted to drink. A much-needed reality check. He straightened and made a silent promise not to cross the line again. Nothing happened, but he'd wanted it to. He had nothing to offer. To act on it would be a selfish move, and he'd come to San Francisco to make things right with her, not fuck them up even more.

****

Once checked into the hotel, he went to his room for a quick shower while Peyton went to her room to freshen up. He stepped out of his room just as her door opened. In dark skinny jeans, sky-high black heels, and a loose-fitting, sheer black blouse, she looked incredible. Her top dipped into a low V across her chest and displayed the edge of a black lacy bra. His self-discipline being tested. Energy crackled in the air when he locked onto her gaze, shifting on his feet and drinking her in.

"Hey," she said. A genuine smile spread across her face. Her long dark hair fell around her shoulders in loose waves. He itched to run his fingers through it.

"Hey. You ready to go? I called an Uber."

"Yes, sounds good."

Once on the elevator, he worked to control the spike in adrenaline. Glancing down to see the lace of her bra against her chest as it rose and fell at a rapid rate. The confined space tested him.

The energy of the city buzzed. People packed the sidewalks, moving briskly, their shoulders brushing one another. Honking horns and commotion sounded around them. A perfect evening, the air warm with enough breezes to keep you comfortable. He helped her out of the car when they arrived at Lago's.

"Wow. This is magnificent architecture," she said

of the contemporary building.

With his hand on the small of her back, he guided her past the long line of patrons who stood outside waiting for a table at the popular haunt. Most restaurants in the city didn't provide waiting areas, using all the space available for seating. Jasmine, the twenty-something hostess, greeted them when they walked in, offering him a warm hug. Many a night here, spent eating, drinking, and picking Roberto's brain.

"Hey, Jackson. Roberto can't wait to see you. It's all we've heard about this week." She winked.

"I'm happy to be here. Can't wait to see him. This is my friend and designer, Peyton Kroft."

"Nice to meet you, Peyton."

"Pleasure to meet you as well." She smiled, her gaze moving around the space. He saw her wheels turning. The restaurant was narrow and long, and the dining room sat off to the right while the bar veered left. Dark woods, brick, and soft lighting set the tone.

"Roberto reserved a table for you in the bar. He assumed you preferred to spend most of your time in there."

"Yes. It'll be great to see it in all its glory on a Saturday night. We'll be back tomorrow afternoon to look around when it's empty."

Jasmine escorted them to their table, and a waiter greeted them to take their cocktail order. He suggested a nice bottle of Chardonnay, and Peyton agreed. She used her phone to snap several pictures of the bar area. The room was packed, filled with people having a great time. Soft jazz played in the background, and large dark brown iron candelabras with white, tall pillar candles hung over the bar.

"I'm so glad we came. Pictures don't do this place justice. I love the exposed brick wall, and the open shelving is beautiful." She typed some notes into her phone before setting it down on the table.

"It's definitely better in person."

Roberto approached, and Jackson pushed to his feet. Happy to see him. He'd missed his friend. The older man pulled him in for a hug. "So nice to see you, my friend. I miss having you around the corner."

"Miss you, too, buddy. Let me introduce you to—" he attempted an introduction, but the older man would have none of it.

Roberto put his hand up and smirked. "No need. Peyton, I've heard so much about you. It's a pleasure to finally meet you."

"It's very nice to meet you, Mr. Grazano, and may I say, your restaurant is gorgeous. It's quite inspiring."

"Well, of course you *may say,* as often as you'd like. Nothing better than a compliment from a beautiful woman. And please, call me Roberto." He winked. His friend would enjoy giving him a hard time tonight. Familiar of his history with Peyton, a topic of conversation many times over the years.

"Thank you so much, *Roberto*," she teased.

A pink hue climbed her cheeks. Not obvious to most, but he didn't miss it.

"So Jackson is ready to take the leap and open his own place. You have no idea how many conversations over the years we've had about this dream of his. I'm so happy to get to see it come to fruition." Roberto smiled as the server brought over the bottle of wine.

"It's amazing. I'm glad he has you as a mentor. Lago's will have a huge impact on the design at PBV

Bistro." He liked hearing the name of the restaurant roll off her soft pink lips.

"I believe Jackson has many inspirations helping him through the process. I'm guessing his designer brings him a ton of support," Roberto said.

"It's all part of the job. I look forward to you coming out to visit the Bay area for the grand opening."

Roberto smiled. "I wouldn't miss it. What do you think of the name PBV Bistro, Peyton? It's got a nice ring, doesn't it?"

He chuckled at Roberto's blatant attempt to make him squirm. But Jackson didn't squirm. He shot Roberto a warning look, which only made the older man's grin spread wider.

"Yes. It sounds great." Peyton fiddled with her napkin.

He stopped pushing, at least for the moment. "Okay, I'll check on you soon. You two enjoy dinner. I'll join you for a glass of wine after."

"Sounds good. We're set for lunch tomorrow? My treat." He wanted to spend some time with his old friend away from his place of work.

"Of course. Looking forward to it."

Someone from the kitchen called for him, and he rushed off.

"What are you hungry for?" he asked, looking over the menu.

"I can't decide between the steak and the salmon."

"Why don't we order both and share?" he suggested. They'd done this in the past many times, so it seemed like the natural thing to do.

"Perfect."

"So do you think you have a good vision for the

bar area now? This is by far my favorite layout."

"I do. I had an idea of what to do before, but now I'm certain which direction to take things. This place has an industrial vibe, yet it manages to remain warm at the same time. I like it. It's unique in the way it brings in so many different elements, yet they all tie together." She hesitated as if she wanted to continue but stopped.

"Something on your mind?"

"Does Roberto know what PBV stands for?" She gathered her hair, pulling it over one shoulder.

He sipped his wine before setting down the glass. "He does."

"I think you need to consider changing the name. Once you do it, you can't go back."

"I'm not changing it."

She blew out a frustrated breath. "So what happens when you get married someday? You think your wife will be okay with you naming your restaurant after an ex-girlfriend?"

He chuckled. "Now you're marrying me off?"

"It's possible, Jackson. You're not thinking this through."

He'd made her a promise. Though a lot changed between them, he'd never strayed from his vision for his restaurant, including the name he'd chosen so many years ago. He understood her apprehension now, but he'd made up his mind a long time ago, and he had no intention of changing it.

"I have thought it out. Hell, I've had years to think about it."

She ran a finger over the stem of her wineglass. "Why not use *your* initials?"

"I don't have a middle name. Are you suggesting I

name it JV Bistro? It would be like asking people to eat at the junior varsity bistro. Would you eat there?"

A grin spread across her face. "You know you're ridiculous, right?"

"I do, and I'm fine with it."

"Seriously, I don't want this to cause problems for you later."

"It won't."

"How can you be sure?"

One thing he remembered about Peyton—she didn't let things go. Ever. She wanted an answer, so he'd give it to her.

"I don't intend on getting married."

She choked on her wine and reached for her napkin to cover her mouth. He offered her help, but she put her hand up to indicate she was okay.

"How do you know you won't get married in the future? You're young."

"It's not something I want."

"Why not?"

Fucking persistent. He cracked his knuckles and shifted in his seat. "Jesus, Peyton. I don't know why you can't leave it alone. I date plenty of women. I don't want to get married. It won't be a problem if I name my restaurant what *I choose* to fucking name it."

She leaned back in her seat. "Okay, if you say so."

He was agitated; it took a minute to control the nerve she hit. He sipped his wine. The truth was, he'd been in love with one girl in his life. And he'd bedded plenty since, so it wasn't like he hadn't tested waters. Peyton was his first love, and he was damn certain she would be his last. And he was okay with that. He'd changed. Like a car after it'd been in a horrible accident. It never truly recovered. The flaws lay beneath the surface. Forever damaged. And it didn't matter how many new fucking coats of paint you tried to use. The dings were too great. And he'd spent years reining in those feelings and locking them away a long time ago.

"You've been through a lot, and I wish I could've been there to help you. I loved Chloe, and I knew her for a long time. She would want you to live your life. You know she would."

Goddamn this woman. Always coaxing and prodding. Needing more. More than he had to offer. He nodded to the waiter to refill their glasses. She deserved more of an explanation for what had happened, and he wanted to give it to her.

"You know, people say sorrow eventually fades. It hasn't faded for me, Pea. Not by a long shot. On days when I don't wake up in pain, I punish myself for not feeling it."

She interrupted, speaking just above a whisper, "Jackson."

Unease rolled through him. Memories flooding back to the day his heart split in half. He put up a hand. "Let me say this to you. It's taken me a long time to get here. Chloe's death changed me. My little sister was murdered. I could have saved her. My fucking selfishness cost Chloe her life."

"What are you talking about? You can't believe it was your fault?"

The concern in her eyes took him back in time. When he was unreachable no matter her efforts. And hell—he still was. He'd played a role in his sister's death and hurt Peyton by walking away, all in one foul swoop.

"She begged me to let her come to your house that night. But I wanted to be alone with you. I didn't want to share our last night together with anyone. Had I said yes, my sister would still be alive right now."

Before he could say another word, she stood, moving toward him. She knelt in front of him; one of her small hands cradled the side of his face. "Don't you dare do this to yourself. It's not fair. Your mom hung out with bad people, Jackson. You had no control over what she did. Ryker Jonze is responsible for Chloe's death. Not you. *Never you.* You protected your sister and loved her. We were young and in love. Who's to say Ryker wouldn't have been there the next day or the day after? You had no way of knowing what would happen. You can't do this to yourself. I won't let you."

Love for this woman hit him hard. Peyton knew him better than anyone did, and though he held himself responsible for his part in his sister's death, it was nice to hear she didn't. He owed her more. She needed to understand why he'd left her all those years ago. Waiting until she returned to her seat, he took a healthy swallow of wine.

"Well, I can't change what happened. I've accepted it. But you need to know I didn't leave you because I blamed you. I never, ever blamed you for any part of this. How could I? I never considered the idea of you thinking I did. I left Tahoe because I couldn't be what you needed anymore. You know, Pea, I believe everyone has one true match. I just happened to meet mine at the wrong time. You were it for me. Nothing in the world could have kept me from you. I would have bet my life on it. Then the fucking unimaginable happened. I put my own personal needs before protecting my sister. This is on me. I was fucking selfish. There's nothing I can do to change what happened. So letting you go was the price I paid for what I did. Not everyone deserves to be happy. But you do, Pea. And it's important you understand why I left."

His words stole the air from his lungs, and a sharp pain hit the center of his chest. Liquid pooled in her eyes. *So fucking tragic.* In the end, he'd hurt everyone he loved. Moreover, his sister, Chloe, had paid the ultimate price.

Her voice cracked with emotion. "Chloe's death was not your fault."

"But it could have been avoided. I left her alone. I should have kept her safe. It's something I have to live with."

She reached across the table, wrapping her hand around his. "But you are not responsible, Jackson. You were a kid. You did the best you could, and Chloe loved you so much. Ryker is responsible, not you. I think you know it deep down. Sometimes things are out of our control. And Chloe's death was tragic and horrible, but it was out of your control."

"The parole board contacted me. The fucker requested early parole. If it's the last thing I do to honor my sister, I will make sure he never sees the light of day." His desire for vengeance at times could be all consuming. His training and fights helped to keep it reined in. Under control.

"He deserves to rot in hell," she hissed, pulling her hand away when the waiter approached their table.

He set down their dinner plates and refilled their wine. Jackson picked up his glass and waited for her to do the same.

"Here's to Ryker Jonze. May he spend the rest of his miserable life stuck in his own little corner of hell."

"I'll drink to that," she said, clinking their glasses together.

"So are you good with the name of the restaurant? I mean, I'm not changing it. But I don't want you to be upset about it."

Her beautiful mouth curved, and he yearned to kiss those perfect pouty lips. Just one taste. Still a selfish prick wanting her the way he did. Didn't have a fucking clue how he'd survive the next few weeks.

"Yes, of course I'm good with it. Thank you for telling me all of this. I'm sure it isn't easy to talk about. But it helps me, you know, to hear what you were feeling. Even all these years later."

"I owed you an explanation. Should have done it years ago."

"It doesn't matter. I'm just glad you told me." Her gaze filled with understanding, softening some of the hard edges surrounding his heart.

"I am, too."

He needed to let go of some of this turmoil. Apologizing was a start.

"So I'm curious. Is this why you came to San Francisco and found me? Why now?"

Goddamn, this woman never stopped reminding him why he'd given her his heart so long ago. She never backed down. Long, dark hair tumbled over her shoulders when she reached over and snatched a piece of salmon. Her blouse dipped low, granting him a glimpse of her black lace bra. He yearned to touch her. To taste her.

"I needed to apologize and make peace with you. It's haunted me for a long time. The way I left. The fact is, I shut you out and gave you no explanation."

It was an honest answer. She leaned over his plate again and forked an asparagus spear. "Well, you set up temporary residence in San Francisco and named your restaurant after me. It's an awfully generous peace offering."

"What can I say, Peanut? I'm a generous guy."

She laughed, and the mood lightened. They visited memories he hadn't allowed himself to think of in many years. The conversation and the wine flowed freely. Roberto joined them, sharing stories from the past. After the short Uber back to the hotel, they agreed to meet in the morning to work out.

Pausing at her door, she slid the key in, before turning to face him. "Thank you for sharing what you did tonight."

He leaned forward and brushed his lips against her cheek. "It shouldn't have taken me this long."

His breath came hard and fast when their skin touched. He'd never wanted anyone or anything the way he wanted her right now. Her phone rang, causing her to jump. He stepped back when she looked down at her screen.

"It's Sebastian. I better take this. He's called a few times."

The douchebag's timing was impeccable. Had to give the guy props. "Sure. See you in the morning, Pea."

"Hey, Jackson."

"Yeah?"

"I'm glad you came back."

"So am I."

She answered her phone, but he didn't miss the heat in her stare when she looked back at him before stepping in her room. Didn't doubt she wanted him as much as he wanted her. However, acting on it would complicate things. She was already getting into places he hadn't allowed anyone in years. And the biggest surprise of all—he liked her there.

Chapter Six

Present

"Remind me again why we had to get up so early to exercise?"

"The early bird gets the worm," Jackson said matter-of-factly while she struggled to keep his brisk walking pace.

"Eww. Some of us don't want the worm."

"Interesting, since you're already dating the worm." His sarcastic tone irritated her.

She glared. "What's your problem with Sebastian? You barely know him."

He ignored her question, pausing to stretch. Navy joggers hung low on his hips, and the fitted white T-shirt stretched across his muscled chest when he bent over. His hair was still rumpled from sleep, yet he managed to look like he graced the cover of *GQ* magazine. The crisp and cool air sent a shiver down her spine. Thankfully she'd planned for it with her leggings, long-sleeve tee and pullover.

They walked to a beautiful park just mere steps from the hotel. A paved path curved around the perimeter, and tall trees hovered above. Runners and cyclists roared by. Dog walkers hurried along. Their pups ran alongside them. The smell of autumn filled the air, and fallen leaves covered the path. Splashes of yellow, red, and orange splattered the ground like a painting. She leaned against a bench, attempting to look like she was stretching, sneaking in a few stolen glances whenever possible. The man so strong and determined. Jackson was *that guy*. You know, the one who liked to put in his eight- to ten-mile run before the rest of the world got out of bed. She didn't work out often, much to the dismay of her two best friends and her sister, who were all on the fitness wagon.

"Okay, you ready?" he asked, guiding her to the path.

"I thought you were going to run?"

"It's a one-mile loop. We can walk one as a warm up, and then I'll run, and you can walk a few laps."

"A few laps? I'm thinking one loop and a bagel break."

"Bagels after."

"So bossy. Do you have loops or laps at every hotel you stay at?" she teased.

"Yep. You get used to it after being at the Naval Academy. It's part of my routine now. And *I* chose the hotel, remember? This is where I stay when I'm in New York." She couldn't help but notice two women turn to gawk at him when they jogged by. She didn't fault them. She had a hard time looking away, too.

"Good point. So what's with the snide remark about Sebastian?"

"I'm kidding. I don't know him." His voice remained low and smooth.

"He's a nice guy."

He glanced over at her. "It's pretty serious with him, huh?"

"Things are good." She cleared her throat. A week

ago, she wouldn't have wavered. Jackson's return was a reminder of the deep connection they'd once shared. Her relationship with Sebastian was emotionally shallow. Physically, there was no spark, but neither bothered her until now. Because for the first time in a long time, she remembered what it felt like to *want* someone. Her desire for Jackson, all consuming.

"Peanut, if we're going to be friends, we should be able to talk about these things. I haven't seen you in nine years, and I want to catch up."

"Okay, since we're friends now, let's find out things friends should know about one another." She huffed and puffed, as it soon became clear his idea of walking and her idea of walking were very different. Her cardio routine included window-shopping and an ice cream cone. She pulled her jacket up and over her head, tying it around her waist. The sun made its way out from the clouds, and she actually broke a sweat. Her phone lit up with a text from Wolf.

I would like to set up a photo shoot with the press the day you arrive home. Let's not plan any more trips until after the election.

She rolled her eyes before shoving her phone in her coat pocket.

"Good idea. Especially since you're already gasping for air, I'll start. How'd you meet Sebastian?"

"We were set up."

"Because he had a reputation for being a player before he started dating you, didn't he?"

"*Yes, Dad.* But he's settled down now."

Sebastian, an infamous playboy before they dated—was oddly the one who continually pushed to move their relationship forward. They were monogamous as far as she knew, and he gave her no reason to doubt him.

"Just want to make sure he's a good guy for you."

Her stomach twisted. Was he a good guy for her? She never stopped long enough to think about it, content with the relationship.

"Okay, my turn. So you and Lana aren't dating?"

"No. We're not dating. We went out a few times. Had some fun. Not much more to it."

Colorful leaves drifted down from the trees above. Fall had always been her favorite season, and experiencing it in the Big Apple made it even better.

"I'm surprised. The woman couldn't keep her hands off you. She's like a cat in heat," she joked, wiping the sweat from her forehead.

"I said I wasn't dating her. I never said I wasn't sleeping with her," he replied without inflection.

"Oh. *Ohhhhh.* Okay. And she's all right sleeping with you and not dating you?" She tried to keep her composure when the air left her lungs. Thinking of him having sex with Lana made her sick to her stomach. Talk about the irony—she wasn't having sex with the man she was dating, but he was having sex with a woman he wasn't dating. Hence, the reason she needed to be cautious. Jackson made it clear he wasn't looking for a relationship. She didn't need to throw away what she had with Sebastian for something she couldn't have—been there, done that. Life was about learning from your mistakes, not repeating them.

"No one's complaining." His voice held a trace of humor.

"Aren't we full of ourselves?"

"Just stating the truth."

"Lana's fine with your arrangement? I don't buy it."

"Says she is."

"At least you're honest."

"Yep. Enough about our current situations. Who was the first person you dated after me?"

The caution in his voice alerted her he was hesitant to ask.

"Benjamin Buckley. Sophomore year, college. Lasted a year and a half."

"Catchy name. You didn't date freshman year?" He didn't hide his curiosity.

"Nope."

"Why did you and Mr. Buckley break up? Kind of a lengthy courtship," he teased.

Why did talking to him have to be so easy? Her other relationships failed comparatively. She never trusted anyone more than Jackson, which seemed odd considering he'd been the man who'd hurt her the most.

"I didn't date freshman year because I wasn't…um, I wasn't in a good place. Benjamin was relentless and pursued me from the first day at Stanford. I gave in after a year of him asking me out. He truly was the sweetest guy, and he deserved better than me. So I ended it."

"What do you mean he deserved better than you?"

She rolled her eyes. "Easy, tiger. I'm not suffering from low self-esteem. He loved me, and I didn't love him back. No one deserves that."

"Well, if he's a good guy, I'm sorry it didn't work out," he said before he flashed her a wicked grin. "Nah, I'm over it. *Fuck Benjamin Buckley*. I'm glad it didn't work out." His laughter was a full-hearted sound.

She punched him in the arm. "Classy. Thanks. My turn. Who was the first girl you dated after me?"

A deep pit formed in her stomach, and her entire body tensed while she waited for his answer.

"I didn't date anyone for a long time. I'm not going to lie to you and tell you I didn't hook up with any girls, because I did. It took a while, though."

She relaxed a bit, hearing he didn't get over her all that easily. "How long is a while?"

He turned to look at her. Raw hurt glittered in his stare. "Seven months and a lot of tequila. I hooked up with some random chick, and I didn't even know her name."

"Eww, disgusting."

"You want me to lie?"

"Nope. Who was the first real girlfriend after me?"

"Not until the second semester of my junior year. Nice girl named Stella. We dated for four or five months."

She tried to appear casual and unaffected, but her chest ached at his words. She couldn't stand the idea of Jackson with *anyone*. It wasn't logical—but it was the truth. "Why did you and Stella break up?"

"Pretty basic. She wanted more, and I didn't."

"Sounds like we both took a while before moving on." Relief flooded her. And why learning he had a hard time getting over her was as good as winning the lottery, she would never know.

"Glad to hear your dad and Jayden don't hate me." A muscle flicked in his jaw.

"Of course, they don't hate you. They knew how close you and Chloe were. Everyone understood why you left. Well, except for me."

The memory hit her like a slap in the face. Such a lonely time. She'd lost both Jackson and Chloe in the blink of an eye. He'd been the center of her universe, and Chloe was like a second sister. The departure so final, she grieved for them both. Barely getting out of bed for days on end after he'd asked her to leave his house. It took her years to really recover from the loss. How could she consider risking it all over again? Being vulnerable was not an option.

"You didn't understand it because I'd promised I'd never leave you, after all you'd been through with your mother. And then I did the very thing I swore I'd never do to you."

"Maybe I shouldn't have expected you to make promises you couldn't keep. We were young." She winced.

"Nah. This is on me."

"You had your reasons." A lump formed in her throat. Hadn't thought about those last few days they spent together in a long time. The hurt. The loss.

"Did you meet Dani and Elle in school?"

Thankful for the subject change, she relaxed a bit. "Dani and I were roommates at Stanford. Been close ever since. We met Elle at Shine, and the three of us became the best of friends."

"You can have them come eat lunch with you at the restaurant anytime you want."

"Thanks. *My turn.* How does someone who's been serving time in the navy have the money to open a restaurant in downtown San Francisco?"

"Ah, I've been wondering when you would ask me this one. Remember how Joseph owned the trailer park in Reno, and the restaurant and the rental homes in

Tahoe?" He stopped when they completed a lap on the mile loop.

"Yes," she said, shielding her eyes against the morning sun, looking up at him.

"Well, his portfolio was quite diverse. Turns out he owned a whole lot of real estate in South Lake. When he passed away, he left me his entire estate. A bit more than nine million dollars. And he referred to me as his only son in his will." His tone reflected his awe and respect for Joseph.

She stared at him. "I'm speechless."

"There's a first time for everything," he teased.

She rolled her eyes. "He never told you he'd be leaving you his estate?"

"Nope. Caught me off guard. Had no idea. He left me a note to use the money to go after my dream."

"And he left you the resources to do it."

"Yep." He hesitated and looked around. She wondered what he was looking for.

"Go. I'll walk another loop. I'm sure you'll run several laps before I finish one."

"I'm not done talking yet. You sure you can't run?"

"This walk is the most challenging workout I've done. Ever." Her reaction seemed to amuse him.

"Okay, I'll find you on the loop."

"Go, I'm fine," she insisted when he finally took off running.

She smiled at a couple pushing a baby stroller when they passed. The mile loop left her hot and sweaty, so she slowed her pace. She walked along the path, looking up where branches joined, creating a canopy above. Little yellow flowers covered the branches. She thought about their conversation. About how much time had passed. A loud ruckus startled her, jaw hitting the ground. She came to an abrupt stop. What the hell? Jackson approached, pushing some sort of stroller.

"What are you doing?"

"I rented a jogger stroller. There's a little rental shack right over there. Now we can keep talking. I'll push you."

Satisfaction gleamed in his eyes, and an easy smile played at the corners of his mouth. She fought the urge to reach up and kiss his soft lips.

"It's for babies, you fool." She tried to suppress the growing desire she couldn't shake.

"The man said it's for toddlers *or* children. You're small. You can't weigh much more than a kid." He showed no signs of relenting.

"Jackson, I'm hardly the size of a toddler."

"With childhood obesity today, trust me, they make these things for all sizes. They can't discriminate against the chubby kids. Get in."

"Are you crazy? What if I break it?" Was she actually considering riding in the ridiculous contraption?

"I'll buy it if it breaks. Get in. If it costs me a couple hundred bucks, it'll be worth it."

"Ah, look at Mr. Money Bags. Big spender, huh?" she said.

"Get in, Peanut."

"Oh, my gosh, this is mortifying," she mumbled, climbing in. The seat ended up being pretty darn comfortable. She pulled her legs up and crossed them, so they didn't drag on the ground. People stared, chuckled, pointed, and gawked. Jackson sported a huge grin. Leaves fell from the trees above, and she reached out and caught one. The smell of New York hot dogs lingered in the air.

"You know sitting crisscross makes you look like a little kid, right?" His laugh rang in triumph.

Finally. Her new favorite workout. The jogger stroller. What a brilliant invention. He even bought her a hot dog on their fourth loop. She'd missed him.

This.

The realization that she still loved him was impossible to deny. Too obvious to convince herself otherwise. Probably never stopped. He was the love of her life. Then and now. Even if she couldn't have all of him, she wanted him in her life. In whatever capacity possible. Logic told her to run, but her feelings for him had nothing to do with logic.

After they cleaned up, she and Jackson met with Roberto, stopping by Lago's to take more pictures of the bar and prep space behind it. She took measurements to reference and scale to the space in San Francisco, which was much larger. Roberto and Jackson discussed installing a cutting-edge point-of-sales solution, the easiness between them impossible to miss. They were very close.

She closed her notebook and dropped her phone in her purse, and Jackson ducked out to use the restroom. She and Roberto were alone for the first time. Warm brown eyes in a still-handsome face studied her.

"I'm happy you're designing PBV for him," he said when he set his phone on the table.

"So am I."

"He's talked about you since the first day I met

him, over five years ago. I feel like I know you because I've heard about you for such a long time," he said. A warm and genuine smile filled his face.

"Really? I wouldn't have thought I'd be a topic of conversation."

"How could you not be? Weren't you two very close?"

"Yes. Of course. Very close. However, when he left, I figured he wouldn't look back."

He chuckled, placing a comforting hand over hers. "My dear, when tragedy strikes, you don't always think with a level head. Running from your past doesn't mean you forget what you've left behind. Sometimes one doesn't feel deserving of the good things in their life when they blame themselves for the bad."

She chewed her bottom lip. His words caught her by surprise. She'd wanted to be there for Jackson. But he'd pushed her away. Refused to talk to her after Chloe's death. How could he not think he deserved the good things in his life? He wasn't responsible for what happened, whether he believed it or not.

"I didn't know how to help him. He's stubborn when he wants to be." She'd tried to get through to him, going to his house every day, bringing food to him and Joseph, sitting outside his bedroom door for hours because he refused to talk to her. He wanted nothing to do with her at Chloe's funeral, and after the service he told her she would only be a reminder of how he failed his sister. In the end, he begged her to leave.

Roberto's boisterous laugh echoed through the bar, snapping her out of her trip down memory lane.

"His stubbornness is what made him an asset to the navy and a champion in his fights. But our strengths and our weaknesses are often one and the same." He inspected the glass votive on the table.

"Have you seen him fight?" she asked.

"Many times. He's magnificent. Nevertheless, I'd like to see him step away. I don't believe he fights because he likes the training. He uses it for other purposes."

There was wisdom and confidence in the older man's voice. He considered Jackson to be family and knew him well.

"What other purposes?" she whispered quickly, as Jackson walked their way.

"I believe he uses fighting as both a form of escape and self-punishment." He pushed to his feet when Jackson approached. A sharp pain took up residence in the center of her chest. If Roberto was right—the reason Jackson fought made her want to wrap her arms around him. Protect him. Love him. Tell him how amazing he was. In a matter of days, she wanted to let her guard down and take a risk. All for the chance to love this man one more time.

They walked into the café up the street. The place buzzed with loud chatter and conversation. Jackson told Roberto he wanted to take him somewhere away from work so he could relax. The smell of warm bread and pastries filled the air. Servers hustled around. When an older woman in her mid-fifties stopped at their table, they took the opportunity to order quickly. She enjoyed watching the two men together and observing their banter. Sitting back in her chair, she took in the boy who stole her heart so long ago. Happiness radiated from him. He'd grown into an impressive man. *A good man.*

Wearing a gray T-shirt and faded jeans, his dark hair tousled. Striking green eyes and a chiseled jaw shadowed with just a bit of scruff gave him a masculine, sexy look. Her fingers burned to touch him.

He caught her staring, his slow grin building. "What's up, Peanut?"

Butterflies fluttered in her belly. She wanted to climb in his lap, wrap her arms around his neck, and pull his mouth to hers. *She'd lost her damn mind.* All thoughts consumed by this man. "Just listening."

"She's beautiful, isn't she?" he asked Roberto.

Her pulse raced at his words. Wiping her now sweaty palms on her jeans.

"Just as you described her." Roberto winked at her.

"Now who's being *ridiculous*?" she teased, trying to hide her embarrassment.

"So Jackson tells me your boyfriend is running for mayor of San Francisco. Very impressive."

"Yes. It's exciting." She forced herself to think of Sebastian. Why couldn't he consume her thoughts?

"Peanut here could end up being the *first lady* of San Francisco." A muscle in Jackson's jaw twitched, yet he appeared unaffected otherwise.

"Let's not get crazy." She hated the spotlight. The campaign alone had grown overwhelming. It wasn't the life she wanted or one she saw herself living. At least not anymore.

****

Davis and Nelson came to the hotel bar to meet them for a drink at nine p.m. She liked them both a lot. They ordered appetizers for dinner and filled her in on their college antics.

"Jackson, being the asshole he is, shaved my left

eyebrow off our sophomore year while I was passed out drunk after finals," Davis said through clenched teeth. Nelson and Jackson fell back in their chairs in hysterics.

"Well, you had it coming. You did write *dickhead* across my forehead with a Sharpie the week before."

Laughter filled the small bar area, and she couldn't help but join in.

"Oh man, remember that? We had a huge wrestling tournament the next day. Coach was pissed." Nelson snorted.

"Yeah. I remember. When I won the match, the crowd cheered, 'way to go, dickhead.' "

Davis cringed at the memory. "Coach made me run laps and do drills for more than an hour in the hotel parking lot that night."

"Serves you right, douchebag." Jackson smirked.

"So, Peyton, tell us about the design for PBV. It's going to be similar to Lago's in the bar area, right?" Davis sat back in his chair, tipping back the last of his whiskey.

"Yes. Lago's will be the inspiration for the bar area, but we will tie in a more urban vibe to give PBV its own unique style. Here are some photos of a few rustic elements I want to bring in to the design." She handed the two men her phone, and they scrolled through the pictures.

"Wow. I'm impressed," Davis said, studying each one carefully.

"You definitely have the right designer leading this project." Nelson winked.

"I told you she's the best," Jackson said, handing his credit card to the server. Her stomach fluttered at his words. Her reaction to him almost overwhelming at times.

"You've been saying it since the day we met you," Davis razzed his friend, and they stood and said their good-byes.

"It was great to finally meet you, Peyton. We'll be flying out for the opening," Nelson said when he pulled her in for a hug.

"If this guy gives you a hard time, you just give me a call. I can fly out any time." Davis wrapped his arms around her and laughed.

"Back off, smartass." Jackson tugged his friend away.

Something had shifted between her and Jackson. She didn't know what it was. Maybe it was the way he looked at her or the way their gazes locked several times throughout the day. She didn't know if he felt it, but she sure did. And she wanted him. In every sense of the word. She would happily end things with Sebastian to be with Jackson. Maybe it was the two glasses of wine talking, or maybe she had lost her mind. For the first time in a long time, she didn't want to think. Only wanted to feel.

The elevator made its way up to the eighth floor. Her phone vibrated in her purse. Sebastian. She replied with a quick text, *busy day, let's talk later*.

He texted back, *I'll pick you up at the airport tomorrow. We'll talk then*.

She replied, *Okay*. She didn't want to postpone the inevitable talk. Dropping the phone in her purse, she looked up. Jackson watched her.

"Who are you texting?" His sharp tone did not hide his sudden agitation.

"Sebastian. He's just checking in."

"He's keeping tabs on you, huh?"

The elevator doors opened, he stepped out in front of her, and walked several paces ahead. What just happened? Why was he angry?

"What's your problem?" she yelled out.

Coming to a hasty stop in front of her, he turned around. "I don't like him."

"Clearly."

"Why are you dating this guy?"

She took a step back. His words stung. He had some audacity questioning who she dated after all these years. He'd left her, after all.

"I'm not even validating your ridiculous question with a response. Good night, Jackson." She pushed past him and made her way down the hall to her door.

"Ah, still a runner, huh, Pea?"

Her hands fisted at her sides. Why was he picking a fight with her? Why now? They'd had a great day together. All of this because Sebastian texted her?

"Takes one to know one, I guess," she hissed, fumbling through her purse for her key.

His arrogant chuckle came from behind. "Yeah, you sure as shit like to point out how I left. Maybe it's time you take a long look in the mirror, sweetheart."

Whipping around, her back to the door, she faced him. "Meaning?"

"You're so busy pointing your finger at me, you don't own your own shit."

She shook her head in disbelief, stunned by his words. "*My shit*? What are you talking about?"

"You heard me. Where the hell have you been for the last decade, huh? Yeah, you tried to be there after Chloe died, for what? Two weeks? Nine fucking years went by. I didn't see you making any attempt to find me."

A gasp escaped, and she struggled to speak. She needed to get away from him. Fury took over, and she turned to open her door before his hand wrapped around her wrist to stop her. Forcing her body back around to face him. "Why didn't you try to find me, Pea?"

Her breaths came hard and fast.

"You told me to stay away from you," she shouted, anger pulsing through every part of her.

"Well, I sure didn't have to work very hard. You never thought to reach out or try again? A year later? Five years later? I'll ask you again. Why didn't you try to find me?"

How dare he throw this in her face? This wasn't her fault. He'd told her to leave. Wanted nothing to do with her. She wasn't going to be a glutton—for what? For him to reject her. Again.

"You didn't want me." Her voice trembled when the painful words left her mouth. She hated how weak and small she sounded.

He pressed one hand against the door beside her head, trapping her there. "I get it, Pea. But this thing you carry around—this fear. You can't run from it. Your mom hurt you when she left, and hell, I know I sure as shit didn't help matters. But aren't you tired of being afraid? You never tried to find me because you were terrified of being rejected. And you're dating a douchebag because there's nothing to lose. He can't hurt you. And playing it safe is not living."

She wanted to slap him. Wanted to hate him. But even now, he still knew her better than anyone. She wouldn't shed a tear over her relationship ending with Sebastian because they never invested emotionally. Nothing compared to the connection she shared with Jackson.

She let out a long sigh. "What do you want from me?"

"I want you to stop being so afraid. I want you to be happy." He reached down and intertwined his fingers with hers. Her hand fit in his like it belonged there.

She looked up at him, wanted to savor this moment.

"Right now, right here, I'm happy," she whispered. A strong, sensuous current surrounded them.

His head tilted, his face close enough for her to feel his warm breath against her cheek. "You make me so fucking crazy, Pea."

Her breath quickened. His steady green stare bore into her in silent expectation. So easy to get lost in the way he looked at her. Her body ached for his touch.

"Crazy isn't so bad," she said, her voice laced with need. His gaze searched hers, and she met it dead on. Sure of herself. Certain of what she wanted. And she wanted him. No doubt about it.

His large hand cupped the side of her face and moved to stroke her hair in a gentle rhythm. Her senses leaped to life. His nearness overwhelming. She couldn't wait a second longer. She traced the rugged line along his jaw; his scruff prickled against her fingertips. His tongue swiped at the corner of his mouth, and desire engulfed her. His thumb stroked her bottom lip, and with silent permission, his mouth covered hers. Her wild-beating heart the only audible sound. His tongue parted her lips, sending shivers of desire racing through her. She tangled her hands in his hair desperate to pull him closer. His hard, strong body pressed her against the door. Her breasts ached with need. His moist, firm mouth demanded a response, and she welcomed it. His lips moved and seared a path down her neck before recapturing her mouth. Her body blazed, returning his kiss with reckless abandon. He pulled his mouth from hers. The move so abrupt it left her burning and desperate. She searched his gaze.

"Fuck. We shouldn't be doing this, Pea. I'm sorry. I shouldn't have let this happen."

She was still breathless. "What? I wanted it to."

Lifting his hands from her body, he placed them beside her head against the door, resting his forehead against hers. His breath came hard while he watched her. Rejection threatened and loomed. She could feel it.

Oh.

My.

God.

This was not happening. She lifted her arms to cover her face.

He pried her hands away, tipped her chin up, insisting she meet his gaze. "Stop. There's nothing to be embarrassed about."

"Why did you pull away?" she asked and tried not to crumble into a million little pieces.

He watched her, didn't speak for a long moment. "I can't give you what you want. What you deserve. I didn't come to San Francisco to mess up your life. You have a boyfriend, and you were happy before I showed up."

She refused to hold back. Fear kept her from

feeling anything for such a long time, and he was the one person she would risk it all for.

Again.

"I've never found anything close to what I had with you. Not with anyone. I'd end things with Sebastian in a heartbeat if it meant we could have another chance. For you, Jackson, I would walk away from anyone." She laid it all on the line.

"No, Pea. This can't happen. You deserve a hell of a lot more than I can give you."

Horror flooded her. Was he seriously going to give her the *it's not you, it's me* speech? She lowered her gaze to avoid his intense stare. How could she allow herself to go here again?

"Damn it, look at me," he growled, and a tear broke free and rolled down her cheek.

"Jackson, you need to leave."

"You think I don't want you? You're upset because you honestly think I don't want you?" He held her face, forced her to meet his gaze.

Umm—seriously? She'd offered herself up on a silver platter, and he turned her down. Now he wanted her to answer this ridiculous question? She moved to put the key in the door. His big body stopped her again.

"Peyton." He placed a hand on her shoulder and turned her to look at him. He rarely used her name, and the urgency in his voice caught her off guard. What more was there to say?

"I want you so bad I'm going out of my fucking mind. Hell, I've wanted you in my bed since the moment I laid eyes on you again. But I'm not a forever guy, Pea. Not anymore."

She let out an incredulous laugh. "But you didn't

push Lana out of your bed, did you? Do you reserve rejection just for me? You've made it clear you've been with many women. It's just me you can't cross the line with, right?"

Shame all but slapped her in the face.

"Yes. You're the only woman I'd refuse to cross any line with. And you *know* why. Hell, I'm naming my restaurant after you. I told you last night you've always been *it* for me. So yeah, this shit is complicated. I can't offer you what you want. What you need. What you fucking deserve. I wish I could. Hell, I don't want you to hate me again, and if this goes any further, I don't think you'll want to be friends with me in the morning."

Ouch. He wanted to be friends. She was willing to walk away from her relationship with Sebastian to see where things could go, and he wouldn't even take a chance on her—on them.

"Yeah, we can be friends. I hear you loud and clear. We're good. I'll see you in the morning. Good night."

He reached for her hand, and she pulled away, rejecting his pity. *Enough is enough.* She tried to close the door, but he put his hand up to stop it.

"I do love you, Peanut."

And this was how he showed her?

"Don't let the door hit you in the ass, Jackson," she said before slamming it hard enough it closed this time.

She wiped the tears from her face, processing what just happened. It hurt, but she was still breathing. And there was no shadow of a doubt now how unfulfilling her current relationship was. She would end things with Sebastian tomorrow—for herself, not for Jackson. And if Jackson Vance wanted to be friends with her, that's exactly what he would get.

He had friend-zoned her.

She would friend-zone him right back.

Chapter Seven

Present

He'd crossed the line last night before putting a
stop to their kiss. What the fuck had he been thinking?
Jesus. Her soft lips had urged him on. He'd wanted
more. Needed more. The hurt in her eyes weighed on
him. She'd actually believed he only rejected her. Only
stopped it to protect her—not hurt her. Doing the right
thing sucked. And it took a shit ton of restraint. The
woman did crazy things to him. Making him lose his
fucking mind.

He took the elevator downstairs to catch an Uber to
the airport, half expecting her to be pissed off, or at the
very least, thought it would be awkward between them.
But instead, she acted as if nothing happened. Appeared
chipper—almost bubbly. Unaffected by the fact he'd
nearly tore her clothes from her body in the middle of a
hotel hallway outside her room. Meanwhile, he hadn't
slept much. The kiss had continued to replay in his head
throughout the night. Three cold showers later, he'd
still been staring at the damn ceiling.

"So I did some research this morning and found
similar candelabras to the ones at Lago's, but these
have the darker wood, which will go better with the
floors you chose."

Huh? She wanted to discuss lighting for the

restaurant?

"Sounds great. Thanks for being so on top of it."
The only thing he wanted to be on top of was her.

"Absolutely. I'm looking forward to getting back
to work."

Once in the car, she focused on her phone.
Irritation flooded him. She sat unfazed beside him. He
didn't feel *unfazed*. Fucking miserable was a more
fitting description.

Once through security they boarded the plane. Not
a word mentioned about the previous night. Was this
the same woman who slammed the door in his face just
hours ago? The conversation remained light, as if they
were casual acquaintances. Like nothing fucking
happened. She opened her book after takeoff and didn't
look up again until the flight attendant came around to
take their drink orders.

"Can I give you a ride home from the airport?"

"So sweet of you to offer, but my boyfriend wants
to pick me up." A wider-than-normal smile spread
across her face, and for the first time today, he saw a
crack in her demeanor.

He scrubbed a hand over his jaw in frustration.
Couldn't have it both ways. He had nothing to offer her,
yet he seethed at the thought of her with the douchebag.

"How generous." His voice lacked any trace of
emotion.

She nodded, her lips pursed, before turning back to
her book and completely ignoring him the rest of the
flight. He'd asked for it. No right to be agitated. But
their goddamn kiss left him frustrated. He hadn't
thought of anything else in the last twelve hours. He
sent a text to his trainer, Mick, and asked to be

squeezed in later today for a workout. In desperate need to beat the shit out of something. Anything.

After picking up their luggage, they exited the airport. "Well, thanks for a great trip. I'll see you later," she said and turned to walk away.

"Where is he meeting you?"

"You don't need to walk me. He's at passenger pickup, and I can manage just fine on my own. I don't need a *friend* to escort me."

Ah, the queen of passive-aggressive behavior just showed her hand.

"I'm walking with you."

She managed to stay a step ahead of him, a big phony smile plastered across her beautiful face when she looked over her shoulder and chuckled. "Suit yourself."

Sebastian's driver stood outside his black Lincoln Town Car in the ridiculous uniform, and the douchebag jumped out when they approached. She patted Jackson on the shoulder the way a dude greets another dude in passing. "See ya, buddy."

Buddy? Seriously?

"Yeah, I'll see you tomorrow, Pea."

She flung herself into the bastard's arms. Sebastian appeared thrilled by her warm greeting. Yeah, he needed to beat the shit out of something. The sooner the better. He got in his car and drove straight to the gym. The next three hours spent pushing himself into a state of fatigue. He needed to get the thought of Peyton and the douchebag out of his head. Sleep would be his only escape.

****

"I don't understand why I can't go with you guys,"

Chloe pushed.

"Jesus, Chloe. I'm leaving tomorrow. I want to spend some time with my girlfriend tonight." He grabbed his car keys off the counter.

"I want to hang out with Peyton, too."

"She's not leaving for school for a few weeks. You'll see her after I leave. This is my last night with her." He walked toward the door.

"It's my last night to be with you, too," she shouted.

Taking a deep breath, he walked back toward her. "I love you, sis. We'll go to breakfast tomorrow, okay?"

She crossed her arms in front of her chest. "Fine."

Her blonde shoulder-length hair resembled their mother's. Her green gaze matched his and shone with a spirit full of fire. Her pink tank top and jean shorts hung on her scrawny stature. At fourteen, she was strong and stubborn and wearing makeup for the first time, an attempt to look her age. He adored her. But he needed tonight with Peyton. He worried about how his girl would handle the separation. Hell, he worried about both of them.

"Joseph's working late. Call me if you need me. Stay here in the house tonight. Mom's in a mood. I don't want you around her."

"Don't tell me what to do. You're not my boss."

Fuck. He didn't have time for this. Not tonight. He set down his keys and walked over to her. Pulling her into a hug.

"I'm sorry. Don't be mad. I'm looking out for you. Joseph said he's going to buy you a plane ticket to come see me at least once before I come home for

Thanksgiving."

Her stiff posture softened, and she wrapped her arms around his middle. "I'm sorry, too. I'm going to miss you. And I'm going to miss Peyton. I wish things didn't have to change."

"I know. I don't want things to change, either. But it's part of life. We'll get through it. Now, promise me you'll stay here tonight. I'll check on you when I get home."

"I promise."

He kissed the top of her head and rumpled her hair. She smiled and wiped the tears from her cheeks.

"I love you," he said, turning to look back at her.

"Love you, too."

The room spun, and he reached for a wall or something to hold on to for balance. When he looked back, his sister was gone. Screams came from his mom's trailer, and he hurried outside and down the driveway.

Chloe.

The ground tilted and turned, making it impossible to stay on two feet. He dropped down to crawl. Gravel and dirt grated against his hands and knees, and Chloe's voice shouted his name over and over. The faster he tried to move, the farther away the trailer drifted. A warm liquid hit his skin. He raised his arm and studied the blood covering his hand. Fear nearly choked him. He pushed to his feet and tried to run, but his legs wouldn't move. Air left his lungs.

"Take me with you, Jackson," he heard Chloe call after him.

He shot to a sit position, gasping for air. The same fucking nightmare had tortured him for the last nine years. It always started and ended the same way. A few months passed since he'd had one, but being around Peyton had him visiting memories he'd avoided for a long time.

His breathing still labored, he pulled the drenched T-shirt over his head and tossed it to the floor. Reaching for the remote and turning on the TV, he desperately needed a distraction.

Damn it. He scrubbed a hand over his face, his thoughts drifting to Peyton. Keeping her at a distance would be in her best interest. He'd never escape this all-consuming hell.

He checked his email, The realtor in Miami had sent him some properties. The sooner PBV was up and running, the better off everyone would be. He went through the pictures of each location and responded to the agent, letting him know which properties he liked and disliked, and asked him to continue the search. He'd be there in a few weeks to check them out, and needed to focus on moving forward. He spent too much time in the past lately.

****

Inundated at the restaurant since he returned from New York. Peyton submerged herself in work as well, and though he tried to keep his distance, an invisible force lived between them. She no longer called him buddy, nor did she bring up what had happened the last night of their trip.

Lana called multiple times, but he found one excuse after another why he couldn't meet her. He went to the gym most days after work and managed to stay busy from morning until night. The woman pushed to have dinner tonight, and he agreed. He could use the distraction. Walking out, he found his decorator extraordinaire putting her laptop in her briefcase.

"Are you leaving?" he asked curiously.

"Yep. I'm meeting Dani and Elle for dinner up the street."

"Where's Sebastian tonight?" He shouldn't ask but couldn't help himself. It drove him crazy night after night wondering if she were with him.

"At a meeting, but I may see him later." She looked away whenever she spoke about Sebastian now. Was she uncomfortable talking about her boyfriend to him after what happened between them in New York?

"Let me walk you to your car. There's been two assholes set up outside the restaurant all day." He hated the way the paparazzi stalked her. Sebastian did nothing to stop it, and it bugged the shit out of him. Jackson warned them to get the hell away from the entrance of PBV, but they'd leave for a few minutes and return. The sidewalk fell under public property, so there wasn't much he could do.

She let out a long, irritated moan. "I'm sorry. I can't wait for this to be over."

"Don't apologize, Pea. It's not your fault."

She hoisted her briefcase over her shoulder, and he slipped his hand beneath the strap to take it from her. The slight brush of contact against her fingers left him regretting the move. *Christ.* His desire for her was a fucking curse.

"Let me carry it out to your car."

"Thank you. Did you get all your work done?" she asked when they stepped out into the cool evening air.

"Yeah, I had a few interviews and feel good about the staff I've hired so far."

119

One of the dirtbag photographers lifted his lens; the camera mere inches from Peyton's face. "I swear to God if you don't get your fucking camera out of her face, I'm going to rip it from your hands and smash it," Jackson snarled at the piece of shit who took a few more shots before he stepped back.

"Thanks for running interference." She took her briefcase and placed it on the passenger seat of her car and looked up at him. The vulnerability in her eyes nearly knocked the wind from him. Was she scared of these guys? How could she not be? They were relentless and aggressive.

"Yeah, I'd like to do a lot more than run interference, but I'd be useless to you if I ended up in jail, right?" he said.

She laughed. "Don't be ridiculous. They won't do anything. It's just more of an annoyance."

"Why don't I drive you to the restaurant? I can come back and pick you up after." He could reschedule with Lana. His concern was Peyton's safety.

"No. I'm fine. But thank you. See you tomorrow." She gave him a quick hug before getting in her car. She drove off before he could argue, and the two guys were packing up their gear when he walked toward the restaurant.

"I don't think the future mayor is going to be too generous with you once he's in office if you continue to stalk his girlfriend," he hissed, hoping it would back them off. Sebastian could make it easy or tough on the press if he wanted to, if he were to win the election. He couldn't figure out why the guy didn't leverage some of his power to protect her.

One of the guys laughed. "If he wanted us gone,

we wouldn't be here."

What the fuck? Peyton said Sebastian had an arrangement with several press agencies offering photo opportunities of them together, and in return they would leave her alone when they were apart. Maybe these guys worked for themselves. He couldn't imagine they were from a reputable organization. He locked up the restaurant and drove the few blocks to meet Lana. Maybe an evening with her would keep his mind off Peyton.

"Hey, handsome," she greeted him at the entrance.

"Nice to see you, Lana." He kissed her cheek.

She wore a red dress, painted on like a second skin. Heads turned as they made their way through the crowded restaurant to a corner table. The woman oozed sex appeal. Unfortunately, she didn't do it for him. It would be a hell of a lot easier if she did. They shared no real connection. Maybe there'd been a physical attraction for him at first, but it fizzled. All because of one fucking kiss? He'd had sex with gorgeous women over the years. None ever rocked his world the way the kiss with Peyton had.

"How have you been? How did it go in New York?" she asked, resting her forearms on the table with complete interest.

Christ. In a way the trip to New York had changed everything. He realized dating other women was not going to be an option while he spent his days with the only woman he really wanted. Hopefully, once he got the hell out of this city, he could go back to his easygoing lifestyle.

"It went well. Peyton liked the design at Lago's, and I think it helped her grasp the vision for PBV." He paused to order a bottle of wine and some appetizers.

"Good. I read an article on her today. Did you know she was awarded designer of the year in San Francisco last year?"

Was she Googling Peyton? The article had come out over a year ago. Obviously she was threatened by Peyton if she were looking into her.

He leaned back in his chair, lifted his wineglass to take a sip before speaking. "I told you, she's the best."

"You did."

She sat in silence for a moment, as if she wanted to say more but hadn't mustered up the courage.

"Something on your mind?" he inquired.

"Are you sleeping with your designer?" she blurted before taking a long gulp of wine. Her ruby-red lipstick marked the outside of her glass.

"No." He ran a hand over his jaw, deciding how to go about ending this.

"Well, it's impossible to ignore there is something going on there. I didn't miss it the night I met her, and you've been distant ever since you went to New York with her." Her harsh tone surprised him.

Wouldn't have guessed her jealous or insecure. They weren't dating, nor were they exclusive. They'd only been out a handful of times. He'd been up-front with her from the beginning. This little tirade came out of left field.

"I've answered your question. You can take it or leave it. But my relationship with Peyton is none of your business."

She huffed, dabbed her mouth with her napkin before placing it back on her lap. "I'm sorry. I believe you. I got a little jealous. You're right, you don't owe me an explanation. But maybe I'd like to change our status."

"Look, Lana, I told you from the start I wasn't looking for anything serious. So let's call this done. End on good terms."

"I'd be lying if I didn't say I'm disappointed, Jackson. I hoped we could give this thing between us a chance."

Her eyes watered a bit. He didn't want to hurt her. He thought they were just having fun.

"I'm sorry if I misled you in any way. It has nothing to do with you. I've got my own baggage, and I don't want to complicate things with a relationship." He hoped this would appease her.

The waiter set down the appetizers and refilled their wineglasses.

"No, you were very clear when we met. I knew you weren't looking for anything. I guess I just hoped your feelings changed, the way mine have."

"I'm sorry."

"It really has nothing to do with your designer? My bat senses were going off the night I met her. She didn't hide her desire to gouge my eyes out," she said with a laugh. Relieved she appeared to be okay with his decision now, he relaxed. Impossible to hide his smile about Peyton's reaction to meeting Lana.

"Yeah, we're old friends. I've known her a long time."

"She's not dating the guy running for mayor, Sebastian Worthington, anymore, is she?"

"Yep." The mention of Sebastian's name agitated him.

"I recognized her the night we met at PBV because

of the pictures I've seen of them in the press. I thought they broke up, which is why I believed something might be going on with you two," she said, reaching for a piece of bread.

"Why did you think they broke up?"

She paused before finishing her glass of wine. "I probably shouldn't say anything. My best friend, Olivia, works at the Windsor Hotel. Sebastian had a few meetings at the bar recently."

"They both have careers. I don't think it's a secret. I'm sure Peyton's aware of his meetings." His gut told him he wouldn't like where this conversation was going.

"Well, he doesn't leave the hotel after. He gets a room and stays the night there," she said, just above a whisper.

"Maybe he's sleeping it off. Had a few too many drinks."

"Oliva said his meetings are with his campaign manager. He's a total creep. Sebastian takes the elevator up to his room, and a woman arrives shortly after and gets a key from the other guy. Security followed her, and the key is for the same room Sebastian stays in. It's happened a few times in the past week. Same woman every time, and it's not his girlfriend. They think they're really sly the way they go about it, but Olivia is dating the security guard."

What the fuck? Was it true? Or could this just be petty gossip people start because he's a public figure?

"There may be more to the story than your friend knows. They're still together, and Peyton wouldn't tolerate any bullshit," he said, defending her, but he didn't trust the bastard, so nothing would surprise him when it came to Sebastian.

"I hope you're right. If you tell her, please don't say where you heard it. I don't want to get my friend into trouble. Maybe it is just a vicious rumor," she said, forking a bacon-wrapped date and popping it in her mouth.

"I'll leave your friend out of it." He didn't have any idea how he'd approach it, but he needed to give Peyton a heads-up. Owed it to her.

"Thanks. I've got to tell you, for someone who insists nothing's going on, your face tells a different story. Are you sure she's just a friend? Nothing more?"

She's everything.

"Like I said, we have a history."

Chapter Eight

Present

Once back from New York, she behaved like the kiss, along with Jackson's rejection, never happened and ended things with Sebastian. He feigned sadness for thirty seconds before voicing his concern about how it would affect the election. Their breakup more like a business meeting. He begged her not to tell anyone for the next couple of weeks and keep it between them. Leaving no doubt she made the right decision.

She agreed to keep up pretenses until after the election, had no intention of dating anyone right now. As if joining Match.com and painting the town red was at the top of her list. She rolled her eyes. The only man she wanted to be with had rejected her for the last decade, so remaining single for a few weeks was hardly a challenge.

Sebastian called last night, pleading with her to come by the office this morning. She cared for him and wanted things to end on a positive note.

The air was chilly as she stepped out of the car with her pumpkin chai latte in hand. The only time she ever strayed from her standard order of black coffee was the month of October. The sun hid behind the clouds, and the street stilled and quiet as the city had yet to rise. A busy day ahead at the restaurant, she hoped this meeting with Sebastian would be brief.

"Good morning, Eloise," she said to Sebastian's secretary when stepping off the elevator.

"Peyton, it's lovely to see you. He's expecting you. You can go on back." The elderly woman was the only warmth in Sebastian's office space. The décor, a mix between contemporary and minimalist, with everything coordinated in black and white—the walls, the desks, and the artwork. The sterile and clean space fit Sebastian to a tee. She listened to the clicking sound of her black stilettos tapping against the white marble. The rest of the building remained completely silent. Pausing at his open door, she cringed to see Wolf sitting in the chair facing Sebastian.

"Hey," she said, leaning against the doorframe.

"Come in, please, sit down," Sebastian said. He hurried around his desk to greet her. He looked a bit disheveled, which was completely out of character for him. He tended to be as tidy as his office space.

"Thank you." She took the seat beside Wolf, wondering why he didn't excuse himself. She glanced in his direction, and he studied her with an intensity that sent a chill down her spine. Questioning her with his cold stare. The intimidating man with broad shoulders stood a bit over six feet tall. His brown hair lighter at the ends and donned blond frosted tips. It didn't look natural, so she assumed he hit the salon often for highlights. His trendy navy fitted suit, crisp paisley dress shirt, and flashy Rolex screamed money—so smarmy. The man made her uncomfortable.

Sebastian sat back down behind his desk. "So I asked you here today because I need your help."

"Okay." Her voice sounded more apprehensive

than intended.

"I'll cut to the chase. Dereck Cane is leading in the polls as of late last night. We need to be very careful this breakup you've sprung on Sebastian doesn't leak to the press." Wolf's voice was cold and accusing.

Dumbfounded, she gathered herself. "Excuse me? How is this your business?"

"He's my business, so unfortunately for you, *you're* my business, too," he hissed.

"Wolf, please don't speak to her with such disrespect," Sebastian insisted.

"I'm sorry if I'm coming off harsh," Wolf replied. "Peyton, everything matters right now. This election may go down as the tightest race in the last decade."

"I understand. I'm not doing anything to bring attention to our breakup. I've agreed to keep it quiet until after the election. I haven't even told my family we aren't together anymore. I'm not sure what the problem is?"

"Well, it may not be enough." Wolf's attempt at being respectful already running its course.

"Meaning?" She glanced down at her phone to check the time. She needed to get to the restaurant, and arguing with Sebastian's campaign manager did not fit into her schedule today. Or any day.

"We need to get a few photos of the two of you together this week. Can you join him for dinner this evening? I can set something up and have the press there," Wolf said impatiently.

"I have to work late tonight, so it will have to be another time. And since you're so comfortable with the press, I'd appreciate anything you can do to get them to back off. There are two men standing post at my office, and now two different men have planted themselves outside the restaurant I'm designing. It's bordering on harassment. They shove their cameras in my face, and they're growing more aggressive as the election nears."

Sebastian's hand hit his desk hard enough to cause her to jump. "This is unacceptable, Wolf. I've asked you to handle this situation several times."

"It doesn't help she's out with this client of hers all the time. I received a courtesy call this morning. This guy is some big name in the MMA world, and the last thing we need is the press to think there's a story there with you two." Wolf glanced down at his phone before he slipped it into his suit pocket.

What the hell? He researched Jackson? She'd kept their breakup from everyone but her two best friends and agreed to come to his office this morning to try to help. This is how he thanked her? She didn't owe Sebastian anything. Enough was enough.

"I've been out with my client? It happens to be the project I'm currently designing. In addition, he's an old friend. And I don't owe you any explanation, nor will I make apologies for going to and from work." She stood, letting them know the meeting was over.

"Peyton, wait. Please. I'm sorry. I don't know what's gotten into Wolf today."

News flash—nothing had gotten in to him today. He'd always been an ass. A bully by nature. Wolf intimidated people as a hobby. But telling Sebastian would be a waste of time. He never listened, nor did he do anything about it.

"I'm sorry if I'm being rude. I've been working on this campaign for almost a year. Night and day. And I won't allow anything or anyone to derail what we've worked for." Wolf stood and faced her, his stance daunting, his stare ice-cold. She forced her chin up and looked him straight in the eyes.

"I don't think anyone wants to derail what we've worked for." Sebastian scowled at his campaign manager and asked him to give them a minute alone.

After Wolf closed the door, Sebastian moved to stand beside her. "Jesus, Peyton. I don't know what's going on with him. I appreciate you helping me out. I'll make sure he handles the press for you. I'm sorry everything has gotten so complicated. Maybe if I weren't running for office, things would have ended differently for us. I'm still not giving up hope I'll win you back after the election passes. Campaigns are not easy on relationships."

Surprised at the sincerity of his words, she smiled. "Thank you for assisting me with the press. I will do what I can to support you through this. You know I want the best for you."

She didn't want to address the elephant in the room. There would be zero chance of them getting back together after the election. To tell him would be cruel, and pretending she wanted more would be a lie. Some things were best left unsaid.

"I do. Thank you for coming this morning."

"Of course."

He walked her to the elevator, and as soon as the doors closed, she let out a sigh of relief. The awkward meeting couldn't end soon enough. When the elevator doors opened, she ran right into a hard chest. Kenny Wolf. Startled, she stepped back in the quiet corridor, but he didn't move aside. Instead, he blocked her path, at first acting as if he were teasing her, then making it known he had no intentions of getting out of her way.

"So I'm glad I have you alone for a moment. I need to know what your angle is. And you're going to tell me." His harsh tone caught her off guard. Icier than usual. The air buzzed with imminent threat.

Her back stiffened, senses on high alert. They were the only people in the quiet lobby aside from two security guards behind the desk, who were quite a distance from her. She could scream if she needed, and they would hear her. Would she need to call for help? What did he want?

"Please get out of my way. I have no idea what you're talking about, and I don't appreciate you ambushing me," she said, trying to steady her voice in hopes of sounding brave, but it came out shaky and nervous.

"Let me tell you what *I* don't appreciate." He wrapped his large hand around her shoulder and squeezed. "I don't appreciate you ending your relationship with the future mayor just weeks before the election."

She wanted to slap his hand away, but the pressure he put on her shoulder left her trembling and unsteady. She sucked in a fractured breath, speaking just above a whisper. "Please let go of me or I'm going to scream."

He looked over his shoulder and smiled an evil grin. "Daryl and Roman are friends of mine. They'd laugh in your face. I have a reputation in the political world. Do you think anyone's going to listen to the decorator/ex-girlfriend? No one will give a shit about you in two weeks. So let's not be so dramatic. I'm here to remind you to watch yourself. You've got a few weeks to keep a low profile, do you understand me?

And don't go running to Sebastian with a story about how I intimidated you. I'll deny it, and since you broke the guy's heart, I'm guessing he'll side with me. You've done enough damage here for a while, don't you think? Keep in mind I have many people working for me. I have eyes all over you, so you better watch your step."

His thumb pressed hard against her collarbone, and her entire body shook. Releasing the pressure, he removed his hand, and a maniacal smile spread clear across his face. He stepped back and hit the button for the elevator. She moved away, and he laughed, maliciously. Shivers ran down her spine.

He leaned closer before letting her pass. "Too bad we didn't meet under different circumstances. I think I would've liked you. We could've had fun together."

Fear and disgust knotted inside. The elevator dinged, the doors opened, and by the grace of God, a man stepped off. The distraction allowed her to hurry past Wolf, and she didn't stop until she slipped inside her car. She gasped for air, as if the man stole the breath from her lungs. Should she report him? Tell Sebastian what happened? Would it make a difference? Sebastian knew of her discomfort, and he continued to work side by side with the guy. He even had Wolf at their meeting this morning, so maybe he wanted him to intimidate her.

She drove to the restaurant, and her hands trembled on the wheel. She thought about calling Dani and Elle but didn't want to tell them this over the phone. They would be upset and want her to call the police. Better to explain it over lunch today. The media would ruin Sebastian if this came out. For now, keeping her distance from Kenny Wolf was her best bet. He'd shown her what he was capable of. She wondered if Wolf hired the photographers outside of the Shine office and the restaurant to keep an eye on her. It was time to be more aware of her surroundings and have a plan ready if this happened again. She knew exactly who to ask for help.

The sound of a horn sounded from the street when she entered the notably quiet restaurant. The place usually buzzed early in the morning, but today it remained quiet along with the rest of the city. The construction crew wouldn't arrive until later, as they had to wait for the flooring to be delivered this afternoon. It would be a late night for everyone. The lights were on, so she assumed Jackson had beat her here. Moving through the bar, she found him staring at the newly installed brick wall. With his back to her, she took a moment to appreciate his male perfection before speaking.

Her attraction to Jackson hadn't simmered at all, and she was on edge from her confrontation with Wolf. Pulling her bottom lip between her teeth, she admired his defined back and broad shoulders. Her gaze scanned down, remembering how his lips had grazed against hers, the way they traveled down her neck, soft and possessive. She'd loved the feel of his hard body pressed against hers. Every square inch of her melting into him. Butterflies fluttered at the memory.

"Peanut," he said. His voice startled her from her stupor. He didn't turn around, yet he knew she was there.

"Good morning." She moved to stand beside him.

A wicked grin spread across his face as if he'd

caught her doing something sinister. His green gaze so magnificent it took her breath away. She understood he'd been through a lot, and she could even accept his reasons for leaving years ago, but she didn't understand why he kept her at arm's length now. He admitted he wanted her, too, but wouldn't allow himself to act on it. It stung, but a part of her didn't want to give up just yet.

"How are you this morning?" he asked while admiring the wall.

"I have a favor to ask of you."

"Name it."

"Well, this is going to be a bit surprising, but I need a trainer. I want to learn some self-defense moves. Can I work with someone at your gym?"

He studied her, impossible to miss the concern in his stare. "Did your asshole boyfriend touch you?"

"What? No. Nothing happened. I want to know how to protect myself. With the election getting closer and the press getting more aggressive, I think it would be helpful." She wanted to go somewhere private, and a big gym would be too public.

He remained quiet. Serious.

"And your boyfriend isn't concerned about your well-being? These photographers are aggressive. He's okay with it?" His voice was harsh. He picked up a water bottle from the table and took a sip.

What a loaded question. She didn't even have a boyfriend, and the photographers were not the ones posing the threat.

"He said he would handle it, but I want to know how to protect myself if I need to."

"I'm training for a fight in a few weeks, so I'm going to the gym six days a week. I'm sure my trainer has someone who can work with you. I'll text him. But if anyone's bothering you, Pea, all you need to do is tell me, and I'll take care of it."

"Thanks. I'd like to think I can take care of myself."

The man was all intense and occupied now. His shoulders tensed when he looked at his phone, staring like his life depended on it.

"Okay. You're coming with me to the gym tonight. Mick has a trainer who can work with you. We'll go together. I'll drive."

So bossy. However, she preferred to ride with him. Her run-in with Wolf left her shaken.

"You didn't just admit your trainer's name is Mick?" she said with a smirk.

He rolled his eyes, as if the memory just hit him. A wide grin spread across his face. "You aren't still obsessed with *Rocky*?"

"The Italian Stallion? Are you serious? I will *forever* be obsessed with him. It's the best movie of all time. And Micky happens to be the name of Rocky's trainer. This is meant to be." She and her father had watched every *Rocky* movie on more occasions than she could count, and she watched them dozens of times with Jackson when they were younger. She'd always ended up standing on the coffee table screaming during the fight scenes. They were her all-time favorite movies.

"It still fascinates me how much you love those movies. Not because they aren't great, but because a few days ago you sat in a baby stroller, so you wouldn't have to walk. You don't like to sweat. But Rocky, he eats raw eggs and beats the shit out of meat. He runs with a dog named Butkis. Your dog has a damn salutation," he teased.

Maybe the threat from Wolf and her unquenched attraction to Jackson caused her to lose it, because laughter escaped her, and she couldn't stop. He watched her with a genuine smile until he joined in.

Finally able to form a coherent sentence, she said, "I want to beat the shit out of meat, too."

He chuckled. "Fucking ridiculous, Pea. Listen to me. This gym is the real deal. He's doing me a favor. You need to go and work hard, or they won't waste their time on you. Mick is as serious as they come. He doesn't joke around."

"I want to learn how to defend myself, and I'm willing to work for it. I need to run home after work to get my clothes. Should I meet you there?"

"No. I'll follow you to your house, and you can drop your car off. I'll drive you home after. I don't want you going alone."

"Thank you for setting this up for me. I appreciate it."

"Nothing I wouldn't do for you." He slipped his phone in his back pocket.

There were a few things he refused to do for her, but she bit her tongue in lieu of reminding him. The rest of the morning flew by, meeting with vendors and opening packages delivered earlier in the week. Voices came from the entrance. Elle's southern accent fluctuated with excitement when Jackson greeted them. Her two best friends gushed over the space, and he brought them back to where she sat at the table he'd set up for them. Dani held up a large bag.

"Please say you brought what I think you did?" she

asked.

"It is. And we brought one for you, too, Jackson," Elle teased.

"Canes? Never had it," he said, grabbing a chair to join them.

"It's only the best chicken you'll ever have." Dani pulled out four boxes.

"It's not the chicken. It's the sauce. It's magnificent." Peyton tore into her box.

"This is some damn good chicken. Thank you for bringing me lunch. I'll let you ladies visit. I have a meeting with my wine rep in a few minutes."

"Jackson Vance, you just might be better than a glob of butter melting on a stack of pancakes," Elle said in a singsong voice.

"I believe this is her way of saying thank you for letting us eat here again." Dani shook her head with an amused smile.

Knocking his knuckles against the table, he smiled before walking away. She appreciated the time with her friends and filled them in on her meeting with Sebastian and what happened with Wolf.

"I don't even know where to start with this. You need to report him. This is not okay. The man is three shades of crazy town," Elle said, unable to hide the concern from her voice.

"She's right, Peyt. You're being threatened by Wolf, and you have no idea what he's capable of. And now you're lying for Sebastian. This is not normal. They are obsessed with this stupid election." Dani scooted closer.

She insisted things were under control and promised to file a police report if he did anything further. She reminded them to keep their voices down as Jackson didn't know any of this.

"You're not going to tell Jackson, why?" Elle whispered.

"He would fly off the handle about what Wolf did, and it wouldn't solve anything. Jackson would get into trouble, and I don't want to involve him. And what if this drama messes up the election? I can't risk it. As far as lying about my relationship with Sebastian, there's no reason to tell Jackson. We're friends. He'd disagree with me keeping up the pretense, and I don't want him to think I ended things with Sebastian for him. I did it for myself. He's not interested in dating me either way." She tried to make light of the sensitive subject with a chuckle, but it still stung.

"You should tell him. He looks out for you, and it doesn't hurt that he's a badass. He could intimidate Wolf and get him to back off. As far as you and Jackson being friends, obviously it's complicated for him. He's been through some serious trauma. We both see the way he looks at you, Peyt. He even told you he still loves you. And anyone who's around the two of you can see it. He's protecting himself, and he thinks he's protecting you," Dani insisted.

"Well, he's protecting himself *from* me for some reason. Anyway, promise me this stuff with Wolf and Sebastian stays between us."

"Promise," they both said in unison.

"Thanks, I'm glad I told you."

"But if anything else happens, we report it," Dani pressed, and Peyton nodded in agreement.

"So any more sexy dreams?" Elle, always the master at finding ways to lighten the mood, added.

"Nope. But the first one revisits me night after night," she admitted before she pushed to her feet and told them it was time to get back to work. She couldn't talk about Jackson without it reminding her of their kiss. The most amazing kiss. Thinking about what could have happened tortured her night after night.

Lust. Love. It was all consuming.

****

Cement floors covered the entire gym. The smell of sweat was overpowering as they entered, yet a faint hint of eucalyptus mingled in the air. A giant cage sat right in the center of the large, open room. Heavyset punching bags hung along the back wall, and sparring mats were scattered around the ring. Jackson gave her a heads-up about what an MMA gym would be like. She was a little nervous, but after the run-in with Wolf this morning, there was no time like the present to learn how to kick some butt. A man walked over, and they dropped their bags on the mat.

"Hey, you must be Peyton. I'm Mick."

"Nice to meet you, Mick. You do know Rocky Balboa's trainer's name also happens to be Micky, right? I'm sure you get it all the time."

An amused smile appeared on Jackson's face. "Fucking ridiculous, Peanut."

"Ummm, you're the first." Mick chuckled at her enthusiasm.

"How is that possible?"

Jackson leaned down and whispered, grazing her ear. The touch of his lips against her skin so overwhelming her legs trembled. "Rocky is a boxer. This is a mixed martial arts gym. Not to mention the movie has got to be thirty-some years old."

"*Classics* are never old. And a fighter is a fighter," she whisper-hissed back to him.

"Sounds like you're ready to kick someone's ass," he razzed.

Mick told them to run a few laps around the perimeter. A rush of nerves hit her hard. Never being much of an athlete and asking for this, she needed to give it her all and not look ridiculous in a gym full of real *athletes.*

They stopped to stretch on the mats. Mick sent Jackson off to do his routine and then spar in the cage with another trainer named Nico, while he worked with her. Running a few more laps in between some drills, she gasped for air. She did push-ups, burpees, sprinted up a set of stairs several times, jumped rope, and learned a few basic moves—she'd never worked so hard in her life. Mick wanted to get her in the cage to try a few of the moves he taught her.

"Vance," Mick called out.

"Yeah."

"Are you up for a little sparring with Rocky, Jr.?" he teased.

"There's no one I'd rather spar with," he said, and the smile on his face weakened her already shaking legs.

"You're not afraid of a girl, are you?" She wiped the sweat from her forehead.

"Let's see what you've got, Pea."

She stepped into the cage with him. Mick and Nico stood on the side.

"She's got a good jab, and I want her to try a few roundhouse kicks," Mick yelled out.

She bounced around, held her arms up to protect

her face just like Mick showed her. Remembering how vulnerable she was this morning, she listened carefully to everything he said.

"Okay, Peyton. Get in close and try out a few jabs on him," Mick coached from outside the cage.

"You want me to hit him?" she yelled, her breathing erratic. Jackson moved around with a smile on his handsome face.

"There's no other way to learn. Channel your inner Rocky."

She threw out a few jabs, surprised at how fast she moved. Mick continued instructions. She pivoted, and her leg came up fast, hitting Jackson in the hip. He jumped back with a chuckle.

"Caught you off guard, didn't I?"

"You're a badass, Peanut."

They went around and around for fifteen minutes, until her energy faded. This was one tough workout. It felt good. He let her jab and kick and try out new moves. Mick told her if she wanted to walk tomorrow, they needed to wrap it up. She reached for a towel, and Jackson dove at her before she could react. He grabbed beneath her knees while bracing her fall. One hand behind her head, he dropped her to the floor, and she let out a loud oomph in surprise.

"Caught *you* off guard, didn't I?" he mimicked her words. A sexy grin spread across his face.

"You did," she said breathless; her chest glistened with moisture, rising and falling, desire so strong her body ached for him.

Without warning, he pushed up. Standing over her, he extended an arm. Disappointment struck, and she stared for a moment before taking his hand. Mick introduced her to Jackson's sparring partner, Nico, another trainer at the gym. They worked out a schedule, and she asked to come five days a week.

"Impressive goal, Pea," Jackson said before guzzling an entire bottle of water.

Mick insisted they cool down before leaving, so they stretched on the mats, and Jackson showed her some of the basics.

"Do you fight so you can protect yourself? What's your motivation?" she asked, twisting her back from side to side.

"I like the idea of protecting myself, sure. I don't think it's my motivation, though. It's who I am. I like the competition. It's ever changing. I have to push myself. It requires control and discipline, which I need in my life. It prepares me for challenging times."

She studied him. "Does it help you cope with your anger toward Ryker?"

He rolled over and pushed to his feet. "I'm sure my anger plays a part in my motivation. It's what drives me. But anger alone wouldn't be enough to make me successful at this sport. It takes a commitment on many levels."

She understood why fighting was an outlet for him. Wished he didn't have so much anger bottled up. He drove her home and insisted on walking her to the door. Wolf texted to set up a photo op with Sebastian. Did he really expect her to reply? The man terrified her, and he'd threatened her this morning. Sebastian asked her to attend one event with him next week, and she agreed to go.

"I'm proud of you, Pea," Jackson said.

She opened the door and turned to face him.

"Thanks. I feel good about this whole workout deal."

"Awesome. Can I ask you something?"

"Of course."

"Is everything okay with you and Sebastian?"

Her stomach dipped. She couldn't begin to answer his question without lying through her teeth. "Yes, fine. Why?"

"I just heard something about him and another woman. It's probably a rumor, as I can't imagine the press wouldn't be all over it."

Sebastian was most likely already back to his old playboy ways, while he insisted she not date anyone until after the election. "Yeah, I've heard these rumors since we first started dating. People just make this stuff up. Everything is good. But thank you for telling me."

"Sure. I'll see you in the morning."

"Yep, good night."

He walked to his car, and she fought the urge to beg him to come back. Yes, learning to defend herself was priority, but lengthening her days with Jackson at the gym was a bonus. The truth—she wanted to help break through all the anger and fear he kept locked inside more than anything. If throwing herself into his passion of MMA fighting proved a means to do so, then she'd roundhouse kick her way right in.

Chapter Nine

Present

The more time spent with Peyton, the more he missed her when they weren't together. He wanted her in every sense of the word. A kick of possessiveness always at the ready when it came to her. She trained at the gym every night, walked real slow after her first workout. It was tough not to laugh at her grimace when she eased into her chair to eat lunch. But she went back for more the next day and every day since. The woman proved to be tougher than nails. It surprised the shit out of him.

He didn't believe her story that she suddenly wanted to learn self-defense. Swore on everything holy to beat the douchebag Sebastian to a pulp if he laid so much as a finger on her. At first he believed it was about the photographers who parked themselves outside her office and his restaurant. Yet her unfazed disposition around them made him wonder if something else had happened.

He spent his days at the restaurant with her, which now extended into the evening at the gym. She and Sebastian weren't in the press at all since Peyton and Jackson's return from New York, which he found unusual. A part of him hoped she went home from the gym exhausted every night. The thought of them

144

together made him crazy. After he told her about the rumor of Sebastian and another woman, she didn't appear concerned in the slightest. She either had a ton of faith in the guy or didn't give a shit about what he did. Neither made sense.

Spending almost every waking hour with Peyton, he needed to get the restaurant up and running and move the hell on before doing something he couldn't take back. But damn. He wanted her. All of her. Yet what did he have to offer? Branded with a forever scar. A constant threat at any chance of happiness. He couldn't afford to get in too deep with her. Being vulnerable was not an option.

Never again.

She deserved a hell of a lot more. He still hadn't told her he was leaving soon after the restaurant opened. His new manager, Ryan Cook, would take over. He asked Ryan to keep the details quiet for now, which proved what a selfish prick he was because Peyton deserved the truth. He just wanted a little more time. Liked having her in his life again. More than he should. He wasn't ready for it to end. Not yet, at least. Not until it had to. The blurred lines messed with his head. Consumed his thoughts. He hoped his life would get back to normal once he left San Francisco. Once he left Peyton.

They were having dinner at her father's tonight, which she'd put off the past few weeks. Something to do with Sebastian and not wanting to complicate things. He didn't buy it. The guy was so self-centered, Jackson doubted he did much of which didn't serve himself. Unless there were photographers set up at her father's home, he didn't see how joining them for dinner would be worthy of Sebastian's time.

Someone knocked at his office door. "It's open," he called out.

Peyton walked in and dropped in the chair across from him. A zip of arousal hit him. It was always in the air when she was around. Thoughts of desire grew more difficult to push away with each passing day.

"What's up, Pea?"

"You want to drive over to my dad's together tonight?"

"Of course. Are we taking ol' Whiskey with us?" He liked to tease her about her dog and his ridiculous name.

She fiddled with a pencil on his desk and chuckled. "Yes. We can grab him on the way."

"What about Sebastian? Is he meeting us there?"

"Nope. It's crunch time for him. The election is only three days away." Her gaze moved from his when she spoke. What wasn't she telling him?

"Okay. I'm looking forward to seeing your family."

He meant it, too. The Krofts were like a second family to him when they were growing up, and he'd missed them after he left Tahoe. Cutting off everyone important aside from Joseph and a few friends he kept in touch with over the years.

****

He and Peyton drove to her dad's after a long workday. Jayden asked them not to be too late, wanting to get Harrison home at a decent time for bed. They approached the entrance to Presidio Terrace, the upscale neighborhood in the city. The home sat at the end of a cul-de-sac, and he pulled into the drive of the grand colonial revival home. Peyton had grown up here. He'd visited dozens of times over the years. Gone to San Francisco to take her to every one of her high school dances. Not much changed on the exterior, aside from the growth of the trees and greenery surrounding the home.

Unbuckling, he turned to find her watching him. "What?"

"You look like a kid in a candy shop."

"I'm excited to see them. It's been a long time. Your family happens to be some of my favorite people."

"Mine, too. Can't wait for you to meet Harrison."

Light-colored cobblestone paved the walkway, lined with white and lavender hydrangeas.

Peyton pushed open the large wood door and called out, "Hello. We're here."

Her pup scampered off like he owned the place.

A high-pitched voice squealed from around the corner. "Auntie P. Auntie P."

She bent down, arms wide as a little boy sprang into her embrace. She scooped him up in a hug. "How's my handsome boy?"

"Fine." His little hand splayed across her cheek. Blond curls bounced atop his head, and large baby-blue eyes framed by long black lashes locked with Jackson's. This kid wearing a long-sleeve white T-shirt and khaki overalls looked like some sort of toddler you'd see on a magazine selling shit. He was *that* fucking cute. His bare feet rested at her waist.

"Just fine, Harrison?" she teased, nuzzled his neck, and tickled him with her kisses.

He screamed and giggled until pulling back. "He's

not yo udda fwend."

"Nope. This is Jackson. Can you say hello?"

"Hello, Thackthon."

This kid. Joy shone in her eyes, her adoration impossible to miss.

"Hey there, Harrison. Nice to meet you." He put out his hand, and the little dude grabbed a finger and shook it.

"Yo vewy tall."

Jackson was puzzled, completely clueless as to what he said.

"He is very tall. You're pretty tall, too, kiddo." She smiled, and he ran his finger down her nose.

Fucking adorable. Both of them.

Her father and his girlfriend came around the corner. He and Thomas Kroft had been close when he and Peyton dated. Jackson regretted the way he'd left them all without a word.

The man didn't hesitate; he pulled him in close for a hug. He held him there for a moment and patted him on the back in a fatherly manner before pulling away. "Jackson. It's great to see you, son."

"It's so nice to see you again, Mr. Kroft."

"Don't age me. It's still Thomas. I'd like to introduce you to my lovely lady, Lael."

They shook hands, and Harrison squirmed to get down. Running off toward the kitchen shouting about something he made for Auntie P.

Thomas chuckled and turned to his daughter with a look of adoration. "How's my girl?"

"Hey, Dad, I'm good."

He hugged her like he hadn't seen her in years, yet Jackson knew they saw one another often. So genuine.

Even though Thomas Kroft had suffered a big blow when his wife walked out on their family, he never let it derail himself or his girls. Jackson admired him. Wished he could say the same. Life dealt him a blow, and the wheels came off the cart. Nothing would ever be the same.

Peyton and Lael embraced. An easiness buzzed between them.

"Jackson Vance. Say it isn't so," Jayden said in a sing-song voice, as she and Zach came around the corner. She greeted him with a warm hug.

"Hey, J.J. So good to see you." Yep. He had a nickname for Jayden Jaqueline Kroft as well.

Zach pulled him in next. "Missed you, buddy. Really happy you're back."

"Me, too," he said, voice filled with emotion.

They made their way into the kitchen; the enormous home managed to feel comfortable and welcoming. Peyton must have remodeled it since he was last here. The white cabinets and white marble countertops gave the room a bright, open feel. The Viking stove held six burners and a griddle in the middle. He knew his appliances, and these were top-of-the-line.

Harrison sat at the island coloring a piece of paper. "Here, Auntie P. It's fo you."

He handed her a drawing of two stick people, one with brown hair and one with yellow.

"Which one are you?" Jackson teased.

"I'm the wewo one."

They sat around a large farm table, and Jayden poured everyone a glass of wine. "Peyton filled us in on the Naval Academy and your service. Impressive stuff,"

Thomas said, and Jackson appreciated it. Approval from a man he admired most of his life meant a lot.

"Thank you. It was a great experience."

"Do you still wrestle at all?" Zach questioned in between sips of wine. Zach, a bit of a sports fanatic, had come to see Jackson wrestle many times in the past.

"No. I do mixed martial arts now. I like the variety you get with it."

"Is it like UFC fighting?" Jayden inquired, pulling her little boy down from his chair and carrying him over to the table.

"Yep. UFC is for pro fighters. I do amateur fights."

"Any plans to enter any fights? I've been to a few. It'd be much more fun if I knew one of the fighters."

"Yes. I have a fight in a few weeks. Ask my training partner over here. She's an animal in the gym."

They gaped at Peyton in surprise.

"You told me you were going to the gym, but I imagined a few minutes on a treadmill followed by a long steam in the sauna." Jayden did not hide her surprise.

"Well, you know I have a thing for *Rocky*," Peyton said.

"Best movie ever," Thomas chimed in, giving his youngest daughter a high five across the table.

"Jackson's trainer's name is Mick. Does it get any better?" She raised her eyebrows and smirked at him. Pain hit him hard in the chest. How would he walk away from her again? They could keep in touch from a distance, sure. But it wouldn't be the same.

Stroking the stubble on his chin, he met her smile. "It doesn't get any better." And he wasn't referring to his trainer's name. Her smile did crazy things to him.

Turned him inside out.

"Where's Sebastian this evening?" her father asked.

"His meetings ran late today." She flinched, trying to hide her discomfort, but he knew her. Knew when she was lying. Knew when she was hiding something. And she was definitely keeping secrets.

Her father nodded. "The election is right around the corner. I'm sure he's under tremendous stress."

"Yes. He's been working a lot."

The air in the room shifted. Why would the mention of her boyfriend be such a touchy subject? Maybe they knew he was a douchebag, too.

"He let you have a night off from the paparazzi this close to the election?" A bite of resentment laced her father's tone as he looked at her.

"We have an event tomorrow evening. I'm sure there will be plenty of photographers," she said.

"It's got to get old, right?" Jayden interjected.

"It comes with the territory."

"Within reason, Peyton," her father said, his voice harsher than before. "You need to make sure Sebastian does what he can to protect *you* from it."

Obviously, her father didn't like photos of his daughter splashed all over the Internet. Afterward, the rest of the evening went off without a hitch. Lael made a delicious dinner, and Jayden brought dessert. They laughed and reminisced, and Harry entertained them throughout the night. Like no time had passed since he'd seen them last, picking up where they left off.

All too soon he and Peyton said their good-byes. Zach and he exchanged phone numbers, and he agreed to send him the details of his fight. Her family members promised to come for the opening of PBV Bistro in a couple weeks.

There was hardly any traffic when he pulled out on the road. "What a great night."

"Yeah. It was really nice to get everyone together."

"They haven't changed at all."

"Neither have you," she said.

"I've changed more than you think, Pea."

"I disagree. Not to me."

"Well, you tend to see things through rose-colored glasses." He didn't want to let the conversation get too serious, because it always led to dangerous territory. Their connection. Their attraction. Always simmering just beneath the surface.

Exactly where it needed to stay.

"So you have an event with Sebastian tomorrow?"

"Yeah. Last one before the big day. It's going to be a relief when it's finally over."

"I'll bet." He wanted to press her but thought better of it. Her dad had given her a hard enough time about the douchebag.

As they walked toward her door, two men sprang from the bushes with cameras. One came so close she stumbled back and almost hit the pavement. He caught her by the top of her arm and steadied her.

"What the fuck do you think you're doing? You almost hit her. This is private property," he shouted, getting in the guy's face, while the other photographer snapped pictures of them.

"He's not worth it. Come on," she said, reaching for his hand to pull him inside.

"You might want to get out of here. The police will be here shortly," Jackson yelled, shielding her protectively beside him with one arm wrapped around her.

"Such a caring client," one of the men taunted, but they were inside before Jackson could respond.

"Jesus, Pea. This is not okay." Agitated, he scrubbed a hand over his face and peered out the window, watching them drive away.

She walked to the back door to let Mr. Whiskers outside. Jackson trailed behind.

"I'm so over this," she admitted.

"I don't understand how Sebastian is okay with them following you. I thought you said he had some sort of arrangement with the press." He paced, running a hand through his hair.

"Some just choose not to listen. I don't know what else he can do."

"What else he can do? Jesus, Pea. How about call them off. Make some goddamn noise. Call their boss. Or punch them in the fucking throat. I'd be happy to assist."

"I'll talk to him. It'll be over soon."

When he opened the front door, apprehension flooded him. But staying wasn't an option; she had a goddamn boyfriend. "All right. Lock up and set your alarm. Call me if you need me. I can be here in five minutes."

"You're ridiculous. They aren't going to break in for a photo. They just like to catch you off guard," she said, leaning against the doorframe.

"Lock the door," he insisted, waiting until he heard the click before getting in his car. Leaving her grew more challenging with each passing day. The more time he spent with her, the more he needed her. Wanted her.

****

The next morning, several text messages lit up his phone. Bob, Peyton, Zach—all saying the same thing. *Read the Chronicle.* One of the scumbags had sold a picture of the altercation from last night. *Jackson saw red.* In the photo, he held Peyton close to him in a protective manner. His finger pointed in the face of the asshole who'd almost hit her with his camera. It would raise some eyebrows. The caption read…

BODYGUARD? CLIENT?
OR SOMETHING MORE…

Fuck. He replied to her text before jumping in the shower.

You okay?

Yes. It's fine. They like to twist everything into a story.

And, he'd sure given them a hell of a story with this photo.

Okay. See you at the restaurant soon.

He walked to the bathroom. His phone pinged with Peyton's response.

I'm leaving now. I want to get an early start because I'll have to leave early for the event tonight.

When he pulled up to PBV, Sebastian's driver sat out front in the car. Her boyfriend so far under his skin, his mere presence aggravated him. He hadn't come by the restaurant in weeks, but one picture of he and Peyton together, and Sebastian came running. The guy always looked out for number one. He'd be lying if he didn't admit to being relieved Peyton's boyfriend was a douchebag. Hated the idea of her with anyone, but if he were a great guy who made her happy, it'd be a hell of a lot tougher to swallow. They didn't seem to spend much time together, and the few times he'd witnessed them in the same room, they were not affectionate.

Hell, he struggled being in the same city with her and not being able to touch her. He couldn't imagine what it'd be like if he could have her the way he wanted to. By his side. In his bed. He'd never take his hands off her.

When he stepped inside, Bob jerked his head toward the dining room and didn't hide his concern. Sebastian's voice boomed, whining how she needed to help him fix this situation tonight. What the fuck did he mean? He didn't like the way he spoke to her and didn't have to tolerate it in his restaurant.

"Everything okay?" His tone was harsh.

Peyton turned toward him with her arms crossed in front of her chest. "Oh, hey. Yes. Everything's fine."

Sebastian glared at him. If intimidating him were the goal, he'd need to work a lot harder.

"We were discussing the photo going viral at the moment," her boyfriend grumbled.

"Yeah? I'm guessing your concern is over the two assholes who jumped out of the bushes and almost knocked your girlfriend on her ass last night?"

A puzzled look crossed Sebastian's face. Something passed between them, but he couldn't make it out. He wanted to know why her boyfriend didn't show more concern for her safety. Her well-being. Jackson didn't give a shit how it affected the election. He cared about Peyton and keeping her safe.

"Of course, I'm not happy this happened. I've tried to rein these guys in, but they're out of control right now. It doesn't help having the press think there's something going on between the two of you. It sure doesn't make things easier for me."

What. The. Fuck. Easier for him? The douchebag was honest, he'd give him that. Yet the paparazzi stalking his girlfriend didn't piss him off? If he were truly concerned something was going on between them, where was the anger? The asshole was more concerned about what others thought was going on between them.

"You don't trust your girlfriend?" Jackson seethed. He wasn't going to watch this worthless prick disrespect her. He took a step toward Sebastian, stood just inches from him.

She moved between him and Sebastian, her voice calm. "Let's all relax. Sebastian is under a tremendous amount of stress. Of course, he knows nothing is going on between us."

Her boyfriend took a step back and ran a hand through his coifed hair. The man unraveled right in front of them. Peyton put a consoling hand on his back, her voice just above a whisper. "Everything will be fine. It's almost over. I'll see you tonight, okay?"

"I'm sorry. I feel like I've sacrificed so much throughout this campaign, and if it's all for nothing, I don't know how I can live with it," he said.

What a whiney little bitch. What had he sacrificed? It looked to Jackson like everyone around him made sacrifices. He didn't seem to do much for anyone but himself.

"It won't be for nothing. It's going to work out. But this is my place of work. We can finish this conversation tonight, okay?" She appeared anxious, desperate to end the conversation.

What kind of fucked-up relationship was this?

"You'll still come tonight?" His words were so

pathetic Jackson had to walk away.

"I said I'd go, and I will." Her tone impatient, she urged him toward the door.

Peyton escorted Sebastian out front. He glanced out the window, glared when she gave the douchebag a quick hug, the kind of hug you'd give to an acquaintance you haven't seen in a while, polite. How was she even with this guy? Sebastian stood there like some sort of lost puppy before she turned and walked inside. Something wasn't right, and he didn't like it. Keeping his mouth shut had never been his style.

"I'm sorry things are such a mess. I did not mean to bring this *here*," she said once inside.

"I don't give a shit about him coming *here* to talk to you. But what the hell is going on? He seems off. I don't like how he talks to you."

"It's fine. It's a stressful time. I really need to get to work."

"All right. You'll let me know if you need anything?" His gut screamed something was off.

****

Peyton's girlfriends entered the restaurant as he walked Calvin, the new bartender, to the door.

"Well, well, well, Jackson Vance. I do declare this amazing picture in the paper has made you famous as all get out," Elle said and gave him a hug.

He didn't care the picture went viral, didn't give a shit what anyone thought. "I think it's caused Peyton trouble. Maybe you can talk to her. Make sure she's okay?"

Dani studied him before giving him an appreciative hug. "You sound awfully concerned, Vance."

"It's because he's all fierce and powerful on the

outside but sweet as apple pie on the inside." Elle patted his cheek.

Elle was like a southern belle on crack most days, and he adored her and Dani. He'd grown close to Peyton's friends, which also wasn't part of the plan. Attachments were not a good idea. Hell, he couldn't deny the bond he shared with Peyton, and the people in her life were pretty damn great, too. The lines blurred between making peace with her, rekindling their close friendship, and wanting this woman in ways he couldn't wrap his head around.

He rolled his eyes at her. "You caught me. I'm one big soft piece of pie."

Both women laughed, walking toward the dining room to meet Peyton. With the flooring newly laid, the natural light caught the cool imperfections in the panels of the dark wood. Everything came together this past week at PBV, and each day brought a new transformation. He left the three women to their lunch, endless giggles filling the dining room.

****

At the end of the day, he walked Peyton outside before heading to the gym.

"Tell Nico I'll be there tomorrow," she said with a smile, slipping into her car.

"I will. See you in the morning, Pea." Noticing she hadn't buckled herself yet, he instinctively reached across and grabbed the strap. She caught his hand to stop him, and he froze when her fingers wrapped around his hand. His gaze locked on the gentle rise and fall of her chest.

"I can buckle myself," she said, her voice strained.

He met her stare, their hands still entwined on her

chest. "It should be the first thing you do."

"You know, for a guy who doesn't want to care about anyone, you sure seem concerned."

Her words surprised him. "I never said I didn't care. I said I wasn't a relationship guy. Big difference."

She removed her hand from his, but he kept his there. His fingers rested on the soft skin where her blouse dipped open. She sucked in a sharp breath. His need to touch her was stronger than his will to stay away.

"So are you going to stop caring once we aren't working together?"

Great question. What the fuck was the plan? How would he turn it off? He'd leave. Put distance between them.

"I don't know how it works. Of course, I won't stop caring about you. Don't be ridiculous. You better get going. You don't want to be late." He pulled his hand away, already missing the feel of her warm skin. The way her chest pounded from his touch, her body struck with the same desire he fought every goddamn second she was near. He needed her to drive away before he yanked her out of the car and pulled her back into the restaurant, where he'd fantasized a million times about having his way with her.

"See you tomorrow," she said, clicking her seat belt in place. The pain in her eyes nearly split him in two. He hated putting it there.

He went straight to the gym. In need of a good ass kicking. Liked the relief he got from being in the cage. He determined his training, his skills, and his abilities in a fight, though he couldn't control his opponents and the force they inflicted. A part of him enjoyed the pain as much as the victories. He thrived off every hit they threw, scrambled to his feet, and then attacked. The more they gave—the more he retaliated. A certain peace always came over him during his fights. Protecting himself, though it didn't mean he could protect everyone in his life.

"Jesus, Vance. What climbed up your ass today?" Mick asked, scrambling out of the cage.

He'd pounded the three sparring partners Mick put in with him. Jackson took things to the next level and it felt good. Fueled by nothing but the need to survive. Fight back. Take control.

"Nothing. I want to up my training with the fight coming up," he huffed out, toweling off the sweat pouring from his forehead.

"Uh-huh. It seemed like something more," Mick said, his voice serious, handing him a water.

"As my trainer, aren't you supposed to want me to beat my opponent?" he snarled, tipped his head back, and downed the entire bottle. He crunched the plastic in his hand when he finished.

"Beat your opponent? Yes. Pummel your sparring partner like your life depends on it? No."

Nico joined them, leaning up against the net surrounding the cage. "Thank fucking God I had a client tonight. I wouldn't have wanted to be anywhere near you or the cage, Vance."

Mick laughed, but his stare remained laced with concern. "I'm sure Conner, Jack, and Lee are wishing they were with clients, too."

Okay. Maybe he'd gone a bit harder than he should have. He needed it. He sure as hell wasn't getting any other kind of release these days. Hadn't been laid since he'd left for New York. Peyton consumed his thoughts. Mind, body, and soul, and it was fucking with his head. The thought of her with Sebastian tonight made him want to climb back in the cage and beat the shit out of a few more people.

"Where's our girl tonight?" Nico asked, watching Jackson as he spoke.

Both trainers had inquired about their relationship a few times. Most people at the gym assumed they were a couple. They had an unusual friendship. Connected in more ways than most. He told both Nico and Mick they were just friends on several occasions, but it didn't stop them from razzing him every chance they got.

"She's with the wannabe mayor tonight," he said, sounding harsher than he meant it to.

"Ah. Is she? Hmmm, and you're in a foul mood?" Mick teased.

"Fuck off. I'm going to take a shower." He grabbed his bag and gave them both the finger, which only fueled their laughter.

Hot water ran down his back, and his head rested against the shower wall. He knew better than to let this shit get the best of him. Needed to focus on getting PBV up and running before he moved on to the next one. He had a huge fight coming up in a couple weeks with a tough competitor and didn't have time for distractions. Peyton Kroft had become a distraction. In the worst kind of way.

Chapter Ten

Present

She had no desire to attend yet another formal campaign dinner, but it meant a lot to Sebastian. Tonight, his team rallied everyone and anyone they could to come out and support him. Votes would be cast in just two days. The picture of her and Jackson going viral caused him a great deal of stress, and she didn't want to do anything else to complicate matters. Leaving him high and dry when he worked so hard would be cruel. She didn't turn her back on people when they needed her most. Least of all someone she cared about.

"You look lovely this evening." Sebastian slipped into the car beside her.

"Thank you. You look nice as well." She meant it. Wearing a tailored black tuxedo with his hair slicked back, he leaned down to brush something from his pant leg. From his silver cufflinks to his black leather Gucci oxfords, the man knew how to dress. His mood better than earlier today, when he'd nearly blown a gasket.

"Sorry about this morning. Things have settled down. I mean, the press obviously likes the idea of you and the restaurant owner slash *cage fighter*." His manner so condescending and arrogant it got under her skin. "Wolf has been on the phone all day cleaning up this mess. There will be photographers set up outside the event tonight to take pictures of us together. We hope when they see you on my arm, it will be the image they remember when they vote."

Of course, Wolf would be all over it. The man so obsessed with Sebastian and this election. "I would hope voters are thinking about what your plans are for the city, not whether you and I are dating."

He appeared surprised by her comment. "Well, of course, in a perfect world they'll care more about my platform than who I'm dating. But we both know my popularity rose when I started dating you. The people of San Francisco view you as the girl next door, and they credit you for cleaning up my act."

"I'd say you cleaned up your own act. It had nothing to do with me."

"Not true, Peyton. You have a lot to do with my turnaround. I guess I didn't do enough to show you, though," he sulked.

Pack your bags, kids. We're going on a guilt trip.

Seriously, he'd been completely unaffected by their breakup aside from any possible fallout it might cause the election. Jackson had heard rumors about Sebastian being unfaithful—hypocrisy at its finest. She didn't want to bring up the rumor, because it would lead him to believe she cared he'd moved on. She didn't. Her gut told her there were ulterior motives where she was involved.

"You didn't do anything wrong. We've talked about this. We're just better as friends."

"It surprised me Vance didn't know we weren't together anymore," he bit out, making his distaste for Jackson clear.

"I told you I haven't even shared the news with my family. You asked me to keep this a secret until after the election, didn't you?"

"Yes. And I appreciate it. But a part of me still believed you ended things with me because of him. I figured he knew."

She didn't want to explain her feelings for Jackson to Sebastian. Hell, she couldn't even explain them to herself.

"I told you we aren't together. You and I ended because we behaved more like business associates, Sebastian. There hadn't been any substance or passion."

"You're in love with Vance, aren't you?" he asked before gulping the tall whiskey he'd poured himself in the back of the car.

What had she ever seen in this man? He lacked warmth and depth when it came to showing emotions. He hardly knew her, and they'd been together for six months.

"Why are you doing this? I came here as your friend. I kept our breakup quiet to support you. Do you think I want to go to some formal event after a long day at work? You're going to grill me when I'm doing you a favor?" Enough of playing by his rules. He preferred her prim and proper, which might be the reason the relationship fizzled. He didn't know her at all.

His smile appeared forced. "You're right. I do appreciate you coming tonight. However, your relationship with Vance bothers me. When you ended things, you assured me it had nothing to do with anyone else, yet you've been different ever since *he* came to town. You do realize you never told me you loved me. Not once in the six months we were together. I've never said those words to anyone before you, and yet you never said them back to me. You can't answer my questions when I ask about him, which tells me you don't want to answer because you know it will upset me. So yes, I'm curious about why you would choose to love the man who you aren't with, but you couldn't love the man who you were with."

What. The. Hell. Weren't they way past this? Things ended weeks ago, and he hadn't put up a fight once. Why had she even come tonight?

"Have you ever stopped to consider why our relationship ended? Do you realize you never took the time to know me or to get to know my friends or family? Did you ever see one of my finished projects? The answer is *no*. You had more important things to do for the campaign. I attended cocktail parties, rallies, photo ops, family functions, anything you asked of me. You attended two work parties with me in the six months we were together. So instead of blaming Jackson for the demise of our relationship, perhaps you should take a look in the mirror."

"Well, I didn't know we were keeping score. Clearly, I failed you."

"We aren't keeping score. But you won't stop obsessing over Jackson, and our problems have nothing to do with him. So I'm laying it out for you." She fell back against the seat in frustration.

"I get it. But are you really saying you have no feelings for Vance? I saw the photo in the paper, Peyton. The way he looks at you." He chugged another glass of whiskey.

She wanted to scream. He wouldn't let it go. "You asked me if I loved him. I didn't want to hurt you, so I didn't answer. I also didn't want to lie to you, so I said nothing. The truth is, I've loved him for as long as I can remember. And I always will. Jackson and I are not together, not in a romantic way. I have a past with him. A history you can't begin to understand. Quite honestly, Sebastian, if our relationship were solid, none of this would be a mystery. I would have told you about my past with him. I don't throw the words *I love you* around unless I mean them. I'm sorry we didn't get there. I care about you. I'd like to remain friends. But I'm not going to be guilted by you or bullied by Kenny Wolf any longer."

He didn't respond. She closed her eyes, and they remained quiet for a few minutes.

"You're right. I don't do relationships, Peyton. I never have. You really were my first attempt. I clearly didn't take the time to get to know you beyond your professional aspirations, and I regret it now. If I've made you feel guilty since our breakup, I apologize. I'm under a considerable amount of pressure right now, and I'm exhausted. How has Wolf bullied you? It seems like a harsh word for someone who just wants you to have some pictures taken on our way into an event. He is quite fond of you. He helped me put together a little surprise for you tonight."

At least he owned up to some of the reasons their relationship failed. She respected his honesty. He copped out about guilting her, continuing to blame the election for everything and anything going wrong in his life. As far as Wolf, it didn't surprise her he had no clue who his campaign manager was. Sebastian didn't have deep relationships. Everything stayed at the surface. He took what he needed from the people in his life and didn't give much back. It's who he was. It took her a while to see it. This surprise he mentioned would somehow benefit Sebastian with his voters. She doubted very much it would be something for her.

They pulled up to the black-tie rally in his honor, and she grabbed her clutch and started to move when the car door swung open. He placed a hand on her arm to stop her. "I'm sorry. Can we have fun tonight?"

The next two days couldn't pass fast enough. She nodded and stepped out of the car. Wolf must have called in a whole lot of favors, because the walkway was lined with every photographer in the city. She took Sebastian's arm, and they made the long trek toward the banquet entrance of the elegant hotel. Flashes lit around them, emulating the night sky as if it were the Fourth of July. It had never been this overwhelming before. Most likely because of the photo of she and Jackson gaining so much attention.

"Why are there so many photographers here?" she asked, squinting against the flashes, a frozen smile plastered on her face.

"I told you, Wolf and I have a surprise for you." He leaned down and pressed a kiss to her lips, causing her to flinch. Kissing was not part of the deal. She agreed to come as a way to keep the peace. Hell, they'd hardly kissed when they dated.

Angry, she hissed a warning close to his ear, "Sebastian, enough."

He paused, pulled her close, and posed for the photographers. "Sorry, I got carried away. Won't happen again unless you want it to."

Had the man heard anything she said on the drive over? The crowd stirred around them. She spotted

Wolf. A Cheshire cat grin spread across his face. The hair on the back of her neck stood on edge. The sight of him terrified her. He nodded to Sebastian, flashes of light blinding her. Chaos swirled in the air.

Sebastian turned her to face him. "Are you ready for your surprise?"

"What? You're doing it out here?" She didn't hide her displeasure.

"Someone wanted to be here to support us these last few days leading up to the election, and I wanted to give this to you for all you've done for me," he said, loud enough for the people surrounding to hear.

The crowd roared, and butterflies took flight in her stomach. Not an excited flutter, but a nervous one. She didn't have a clue what he had up his sleeve. Why did it feel like the rug was about to come out from beneath her feet? Wolf led two people toward her. She couldn't make them out. So many bright flashes made it difficult to see.

Her eyes adjusted to the light, and she met a dark brown gaze resembling her own. Her mother's gaze. Beside her, Brad Boone, one of Nashville's biggest country stars, smiled. Her body froze, and her mind spun. How in the world could this be happening?

"Baby girl," her mom shouted, sure to allow everyone around to capture the moment on film. She pulled her in for a hug, and within a heartbeat, turned them both to face the photographers.

Brad hugged her from the other side, and flashbulbs lit up the darkness like a lightning storm—in more ways than one. Thunder boomed and scattered inside her. She didn't speak. Couldn't form a coherent sentence.

Photographers shouted questions. "Why hide the fact your mother is married to Brad Boone?" "When was the last time you saw her?" "Are you and Jackson Vance having an affair?" Numbness set in as she turned to pose for pictures with her mom and stepdad.

Sebastian answered their questions while lying through his teeth. "Peyton did not want to overshadow the election with news of her mother being married to Brad Boone. *We* share a close friendship with Jackson Vance. He saw her home safely while I took care of business at the office." Lie after lie. The last nail in the coffin came when he shared how close she and her stepfather, Brad, were. How he played a huge role in raising her.

Raising her.

The air around her vanished. The questions came fast. They walked toward the door, and she didn't feel her feet touch the ground. Her breathing shallow, she tried to process what happened. The betrayal unbearable.

They stepped inside the ballroom entrance. The commotion continued. Guests asked Brad to sign autographs while his wife stood beside him, beaming with pride. Bile rose in Peyton's throat.

"How could you do this?" Not hiding her contempt. She didn't care who heard at this point. She found her voice, and it was damn well time to use it.

His puzzled expression infuriated her. "How could I do this? Your mom reached out to Wolf and said they stayed in the background out of respect for me. She misses you and wanted to surprise you. They wanted to be here for the election."

"Do you think it's odd I've never spoken about my

mother to you, Sebastian? I haven't seen her in almost five years, and when I have, it's been for an hour at the most. We talk maybe once a year. This is a publicity stunt for both of you." She knew it in her gut. Why wouldn't he have asked *her* about her mother when she reached out to Wolf? Why would he surprise her in front of the press? They called all these photographers here to put on a show. A lump so large it threatened to choke her formed in her throat. He used her the same way her mother did. Her hands fisted, and rage engulfed her.

"So maybe this helps fix the mess *you* made last night with Jackson. It comes with the territory, Peyton. You were aware I was a public figure when we started dating. And if this little reunion allows people to believe I did something nice for my girlfriend, what's the harm? It's a win-win." Sebastian's eyes were cold and angry. He'd put on a good show to get her here. This had all been a setup for his own personal gain.

"A win-win for whom, Sebastian?" she asked. They stood off to the side, away from the crowds bombarding the country singer.

He held up his phone, showing her a picture of her, him, her mother, and Brad. Already going viral on social media. It looked like they were one big, happy family.

Sebastian Worthington surprises his girlfriend with her mom and stepdad, who is none other than country's favorite singer, Brad Boone.

"We are blowing up on social media right now," Sebastian boasted, unable to pull his face away from his phone long enough to notice her devastation.

Betrayal at its finest. He revealed his true colors.

She looked around the large white marble entryway. Her mother laughed and took pictures with some of the guests, going on and on about her happiness over her daughter dating the future mayor. Peyton needed to get away from these people.

She walked to the bathroom. Her departure appeared to go unnoticed. Her head spun over the events leading up to this moment. Her mother and Brad Boone were here. Peyton had never spent any time with Brad. Never visited them in Nashville and only met him once in passing. They'd never had a conversation. Both Sebastian and her mother had deceived her. Sebastian had done it for political gain, and her mother had done it to boost her husband's popularity before his new album released next month. They'd both used her.

Her phone vibrated nonstop in her purse. Friends and family must have seen the pictures on social media. Jayden. Damn it. She would be furious their mother showed up and caused a media frenzy.

She locked herself in a bathroom stall and reached for the tissue. Tears streamed down her face. Skimming the texts from her sister, Dani, and Elle cursing out her mother, she opened the one from Jackson. Staring at her phone through blurry tears.

Hey, you okay? I'm here if you want to leave. I'm parked out back.

How would he know to come here?

You're here?

Her heart raced while she waited for him to respond.

I'm here. Saw the pictures on the Internet. I figured you'd want to get out of there.

She swiped her cheek again. Why would she stay

here? Sebastian and her mother did this for their own gain. Neither cared about her.

I'll be right out.

She dropped her phone in her purse and left the restroom. A waiter stepped out into the long hallway and moved toward her. "Excuse me. I need to find the exit at the back of the building. Can you show me where it is?"

He gave her a sympathetic nod. Her tear-streaked face impossible to hide. "Of course. Follow me."

They didn't speak as she strode beside him down a long corridor. The waiter opened the door for her; Jackson waited beside the vehicle and walked toward her when she exited the building.

"Come here, Pea." He pulled her into his arms for a quick hug before he guided her to the passenger side and helped her in. He leaned over and buckled her seat belt. She didn't fight him this time.

"How did you know where I was?"

"I texted Jayden. She told me."

"How'd you know I'd want to leave?" Her voice shook, on the verge of a full-blown breakdown.

"Because I know you."

The car pulled away from the building, and tears threatened once again. "I can't believe they did this. They used me for a publicity stunt."

"I'm sorry. You don't deserve this."

"And Sebastian. He didn't think to tell me?" She reached in her purse for a tissue and blew her nose.

"Does he know you and your mom don't speak?" he asked, grasping her hand.

She leaned back against the seat, exhausted, her hand intertwined with his.

"No. We've never talked about her. He said she reached out to his psycho campaign manager, Kenny Wolf, which might be true. But he should have thought to inquire. I've never mentioned her. Who plans a public reunion and calls in dozens of photographers? He wanted it to look like he did this grand gesture for me. After the photo of you and me received so much attention, I think the timing says it all. He totally used me."

"He's a piece of shit. I don't know what you're doing with him," he said. His harsh tone did nothing to hide his anger. He pulled in front of her house and got out of the car. She wanted to tell him the truth, admit her relationship with Sebastian was a farce, but the humiliation of the situation was too much right now.

"Thanks for coming to get me. I wonder how long it will take them to realize I'm gone." Putting the key in the door, she turned to face him.

"I'm not leaving. I'll sleep on your couch. I don't want you alone tonight. They've posted this shit all over social media, and I'm sure Sebastian is going to be questioned once news of your absence spreads. You may end up with a swarm of nosy reporters outside your house."

She led him inside, and Mr. Whiskers ran circles around them, excited.

"Thank you. You being here means a lot to me."

"There's nowhere else I'd rather be right now."

Aside from him leaving her after his sister's death, she trusted him immensely. Without question. That hadn't changed.

She walked toward the kitchen to take her pup outside. His hand gently grasped her shoulder. "I'll take him out. Go take a bath. I'll find us something for dinner. I'm sure you're starving."

He'd remembered how much she loved baths. And she *was* hungry. He knew her. Maybe better than anyone. Even after all these years.

"Thank you. I won't be long."

Tying her hair up, she slipped into the hot water. A moment to let it all out. She sobbed, cried, and sobbed some more. The betrayal from her mother—it still hurt to this day. Endless disappointment. She pulled her knees up and buried her face in her legs.

Why couldn't her mom have baked cupcakes for her on her birthday or done her hair for dances? The things a mom was supposed to do. But Monica Boone, she planned a public reunion for the paparazzi. A surefire plan to drum up gossip and sell albums. The timing couldn't be better. Brad Boone was famous. People swarmed him. This little publicity stunt was completely unnecessary, but nothing was ever enough for her mother.

And Sebastian, what a self-serving bastard. He'd most likely used her the whole time. He'd gone out with a bang tonight. Supporting him was no longer an option. He could tell the press whatever he wanted. She would not attend election night nor lie about their relationship any longer. It was time to tell Jackson the truth.

She dried off and slipped into comfortable pajamas. Her stomach growled. The divine smell of bacon made its way through the house, leading her down the stairs. She dropped down to sit on the bottom step and listened to Jackson speak to Mr. Whiskers. He explained all the reasons her pup needed to stop whining. Of course, he also told Mr. Whiskers the odds were stacked against him with his ridiculous name. Smiling for the first time this evening, she pushed to her feet and moved toward the kitchen.

"My mouth is watering. What did you make?" There were several pans sizzling on the stove.

"Good. Do you still like breakfast for dinner?" He tossed a scrap to the desperate dog at his feet.

"Yep, it's still my favorite."

He served up two plates and sat down across from her. "How are you feeling?"

"Aside from feeling like I've been kicked in the gut, I guess okay."

"Well, all your training will help you recover quickly," he teased.

"There's something I need to tell you," she said after she took a bite of bacon and savored the taste.

"Okay."

"Sebastian and I haven't been together for a while. I ended it when you and I returned from New York."

He didn't hide his surprise or his relief. "Why did you pretend you were still with him?"

"He was worried our breakup would affect the outcome of the election. I didn't want to hurt him. He's worked hard for this."

He cursed under his breath. "He's a pussy. Who asks a woman to keep up the pretense of dating because it might affect how people vote? What a whiney bitch."

She laughed. Because it was the truth. And he'd manipulated her for his own gain.

"I didn't tell you because the fewer people who knew the better. My family didn't know either. They wouldn't have liked it. I didn't want you to think I did it

175

for any other reason than me not being happy."

"I get it. You're a good person, Pea. But I'm glad you ended it. He doesn't deserve you."

She helped him clean up the dishes, and they sat on the couch and talked. Exhaustion swallowed her whole.

"Thanks for staying over. You don't need to sleep on the couch. There's a guest room upstairs." She didn't want to be alone, wanted to ask him to sleep in her bed. But tonight his rejection would be more than she could handle.

"Of course. I'm glad you didn't throw me out," he teased.

He followed her up the stairs, and she showed him the room next to hers before saying good night. Climbing into bed, she hoped sleep would come fast, not wanting to think about the events of the evening or about Jackson being just a few feet away. Making the mistake of scrolling through her phone, she read the texts from Jayden letting her know their mom and Brad did numerous interviews this evening. Shared how thrilled they were to stand beside their daughter—yes, *their daughter*—at this exciting time for her and Sebastian. Her mother told the press staying away from Peyton during the campaign proved difficult but agreed per Peyton's request. What a slap in the face. The woman had no shame. Add compulsive liar to her list of unimpressive attributes.

Their mom never wanted to be a part of her or Jayden's life. Now she portrayed herself as mother of the year with a sappy story. Sebastian also gave an interview and shared how he'd looked forward to this surprise for some time. Making up a story about how much she missed her parents. Unbelievable. But the final text from her father put her over the edge. The man who raised her. Who had always been there for her.

Don't let anyone get you down, sweetheart. You know who you are, and so do I. You're stronger than you think. I love you.

Pulling the comforter over her head, she tried to contain her sobs. Her hands came over her mouth to muffle the sound. The wood floor creaked, and she froze. Did he hear her? She wiped the tears with the butt of her hand and stayed completely still. The bed moved, and two arms pulled her close.

Jackson.

He pushed the comforter back and forced her to come out of hiding. He stared down at her; the look on his face nearly broke her. He loved her. It shone in his beautiful green gaze.

"You okay, Pea?" His large hand came down to rest on her cheek. His thumb swiped at the falling tears.

She didn't answer but moved closer. She laid her head on his chest, happy to be in the safety of his arms. The sound of his heartbeat calmed her. She closed her eyes, and though the tears continued to fall, she drifted away. And even through today's darkness—there was light.

There was Jackson.

Always Jackson.

Chapter Eleven

Present

He flipped the ham and cheese omelet in the pan before opening the back door to let out the world's most needy mutt. *Christ.* He'd spent the night in her bed, woke up to make them breakfast, and became wet nurse to her high maintenance dog.

Nothing was going according to plan anymore, and he didn't give a shit. She and Sebastian weren't together, and all he felt was—relief. Sure, some of it was because he didn't want her with the selfish prick, but mostly it was because she wasn't with anybody. As if she still belonged to him.

Yep. He'd gone batshit crazy. When he heard her crying last night, he'd decided to help her through this mess. Owed it to her. If he happened to enjoy himself in the process, it was the icing on the cake.

"Are you cooking for me again?" She sauntered into the kitchen in a white bathrobe, hair piled on top of her head in a messy bun, and eyes puffy from the emotional roller coaster ride her douchebag ex-boyfriend had taken her on.

Fucking gorgeous. No other way to describe her. Who looked this good after a night spent crying?

More importantly, how the hell had he survived a night in her bed without touching her? Held her while she slept, inundated with the lavender bubble bath she must have used in the tub as she snuggled against him. He'd wrapped her up and kept her close all night, unsure who needed it more, him or her.

"I wake up early. Figured you'd be hungry when you got up."

"I don't even eat breakfast most days, but this looks amazing. So yes. I'm definitely hungry now." She laughed.

She was lighter this morning. Hopefully she'd shed her last tear over both Sebastian and her mother last night, but he doubted it.

"Good. We're staying here today. I called Ryan, and everything is covered at the restaurant."

"What? No. I'm going to work."

"Listen, the press is aware you left the event early. Four guys are staked out at the restaurant according to Ryan, so you can work from home. I'll stay with you. We'll keep the blinds closed, watch movies, and play hooky," he said with a laugh, setting both plates down.

"So bossy." She forked a bite of eggs. A long moan from her sweet lips followed, causing him to push to his feet in desperate need to put some space between them. Yeah, an ice-cold shower would be fucking helpful about now, but he'd settle for a cold glass of water.

To say he'd been uncomfortable this morning after having her body pressed against his all night was an understatement. Now she moaned while she ate? His body buzzed with anticipation.

"I am technically your boss, right?" He drank the entire glass of water before returning to his seat.

"You're my client."

"Who you work for."

"Touché, boss-man," she said with a laugh.

She agreed to turn her phone off after touching base with her dad, Jayden, Camille, Dani, and Elle.

They worked on their laptops most of the morning and took a break to watch a movie after lunch. Of course, it turned into a full-blown *Rocky* marathon with Peyton standing on her coffee table screaming during every single fight scene. Took him back a decade to a time he'd worked hard to forget. She reminded him of the parts of his life that hadn't revolved around the night Chloe died. A good time in his life. Happy time.

"I wonder if I'd be a good female boxer?" she asked, grabbing a handful of popcorn.

"Hmm, I don't know, Pea. You've got the whole lapdog thing going. You like to be pushed in a baby stroller. I don't see you lasting more than a round."

A pillow came at him so fast he barely managed to catch it. He dove in her direction, and she tipped back beneath him on the couch. He fought the urge to cover her mouth with his. Her scent. Her laugh. Her witty banter. The girl drove him out of his mind with need. He wanted her. So fucking bad. He'd mustered all the restraint a person could manage for one day. He pushed up to stand over her, in desperate need of space. A dip in the Arctic Ocean didn't sound bad right about now.

"I'm going to run to my place, take a shower, and grab some clothes." He moved toward the kitchen to grab his keys. His sudden urgency about leaving left her jumping to her feet.

"You're leaving?" She followed him to the next room.

"Yeah. I'll be back in a while."

"You're coming back?"

"I don't want you to stay here alone tonight. I don't trust Sebastian or those stalker photographers."

He moved around her and hurried for the door. *Space.* He needed space.

"Okay. But you're not cooking tonight. I'll handle dinner."

"You're going to thank me by torturing me?"

She rolled her eyes and laughed. "I'll order takeout."

"Ah, good. Lock the door," he said before getting in his car and putting some much-needed distance between them.

****

Feeling like a new man once he toweled off, nothing beat an ice-cold shower when trying to tamp down a raging hard on. He sent Peyton a text.

Be back soon.

Changing into clean clothes, he dug in the back of his closet for a heavier sweater. The temperature outside had dropped in the past few days. Reaching for his warm black pullover, he knocked it off the hanger. He bent down to find it.

A small-sized moving box tumbled from a stack and fell at his feet. Pulling it out, he dropped down to the floor to look through the box Joseph had left for him after he passed and had yet to open. Hell, no time like the present.

It didn't weigh much for its size, so he assumed it was filled with photographs. Surprise hit when he opened it to find an envelope with his name sitting on top. A letter from Joseph. The attorney for his estate had given Jackson a note he'd left for him when they reviewed the will. The napkin with Peyton's drawing also included with the brief note. It basically told him to pursue his dreams with the money he'd received. Short and to the point. Just like Joseph. However, this letter appeared longer. Not anything he expected, or he would have opened it sooner. He leaned his back against the bed and read the letter.

Jackson,

I'm sure I've been gone for a while if you're finally reading this, as you've probably avoided this box for a good year or so. I know you, son. Maybe better than you know yourself sometimes. There are a few things I need to say to you, and when you're ready, you'll understand why.

First, I want to thank you. Thank you for giving me purpose after I lost my Rose. Losing her, after so many years of marriage, wasn't easy. There were days when I struggled to make myself get out of bed, until the day I met this bright-eyed little boy. You had a confidence I'd never seen in a kid. I don't know if you remember our first meeting. You had just turned seven years old. You were walking two dogs in the trailer park for your neighbor. I asked you if they were paying you to do their chores for them, and you responded, "Yes, sir. I'm earning my own money." It was the first time you impressed the hell out of me but certainly not the last. You've continued to do so every day since.

You took care of your sister every day of her life. I need you to hear me, Jackson. I've never seen a kid step up and be there for his sibling the way you did. Even at a young age. I loved that little girl like crazy, and losing her the way we did was the most difficult thing I've ever dealt with—almost. Because seeing what it did to you, well, son, it was worse. It brought me to my knees many times. You took the weight on your shoulders when you had no business carrying the guilt or burden of what happened. It's been difficult for me to watch you shut everyone out and punish yourself for something you weren't responsible for. It was out of your control. I hope you have come to a place where you can let go of it.

Jackson, sometimes life isn't fair. You can't make sense of things, but you can choose to keep living and keep fighting for what you want. I know my time is limited now, and I need you to know—not a day has passed, from the moment we met, when I haven't been proud of you.

I'm proud of the little kid I met so many years ago, kind, hardworking, humble, and strong. I'm proud of the teenager you became, loyal, smart, determined, and full of fire. Not to mention a four-time state champion wrestler who received a full-ride scholarship to one of the most prestigious academies in the country. It's all you, son. You were born with a work ethic most people never acquire. Lastly, I'm most proud of the man you are today, the one who visited me just two weeks ago. Son, you graduated from college with honors, you wrestled four years with the highest achievements one can receive at the collegiate level, you make time to see me twice a year and call me every week. They don't make better men than you, Jackson. The joy you've given me watching you grow is something I could never repay you for. You are my son, in every sense of the word. A son I never even realized I wanted or needed…until the day I met a special little boy so many years ago. You know I'm not normally an overly sentimental guy, but sometimes things need to be said.

My wish you for you, Jackson, is that you allow yourself to move out of the darkness you've been trapped in for far too long. Son, your job isn't to save the world, but it is your duty to save yourself. Though you weren't responsible in any way for what happened to Chloe, you have been living in your own kind of prison for far too long. People who didn't know you before Chloe was killed wouldn't know what I'm talking about. But you know...and I do, too. On the outside, your life looks damn good. But you've stopped allowing yourself to love, son, and it's not healthy. I know how big your heart is, and you've got it tucked away for safe keeping. I hope you find someone who helps you open your eyes to see the man I see, and helps you find your way back to the life you deserve.

I want you to start living the life you were meant to live. Make peace with the past and leave it where it belongs. Behind you. Allow yourself to love and be loved, Jackson, and everything will fall into place.

Love you, son,

Joseph

He sat there for minutes staring at the letter. Was he living in a prison this whole time? Maybe in a way, but there were reasons he'd put himself there. Reasons most people couldn't understand. And his sister paid a far bigger price than he had.

He glanced down at the letter before folding it up and putting it in his nightstand drawer. Joseph's approval meant everything to him. Making him proud would be one of the greatest accomplishments of his life. The past came at him from every direction lately. His phone vibrated with a text from Peyton.

Enough Chinese food to feed a small village is on

the way. Rocky Five is paused until you get here. Admit it, you're dying to come back.

He laughed. Wouldn't admit it, but he couldn't wait to get back there. To her.

How much Rocky *can one woman watch? Heading back now.*

One can never get enough of the Italian Stallion. See you soon.

When he walked into her house, he laughed loud enough for Ol' Whiskey to start barking. Boxes of Chinese food covered the coffee table. Far too much for two people to eat, even with his appetite. He sat beside her on the couch, eating right out of the carton, and passed containers back and forth. They watched yet another *Rocky* movie as if it were the first time she'd seen it. He wondered how he'd survive another night in her bed without touching her. Or would she banish him to the guest room since she seemed to be feeling better? Why did the idea bother him so much?

He thought back to the last time he'd touched her. Really touched her. The last night they'd been together. Then he wondered how he'd endured being away from her all these years, because the last time they'd been together, he'd thought they were unbreakable.

Chapter Twelve

Nine years ago

Peyton met him at the front door with a hug, and his mouth crashed into hers.

"Hey, Pea," he said, pulling back to look at her.

"Hey. Come on. You carry the basket. I want you to open your surprise down on the beach."

The thin white sundress hit her mid-thigh. Golden skin stood out against the bright white fabric. He itched to touch her. Always did. Scooping up the oversized basket, he followed her out to the beach behind her house.

"What's in this basket?" he asked when they sat down on the warm sand.

"It's your going-off-to-college care package," she said. The sun reflected off the water, hitting her just so, causing gold speckles to dance in her dark brown eyes.

"I thought care packages were for after you were in school?" he teased, grazing his knuckles against her cheek.

He couldn't remember a time when he hadn't love her. It didn't exist in his memory. The girl who he'd move mountains for if she asked him to.

"Hey." His finger traced her bottom lip. "It's going to be fine, Pea. I promise."

"I know," she said, but he saw the fear in her eyes.

He leaned down to tickle her neck with his lips. "Do you?"

Falling back in the sand, she tried to suppress her giggles. "You're worried I'm going to freak out, aren't you? What do you call me, a flight risk?"

He stared down at her before bursting out in laughter. "Not a *flight risk,* Pea. It's the fight-or-flight response. You like the flight."

She pushed to a sit position. Her hair moved in the breeze. "And you like the fight."

"Yep. Which is a good thing since I'm a wrestler," he teased.

"I'll work on my *fight* more and my *flight* less this year, deal?"

She'd shared her concern about them going to school across the country from one another. Her mother's abandonment influenced her ability to trust people. He'd worked hard to break through the boundaries surrounding her over the years. He loved her cautious nature. Part of what drew him to her. Always the observer—a thinker, but once she loved you, nothing in the world compared to being on the receiving end of it. When she felt threatened or afraid, she was quick to run. Leave before she got hurt. He'd been chasing this girl for half his life, and he'd never stop. But when she wanted something, she was a fighter. She had it in her.

"Deal. So tell me about this care package," he said, attempting to distract her.

She wiped a single tear rolling down her cheek. They'd both dreaded the end of summer, and here they were, spending their last night together. "So I've been working on this for a while. I don't like the idea of you going to school alone. You should have these things before you get there. I wish I could go with you and help you get settled."

He pulled her into his arms, sitting her on his lap, her back against his chest. "How'd I get so lucky to fall for the sweetest girl in the world?"

The sound of water lapping against the shore soothed him. They sat quietly. She pressed her feet into the warm sand. The little beach at the edge of the lake in her backyard had always been their spot. They'd spent every summer there since the day they'd met in South Lake, with many weekends in between, as they got older. They'd grown up in this very spot. Made love for the first time here only a year ago. And many times since. Any chance they could sneak off alone, they did. The smell of pine lingered in the air, and the tree branches rustled above each time the breeze came through. The crystal-blue water so magnificent just before the sun went down.

"So—" she said, tipping her head back to look up at him. "You have everything you need when you first get there. You know, all the pharmacy-type stuff. Ibuprofen, peroxide, Band-Aids, toothpaste, your favorite shampoo, and body wash. The basics."

He whispered against her ear, "So thoughtful, Pea."

She never stopped praising him for the full-ride scholarship he received to wrestle in college at the Naval Academy. He wished he had the resources to choose a school closer to Stanford where Peyton was going, but he went with his best offer. He had some big dreams, all of which included Peyton, and this was his chance to go after them.

It didn't make leaving any easier. He worried about

his girl and his little sister. Chloe continued to try and rescue their mother, and it would be a lot for Joseph to handle alone. His mom ran with a rough crowd, doing drugs daily. She and her boyfriend, Ryker, had a volatile relationship. Go figure—a drug dealer and a junky. Joseph threatened to kick her out if she kept bringing him around, but he never followed through because Chloe would leave with her. His sister was loyal as shit to their deadbeat mother, who'd gone to rehab twice in the last five years, and neither attempt lasted after returning home. Chloe wouldn't give up on her. He had incredible guilt about going so far away, but Joseph encouraged him to take the offer and pursue his education.

She pushed herself off his lap and reached for the basket. "This picture frame has two sides to it. You see? Do you know what this one is?"

He laughed. "It's the picture your dad took of us the first day we met. I remember how surprised he'd been at the twelve zillion trash bags we'd filled with pinecones."

"Um...I just held the bag. You did all the work while I took in the sights." She wriggled her eyebrows at him.

He lunged at her, tipping her back on the sand. "You were ten, Peanut. You weren't taking in the sights just yet. It took you about six more years. I got there loooong before you did."

"You did get there quicker, perv."

His breath blew against the sensitive part of her neck. Unable to control her giggles, she begged him to stop. "*Perv*? Because I lusted after you long before you even knew what it meant?"

She smiled up at him. Their gazes locked. Their breaths came in unison. "What can I say? I'm a late bloomer. I loved you before I lusted for you."

"I loved you first. Trust me." His voice was husky.

Lifting the picture frame, he studied the photo of them as kids. "I may have even loved you here. In this picture."

"Love at first sight, huh?"

"Without a doubt." He flipped the frame to see the other side, propping himself above her with one arm. In the photo, Peyton sat on his lap; his arms encircled her, his mouth open in laughter. With her bottom lip pulled between her teeth, she gazed up at him with mischief in her eyes, her cheeks flushed and hair blowing. It wasn't a posed picture, but it captured them. The connection they had. It was undeniable.

"Where did you get this? I love it." He pushed to a sit position, pulling her with him to study the photo.

"The other day when we were out here with Jayden and Zach. She snapped it on her phone when we weren't looking. I loved it, so I had it printed."

"Jesus, Pea, do you have any idea how beautiful you are?"

She leaned forward and grazed her lips back and forth against his. The simple touch sent a shock wave through his body. He trailed his hand up her back and tangled it into her hair, pulling her closer.

"No, I don't. Why don't you tell me?" she teased, urging him on.

"Let's start with this perfect mouth," he whispered before nipping at her bottom lip.

Her head fell back with a laugh, and her hands caressed the back of his neck. Moving onto his lap, she straddled him, her chest pressed against his. His fingers moved beneath her dress to skim her hips and thighs.

"Peyton," her sister yelled from up at the house.

They scrambled to their feet within seconds, panting and laughing. They walked up the steps toward the house, hands intertwined. Strolling through the grass, he saw Jayden standing on the patio.

"What's up?" Peyton asked Jayden as her boyfriend, Zach, stepped outside and gave Jackson the handshake-man-hug thing they did.

"Do you guys want to come with Zach and me to dinner?"

Peyton's answer came quick. "No. We'll eat something here. We're just going to hang out by the water."

Jayden's eyes were glossy with emotion when she looked at Jackson. "You're leaving in the morning, right?"

"Yep. Are you getting mushy, J.J.?" he teased.

She elbowed his side before opening her arms for a hug. He and Jayden had grown close over the years.

"I love you, Jackson."

"Love you, too," he said and kissed her cheek.

"We'll see you at Thanksgiving. Miss you already, buddy." Zach patted him on the shoulder.

Returning to their spot by the water, Peyton helped him finish going through his basket. He fell back laughing after pulling out a can of pepper spray labeled *chick repellant*. A fish and tackle box packed full of his favorite candies: Gummy Worms and Swedish Fish. A large sucker bouquet wrapped in ribbon, and a tag reading: LIFE SUCKS WITHOUT YOU. He loved it.

"This is by far the best care package anyone has

ever made," he said, kissing her neck and wrapping his arms around her.

"I'm glad you like it."

"You know there's nothing I'd ever do to jeopardize what we have, right?" He looked up at the stars moving across the dark sky.

"I do. And you know I wouldn't, either, right?"

"Yep. And we'll talk on the phone every day," he teased.

She lay back on the blanket, rolling onto her side. "Thank God for Facetime."

"You're it for me. Forever. I need you to trust me. I know you worry, Pea. But I'm not going anywhere. Ever. Okay?"

Her eyes grew bright again. "I'm not worried. I have complete faith in you. In us. In this."

"Me, too."

"Are you worried about Chloe?" she asked.

"I'm terrified for her. I don't know what I can do to keep her safe from this shit." He intertwined his fingers with hers.

"I'm here for a couple more weeks, so I'll check on her daily. I promise," she said. Peyton loved his little sister. They were very close.

"Listen, you go to school. Do your thing. You're the smartest person I know. I want you to have a great college experience, okay? Don't worry about Chloe. Joseph said he's got it handled. I just wish fucking Ryker would stop coming around. You had lunch with Chloe today, right? Did you see him when you went to the house?"

Her posture stiffened. "Yeah. I went over at noon with lunch for the both of us. He was leaving when I pulled up."

Peyton treated Chloe like a little sister, helping her with her hair, taking her shopping, and polishing her nails. Spending time with her while Jackson worked during the day at Langford's, Joseph's restaurant.

"Did he say anything to you?"

She looked away. The piece of shit had done something. He swore most of the time it felt like he could see into her soul.

"Yes. He said something disgusting, and I flipped him off."

"Motherfucker. What did he say?"

She slid closer to him and put her hand on his cheek. "Come on. He's a pig. Do you really want to know what he said? I don't want to spend your last night talking about a drug dealer. He's disgusting. I handled it, and he walked away."

He moved closer, his lips grazing her ear. "I'm sorry. I wish I'd been there so I could've beaten his ass."

She laughed softly. "I don't want you to get into trouble over some loser. You are on to bigger and better things, Jackson Vance. Don't let anyone derail you. Promise me."

He smiled, his hand playing with her hair. "I won't do anything stupid. I promise. I just want you to be careful if you see him around. Stay away from him. Joseph is working on getting a restraining order against him so he can't come on the property. They've had some run-ins, and he thinks they can use it to file the paperwork."

"I hope it works. I don't want him around Chloe."

"Me, either. I feel like shit, too, because she

193

wanted to come here with me tonight," he said, guilt flooding him.

"She did? You could've brought her. I love having her here."

"I know. But I'm an asshole. I wanted to be alone with my girl." He nipped at her bottom lip. "Doing just what we're doing. In our place. I needed this. I'm not going to see you until Thanksgiving. So I guess I'm a selfish prick, huh?"

"Well, it's not like we didn't already know it, right?" she teased.

He flipped her on her back and pinned her arms to the sand, smiling down at her. She laughed and writhed beneath him. "What am I going to do with this mouth of yours, Peanut?"

"I have a few ideas." She lifted her head, attempting to reach him.

"Is this what you want?" His lips dropped to her jaw, kissing down to the pulsing hollow at the base of her throat.

He raised his head, breath coming hard. "I love you, Pea."

"I love you, too."

He brushed a gentle kiss across her forehead, and her fingers tangled into his hair, urging him closer. His thoughts spun. Emotions whirled and skidded. He wouldn't see her for a while. His girl. The girl who set his world on fire. Their kiss grew frantic. Her dress crept up her thighs, and she pressed closer to him, trailing tickling fingers up and down his back, the sensation making it difficult to take things slow.

Lowering his head, he sealed his mouth over hers, wrapped his arms tighter, wanted to keep her close. Her hands slipped beneath his shirt and ran up his back and shoulders. Her touch sang through his veins. He skimmed the curve of her hip and thigh and kissed her deeper. To kiss her forever would never be long enough. His heart thundered. Their breaths came faster.

"Jackson. Condom," she said, her words coming out in gasps.

He reached in his back pocket. The last thing he would ever do is derail her life. He quickly took care of business before he stared down at his girl. He couldn't wait a second longer. She reached for him, and his mouth covered hers. They surrendered to desire and erased all distance between them.

He loved her under the twinkling stars while the water splashed against the shore. He looked down at her, aware that there would never be a more perfect moment than the one they were in right now.

****

Her dad was back in San Francisco, so they spent the night out on the beach, camped out on blankets. He held her in his arms until the sun came up, until they both finally dozed off.

She rolled onto her stomach. "Good morning, sunshine."

"Mornin', Peanut."

"Big day today." Her smile appeared forced.

"Yep. Big day." He brushed the hair back from her gorgeous face.

"Thanks for spending your last night with me."

"Nowhere else I'd rather be."

"Me, either."

"I love you," he said, pulling her back down to kiss her thoroughly.

"Okay, we're not saying good-bye; we're saying *see you soon*, remember? You'll call me when you get there, right?" she said, her voice shaky while she rambled on, trying to avoid the inevitable good-bye.

They walked out to his truck. The light breeze rustled in the trees around them, the air crisp and cool. The orange and yellow hues reflected off the lake as the sun came up. His gray hoody draped over her white sundress, and her hair tousled around her beautiful face.

"Love you, Peanut."

"Love you, too."

He kissed her good-bye and jumped in his truck. Dragging it out would make it worse. A pit formed deep in his stomach and churned when he put his window down and looked at her one last time before pulling away. Tears streamed down her face, and his heart wrenched.

"I'm fine," she yelled, waving from the driveway, swiping at her tears.

"Love you," he called out one last time before turning onto the road.

Fuck. He hated leaving her. Dialed her the minute her house was out of view, his Bluetooth ringing.

"Hello," her response half sob, half laugh.

"You okay?"

"Yep."

"Be strong, Pea. We're going to be fine."

"Promise?"

"Promise."

Chapter Thirteen

Present

The last twenty-four hours had been a complete whirlwind—for good and bad. Sebastian and her mother were relentless about reaching her. Not because they noticed she'd left the event before it even began. Not because they were concerned with how their little show had hurt her. And most definitely not because either of them wanted to apologize for what they'd done. No. They wanted to set up the next photo opportunity. They called and texted with merciless determination to see when they could meet with her; in a public place, of course.

Jackson had held her all night after he picked her up from the hellish evening. They'd spent the day together. Just like old times. He'd stayed the night again last night, slept in her bed for a second time, insisting he didn't want to leave her alone for fear of the press stalking her house. The press never came knockin', but she sure wasn't complaining. She loved having Jackson there. Didn't know what was happening between them, but whatever it was—she'd take it.

He'd stayed with her two nights in a row and slept in her bed both nights. And yet nothing had happened. *Nothing physical.* So much had changed between them otherwise. Almost like they picked up where they left off nine years ago, with the exception of their physical relationship. It was torture. Being so close to him without being able to touch him. Kiss him. But being with him. It was enough. At least for now.

She had multiple meetings scheduled first thing this morning. Her fabric rep stopped by with swatches. Details still needed tweaking with Bob and his men, not to mention going through the piled-high boxes of deliveries stacked in the corner. She and Jackson agreed to go to the gym after work.

Tension filled her each time her phone vibrated with a new message. Messages she ignored. Tomorrow was election day. She had no intention of attending the event with Sebastian or putting on a show for his benefit. Her mother would be disappointed, of course, but she didn't care to please her mom anymore, either. Enough was enough.

She sent Dani and Elle a quick text, touched base with her father and Jayden about her decision not to attend election night, and turned her phone off. The constant texts were a distraction.

Bob called her over to see the barn door the guys hung, leading to the wine cellar.

"It's perfect," she said, admiring the magnificent vintage door from her favorite antique shop.

"You've sure got an eye, Peyton. I couldn't visualize it when you first told me what you wanted, but seeing it up, it looks incredible."

"Ah, ye of little faith. Never underestimate the power of a vintage piece," she teased.

The main door swung open, and she startled at the sight of her mother. Monica Boone wore a sleek cream pantsuit, a blush-colored blouse, and her hair swept back into a fancy chignon. She was modern, elegant, and beautiful.

On the outside.

Peyton froze. They hadn't spoken the other night due to the show, orchestrated by the very woman herself. Hadn't been face-to-face with her in many years, and a mixture of pain and sadness hit her hard. The building anger allowed her to square her shoulders and meet her mother's glare head on.

"Peyton." Her mother's harsh tone caught her off guard, and it was impossible to miss the disdain in the glare aimed her way. *Unbelievable.*

"Monica," she said, knew this would infuriate her—but also kind of the point. She wanted to stick it to her after the stunt she'd pulled. And truth be told, the woman had lost the right to be called anything else long ago. But the most consistent thing about Monica Boone, her belief she was entitled to what she wanted. And she usually got it.

"Are you really this childish?" she hissed.

"I really am." Peyton smiled proudly. Bob excused himself, looking back at her with a questioning gaze. She nodded to let him know it was fine.

Because she was fine. This woman couldn't hurt her anymore.

"Well, I'm sure your father would be very proud of your lack of respect for me."

"I think he's proud of who I am."

She huffed, setting her Birkin bag down on the bar and crossing her arms in front of her.

"Can we talk?" Her tone softened.

"I don't know what we have to talk about, and I'm swamped today." She led her mother to a table in the corner.

"Yes, you do. There's an election tomorrow, and you need to be standing beside your man. Don't punish him for allowing me to come here and support you both. It's not right."

She nearly choked on her mother's words. Seriously? She understood her attempt to sell the fairy-tale mother-daughter reunion story to the press, but did she think Peyton would buy it?

Bitter laughter rolled off her tongue before she spoke. "Are you kidding me? First of all, you know nothing about me. Sebastian is not *my man*, nor am I interested in your bullshit story about coming here to support us. You don't know him. You don't know your own daughters. You've never even met your grandson. You're here because it's a brilliant publicity stunt, and well, let's face it—Mrs. Boone likes to promote *her man*."

Her mother gasped with shock. Her natural abilities in theatrics were impressive. Peyton studied her. Hadn't seen her since the day she graduated from college. Her mom and Brad had been in town for a show, though they didn't make it to the ceremony to see her receive her diploma—they did send backstage passes to his concert later that evening as an apology. Peyton and Jayden had attended the show just long enough to tell their mother they were no longer going to make any effort to have a relationship with her. It was the straw that broke the camel's back.

Monica aged well, no denying it. Obviously, putting herself first her entire life had paid off when it came to getting old. Her flawless tanned skin glowed, her makeup perfected to show off high cheekbones, and her dark eyes were framed in a smoky liner and shadow.

But when she opened her mouth, her beauty dissipated. "You want to play it straight. We can do that. This little show benefits both Brad and Sebastian, so I assumed you would be on board. Your anger for me is clouding your judgment at the expense of two good men. When did you become so filled with hate? I'm disappointed in you. You've become very selfish, darling."

Her jaw dropped, but humor filled her voice at the ridiculousness of her mother's words. "Well, maybe the apple doesn't fall far from the tree, after all. You have the audacity to come to my workplace after you staged a reunion playing the doting mother? I guess we best not mention the last eighteen years of absence from both mine and Jayden's lives. You are the most selfish human being I've ever known. You think I'd do you a favor after what you did to our family? Have you ever thought about the damage you leave in your wake? How dare you come and try to prey on my weakness to get what you want? We're done here. I'm sure you can find the door."

Her mother stood and took a couple steps before stopping. She didn't turn around when she spoke. "I understand you and Jayden hate me. The simple truth is, I never wanted children, Peyton. Your father did. I hoped after all these years, maybe we could be friends."

Her stomach twisted, caught off guard when her mother's voice broke on her own words. A lump formed in her throat, and emotion welled. "I needed you to be my mom, not my girlfriend. And friends don't *use* one another. At least not the friends I have."

"I'm sorry this is how you feel. I'd like to have lunch with you and Jayden tomorrow before I leave, if you'd consider it."

A part of her wanted to believe her mom was trying to mend the fence. Pick up some of the pieces she left behind. A little voice in the back of her head warned her not to trust this woman.

"Would you be willing to meet at my house for lunch? You've never seen where I live. I could have Jayden come there, and we could avoid being out in public."

Her mom frowned at the idea. "It's just—I'm very particular about the food I put into my body. I don't want to be cooped up in a house. I'd prefer a restaurant, so you don't have to fuss, and we can just spend the time together."

The second most consistent thing about Monica Boone—she never hid her true colors. Over the years Peyton learned that disappointment was just unfulfilled expectations, so best to keep her expectations low. Monica Boone would not be meeting her daughters for a private lunch because there was nothing to gain by doing so. She'd choose the restaurant, place the call to the media, and turn it into her own little reality show.

"Let me think it over, okay."

"Okay, well, let me know right away, because I'd need to set things up at a restaurant and rearrange Brad's schedule," she said, leaving off the part about calling the press.

"Take care, Mom."

"All right then. I hope to hear from you. We'll stick around to support Sebastian at the election. I hope to see you there."

She nodded. Her mom walked out the door. It didn't hurt to see her mother walk away. Not anymore.

"You all right?" Jackson's deep voice came from behind her. How long had he been standing there?

She turned to see him leaning against the wall near the hallway. "I am."

He walked closer, and everything else evaporated around them. She wanted him. All of him.

"She wants you to go tomorrow night, huh?" His beautiful green stare studied her, as if he could see into her soul.

"Yep." A thought hit her. "Hey, do you think Ryan could handle things here for a day or two?"

"Sure. He's a capable guy."

Her need for him grew with each passing day, and she didn't know how to stop it anymore. *She didn't want to stop it.*

"Let's go to Tahoe tomorrow. We can stay at the house. It might be good for both of us to go back there after all this time. I need to be out of sight. I don't want to be stalked by the press when I don't show up."

His hand scrubbed along his jaw as he thought it over. He looked conflicted but nodded. "I think we should do it."

She lunged at him and buried her face in his chest. His arms came around her. His head rested atop hers. Pulling back, she looked up at him. He wanted her as much as she wanted him. It was evident every time he looked at her. For some reason, he wouldn't allow himself to go there. She didn't understand why. But she'd take any part of him she could get.

"I'm glad."

"Me, too. Gym tonight?"

"Yes. I promised Nico I'd be back today."

"Sounds good, Pea. I have a few more meetings, so I'll be in my office."

The rest of the day blew by at a rapid pace. After avoiding her family lake house for the last decade, the thought of going back excited her. Jackson had gone back a few times to see Joseph and admitted he, too, had stayed away from his hometown whenever possible. South Lake had been their favorite place in the world at one time. It was time to remember all the good times they'd had there.

When she turned her phone back on, there were a slew of vicious messages from Wolf and some not-so-friendly texts from Sebastian. They wanted her standing beside Sebastian tomorrow on election night, and they weren't backing down. She responded to them both with the same text:

I'm sorry, but I won't be in town tomorrow.

Wolf responded within seconds.

Do you have any idea who you're fucking with? You better change your plans.

Her stomach dipped. The man scared her. The way he'd confronted her by the elevators—something told her it was just the tip of the iceberg. He had already shown her his dark side. How far would he take it? After tomorrow, she assumed his interest in her would end, so leaving for Lake Tahoe couldn't come soon enough.

"You about ready?" Jackson's voice startled her, causing the phone to slip from her hands, shattering the screen when it hit the floor.

Telling Jackson about the text from Wolf was a bad idea. He would insist on confronting both men. She wanted to get away from the drama, not feed the flame. She turned her phone off and dropped it in her purse.

He studied her. "Everything okay?"

"Yes. Everything's fine. Give me a minute to get ready." He'd already changed into his workout clothes, his fitted T-shirt showing off every line and muscle on his shoulders and abs.

On the way to the gym, they chatted about the things they would do in Lake Tahoe. He wanted to check out Joseph's old restaurant, and she planned to sit out on the lake and walk on the trail where they'd met. He found it hilarious that Mr. Whiskers loved the outdoors, so they were taking him along. He made some joke about her pooch not even being a foot tall, so how much of the outdoors could he even see? She laughed on their way into the gym.

"I can tell you this for sure—Rocky would never have named his dog Mr. Whiskers," he said, dropping his bag on the mat.

"Well, I may be a diehard *Rocky* fan, but not every dog can pull off the name, Butkis. I mean, Mr. Whiskers does not look like a Butkis."

"He doesn't look like a Mr. Whiskers, either." He raised his arms and intertwined his fingers behind his neck. His T-shirt lifted, allowing a small tease of his abs, leaving her sweating within seconds. They hadn't even started their workout yet.

"Yes, he does. The name is very fitting."

"He has *average* whiskers at best," he said. His laughter rang through the gym, and she couldn't help but join in.

The good news—she wasn't thinking about Wolf. Or Sebastian. Or her mother. Only Jackson.

Always Jackson.

"What's so funny over here?" Mick walked toward them.

"Peanut's being ridiculous. Hey, let's do a tough workout tonight. We're going to Tahoe tomorrow for a night, so we won't be here."

"Really?" Mick looked back and forth between them with a smirk.

She didn't care—too happy to be embarrassed. Of course, Nico walked up and asked what was going on. Mick informed him they were going to Tahoe tomorrow. Together.

He whistled like a fool.

"Really?" His grin was so wide it made everyone chuckle.

"Okay, not sure why you guys are acting like shitheads, but I'm ready to work out," Jackson said, making an effort to sound annoyed, but he didn't hide his smile.

Nico ran her through a ton of drills, and she gasped for air by the end of the workout. Collapsing on the mat, she guzzled an entire bottle of water. Jackson sparred with another guy in the cage. Impossible to pull her gaze away from his magnificent body. His movements were deliberate. He stalked the other man and forced him back.

"So nothing's going on there, huh?" Nico dropped down beside her on the mat and tilted his head in Jackson's direction.

"I told you, we're old friends."

Nico was one of those people who you could spend just twenty minutes with, and it was like you'd known him your whole life. Open and honest. Easy to talk to.

They'd struck up a friendship right off the bat.

"Uh-huh. Now you two are going to Tahoe tomorrow? Isn't it the douchebag's election night?" He'd inquired about Sebastian before. Apparently, Jackson's nickname for him stuck at the gym.

"Sebastian and I aren't together anymore," she said, still unable to look away from where Jackson sparred in the cage.

"You don't say?" Nico's sarcasm was impossible to miss.

She fiddled with her water bottle before narrowing her eyes on him. "You know you're acting more like the host of *The Bachelor* than an MMA trainer, right?"

He fell back on the mat and cackled. "You got me."

She rolled her eyes and smacked his shoulder with the empty water bottle. "I'll be right back. I left my poor, broken phone in the car to charge, and I need to see if my dad responded about the lake house being ready for us."

She grabbed Jackson's car keys from his bag and jogged out to the parking lot behind the gym. The cell phone screen had fractured the way a windshield shatters when a rock hits it like one giant spider web. Though challenging, she was able to make out the text from her dad saying the house was stocked and ready. She stepped back and shut the car door as something tight wrapped around her neck, jerking her off her feet. Her mouth went dry. She gasped for air before realizing it was rough hands gripping tight against her throat. Her body wrenched and twisted before her head slammed against the brick wall outside the gym. She couldn't move, her arms immobile. Her feet struggled for traction. Her sneakers slipped against the loose gravel. *Focus.* She met the gaze of Kenny Wolf; he looked far from sane. His distant and cold stare so full of hate. Strong hands wrapped around her neck tighter. She struggled for air.

"Did you really think you could just blow me off? Did this seem like something I'd be okay with? Didn't I warn you not to fuck with me?" he said, his mouth so close to her his spit splattered against her cheek.

Long, shallow gasps escaped her throat. He loosened his hold just enough for her to inhale much-needed air.

"Nod your head if you're hearing what I'm saying, you worthless bitch."

She nodded. His thumb pushed hard under her jaw, and a sharp pain traveled up her cheek. Everything went dark around the edges.

Not enough air.

The breeze whistled around them. Something clanked against the gravel, moving in the wind. Trying to concentrate on the surrounding sounds, she squeezed her eyes shut.

Breathe.

Think.

React.

Instinct kicked in. Her knee came up hard, a defensive move Nico taught her a few weeks ago. Wolf sucked in a harsh breath and jumped back just a little. Her knee didn't hit its mark, landing high on his upper thigh. It didn't drop him to the ground, but there was impact. He moved back enough to allow her to gulp in oxygen. She raised her arms before he came at her again.

Protect your head. Play defense. Get in a hit when you can.

All the instructions flew through her mind, but she hadn't prepared to be hit so hard and so fast it would drop her to the ground. Unable to register what happened. A slap? A punch? Her face throbbed in pain, as if it were split in two. She scrambled to her feet.

"You fucking bitch. I should have known better when we picked you. I told Sebastian I thought you might be a pain in the ass, but he insisted you were perfect. Such a dumb ass. So you want to fight, do you?"

Her back pressed against the brick wall. A profound pain pierced her cheek. The world around her blurred. Using her hands to cover her face, she prepared to kick. He lunged at her. Adrenaline pumping, she turned her body and kicked with all her might. She made contact with him. The force of the kick caused her to fall to the ground again, but now they were no longer alone. Voices in the distance shouted jumbled words.

Fists cracked against bone. Grunts and gasps surrounded her. She struggled to see in the dark parking lot. The dirt beneath her hands formed a cloud of dust, making it difficult to make out what was happening. Light coming through the back door of the gym revealed a reprieve. A strong arm pulled her to her feet. She startled, throwing a punch before realizing it was Nico.

"Peyton, relax. It's me."

Jackson sat atop Wolf, throwing punch after punch. Mick dropped his phone and raced toward him, pulling Jackson off her attacker. She was shaken to her core.

The unbelievable scene left her speechless.

"The police are on their way, Jackson. Stop. Let them deal with this piece of shit," Mick shouted, pressing a foot to Wolf's chest to keep him in place.

He whimpered, rolled around on the ground, unable to get up given Mick's foot held him there. Blood and dirt smeared all over his face and shirt. Her gaze moved to the man staring at her. Just a few feet away, she saw the panic and rage in his emerald-green stare.

Her gaze never left Jackson's until Nico took her by the shoulders. "Damn it, Peyton, are you okay? Say something."

She blinked a few times, processing it all. Her jaw ached. Eyes burned. Jackson's long strides closed the distance between them in seconds.

His hand rubbed her shoulder, gentle, cautious. "You okay, Pea?"

Her throat was dry. She looked up at him. "I think so."

"Did he hit you?"

"Yes. My face hurts." He angled her toward the light shining through the doorway, pulling her hand away from her aching cheek.

"You son of a bitch." Jackson lunged toward Wolf.

"He's not worth it, Jackson. Let him rot in jail." Nico grabbed Jackson's arm and forced him to stay put.

"We need to get some ice on this right away." Peyton didn't miss the concern in Mick's eyes as he assessed her face.

She didn't move. Not ready to put ice on her face. Not ready to look in the mirror. Not ready to sit down and think about what just happened. Her pulse raced.

Sirens blared down the alley. An ambulance arrived along with police cars. Doors flew open, flashing red lights bounced off the brick walls, and a woman's voice came over the police scanner. So surreal. Like watching the events take place from outside her body.

Two police officers lifted Kenny Wolf from the ground and handcuffed him. Jackson, Mick, and Nico took turns explaining what had transpired.

"I'm officer Landowski. Can you tell me what happened?" the older man asked her.

"He attacked me from behind," she said, lifting her hand to her neck, as if trying to protect the fragile column from another assault. Swiping at the tears streaming down her face, she described every detail of the encounter. Jackson stood beside her, wrapping a protective arm around her shoulder.

"And thankfully Jackson, Nico, and Mick came out and found me." Her voice was raspy and dry.

"All right. Thank you. Has Mr. Wolf ever bothered you before?" Officer Landowski asked, and her gaze moved to Wolf sitting in the back of a squad car shouting about his rights being violated.

"Yes."

"What? When?" Jackson crossed his arms over his chest, narrowing his gaze in her direction.

"I didn't want to tell you because I didn't want you to get into trouble over this."

"What exactly happened, Miss Kroft?" the officer pressed.

"A few weeks ago, he cornered me in the lobby of Sebastian's office building. Warned me to play by his rules and then sent a few threatening texts over the last few weeks."

"What the fuck, Pea," Jackson said, scrubbing a hand over his face.

"You didn't report it at the time?" Landowski jotted in his notebook, pausing to look up at her.

"No, it would have gone public. I didn't want it to hurt Sebastian's chances in the election."

"That's why you started training with us?" Nico asked.

"Yes."

"Christ. You should have told me." Jackson shook his head.

She studied him while he hovered over her. He appeared—devastated? Wrecked?

The paramedics examined her and offered to take her to the hospital to be checked out, but she turned them down. The officers said they'd be in touch. She wanted to go home and lay her face in a tub of ice. Jackson walked her to the restroom in the gym to get her cleaned up and propped himself against the doorframe.

"Are you going to hold the door open?" she asked with surprise.

"Yep."

"You're going to stand in the women's restroom?"

"Yep."

Always the protector. She wanted to thank him right then but needed to compose herself. Holding back a tsunami of emotion, she met her gaze in the mirror, startled by the bruising already forming on her neck. Light blue welts scattered her throat. Her cheek swollen and red.

She opened her mouth wide to see if all her teeth

were still in place. A soft chuckle came from the man standing behind her, but he wasn't smiling.

"It's going to be worse tomorrow. The bruises are going to get darker." His voice broke a bit.

She couldn't prevent the urge to go to him. Her emotions barely in check. "Well, at least I have all my teeth." Throbbing pain pulsed in her cheek.

"Why didn't you tell me the fucker threatened you before?"

"I thought I could handle it." Her voice trembled.

His arms came around her, and the built-up anxiety and fear erupted. He held her while she sobbed and quaked and shook. Let it all out.

"I'm here, Pea. I'm not going anywhere."

She gripped his T-shirt, needed to get closer.

He said he wasn't going anywhere. Did he mean it? If so, how long would he stay?

Chapter Fourteen

Present

Anger threatened to engulf him. When he found her with Wolf—his fucking life had flashed before his eyes. She was everything.

Every. Fucking. Thing.

All he ever wanted. His girl, so small and mighty. Feminine and fierce. Soft and strong. A walking contradiction. He didn't know who the piece-of-shit coward was until the police questioned her and the whole story unraveled. The scumbag worked for her douchebag ex-boyfriend. Why hadn't she come to him? Told him the guy threatened her?

Goddamn, the girl was so stubborn, trying to handle a guy twice her size all on her own. It was part of what he loved about her.

He was in over his head. Still hadn't told her he'd be leaving after the restaurant opened. And now, they were going to Lake Tahoe together, and he didn't want to let her out of his sight. So fucking thankful she was okay.

"Are you ready?" she asked, her voice hoarse. It didn't surprise him with the bruises on her neck. He held her while she sobbed. Her pain fueled his anger. He wanted to find Sebastian's sorry ass and make sure he knew what his campaign manager had done to

Peyton.

"Yeah, let's get out of here." He wrapped one arm around her shoulder and led her toward the door.

He thanked Mick and Nico, both still notably shaken. Peyton hugged them good-bye. Although they were badass dudes, they had a soft spot for her. It would be difficult not to. She remained quiet on the drive to her house.

He walked beside her up the steps to her front door, and she paused. "Let's leave for Tahoe tonight. This way we'll get to stay two nights, instead of just one. I'm not going to be able to sleep. Let's grab Mr. Whiskers and some clothes and just leave."

He put a hand on her cheek, saw the fear in her eyes. It'd been there since he'd pulled the asshole off her. He hated it. Hated she had to feel that. Though he'd done all he could not to cross the line physically with her, he couldn't stay away any longer. Wanted to comfort her. Needed to. He'd tortured them both long enough. Suffered for weeks, fighting the urge to touch her. Kiss her. Make her his in every way. He had no fight left. Not when it came to her.

His mouth came over hers. His hand tangled in her silky hair, urging her closer. Sweet sounds of pleasure escaped her. He savored them. She was everything he'd ever desired. So soft. So sweet. A soul-deep need for this woman fueled him. Now that he'd allowed himself a taste, he wouldn't hold back. But he had to be gentle. She'd just been through a horrible ordeal. What the hell was he thinking? He pulled back, and she whimpered, her hands clutching his T-shirt, her eyes fluttering open.

"Please, don't stop," she whispered.

"I don't want to, but you've been through a lot

tonight, Pea."

"It has been an exhausting day." She pushed up on her tiptoes, planted a soft peck on his lips before wrapping her arms around his middle and hugging him. So fucking sweet.

He groaned against the top of her head. He'd opened the floodgates. Controlling it wouldn't be easy. "Let's grab your *average-whiskered* pup, throw some clothes in a bag, and head up to the lake."

She laughed before pushing inside. "I'm on board with everything except your snarky comment about my beautiful boy. Those are some magical whiskers right there."

They were on the road in less than an hour, and for the first time in a long while, he looked forward to going to Tahoe. Lake Tahoe had been his favorite place in the world for most of his life, until it became dark and grief-filled. In reality, he didn't hate Lake Tahoe but hated the memory of what had happened to his sister there.

His mother moved back down to Reno after Chloe died, and he hadn't seen her in years, nor did he have any desire to. She texted for money, and they had no relationship otherwise.

He and Peyton talked and laughed on the drive, which he found miraculous considering what she'd endured just a few short hours ago. She didn't talk about what happened. He understood. Hell, he'd done it himself for years but needed to know she was okay.

"Do you think Sebastian knew Wolf was coming to see you tonight?"

She thought for a moment, stroked her sleeping pup lying in her lap.

Lucky bastard.

"No. Sebastian would never be okay with what Wolf did."

"So why did you two end things? Obviously, he didn't want it to end, because he asked you to keep up the pretense you were still together."

"There were a few reasons. Our relationship was very, hmm—*surfacey.* You know, Wolf said something when he pinned me to the wall. It just came to me. He said they'd *picked* me? I don't know exactly what it means, but it sort of makes sense now. Sebastian needed to change his image and found himself a girlfriend he thought would fit the requirements. I come from the right family, went to the right schools, don't go out a lot. It's disgusting if it were planned out before we even met. He pursued me after our first date. Always wanted to take things to the next level. When you came back, I realized how abnormal our relationship was. He knew nothing about me. Case in point—he brought my mom to San Francisco to surprise me. I think it worked for a while because we were so perfect on paper. But there was no depth—no risk of getting hurt. I'm probably not making any sense," she rambled, fiddling with her dog's collar.

Her words hit him hard. It made perfect sense. He'd never had a connection with anyone else that came remotely close to what he shared with Peyton. Not even in the vicinity. He understood.

"I get it. *Safe* has its benefits. How did they pick you, though? What does that even mean? They chose you to date him? Jesus. The guy is a bigger douchebag than I thought. Well, this shit is about to blow up in their faces because Wolf's arrest is probably going viral

217

on social media right about now."

"I'm sure you're right, and Sebastian is most likely doing damage control. I don't want to have a role in affecting how the election plays out. It means everything to him, and I thought if I could keep the peace and he won the election, they'd leave me alone after. But this is on them now. Whatever happens has nothing to do with me. They just used me as a pawn to get what they wanted."

"They're both fucked up. But you should have come to me after Wolf cornered you, Pea."

"I know. I didn't tell you Sebastian and I weren't together, and I would have had to share the whole truth. I wasn't ready."

"Why?"

"Because you'd made it clear nothing could happen between us. You weren't a *forever guy.* I didn't want you to think I ended it with him because of you. I thought it would scare you off even more."

"But you did end it because of me, didn't you?" he teased, reaching over to tuck a piece of hair behind her ear. The slight contact sent a zip of arousal through him. No one ever affected him the way Peyton did.

"So humble," she teased. "Yes, you definitely had a lot to do with it. But the truth is, I should've done it sooner. I hadn't been happy for months. I just couldn't see it until you came back."

He squeezed her hand. Wanted to let this happen. Fear threatened to take him over, the way it usually did when things felt too good. The calm that came just before the ground disappeared from beneath his feet.

"I don't know what I have to offer you, Pea. But I'm done fighting it." He needed to say it. Warn her about what she'd be getting into before this avalanche of need took them both under.

"You said you loved me. Did you mean it?"

Hell, it was an easy question. The only easy question. He loved her. Always had. Always would. "Yes. It's about all I do know."

"Well, it's enough for me."

"Yeah? You sure?" He should tell her everything right now. He wouldn't be staying. This was temporary. He hadn't been lying when he told her he wasn't a forever guy.

"I'm sure. Because I love you in a way I've never loved anyone else. It's always been you. If there's a chance to have it again, I'm in."

Affection stabbed him in the chest. Damn this girl. She'd found a way in—somewhere she could never stay. But he'd let her in, for as long as he could have her.

"I love you, Pea," he said, voice gruff. Her eyes were bright with emotion, and damn if he didn't like being responsible for the grin spreading across her gorgeous face.

He pulled in the circular drive in front of her family home in South Lake. "When were you last here?" he asked.

"I didn't come back for a long time after I left for college. My dad begged me to redecorate the house two years ago, so I came up a couple times to meet the delivery guys and set it up for him and Lael."

"Over the past nine years, you only came to decorate it two years ago?"

"It reminded me of you. You know, I met you the weekend we moved into the house. Right after my dad bought the place. I'd never been there without you. Every summer, every weekend I went up, we were together. It wasn't the same. And after what happened to Chloe, I never wanted to go back," she said, her voice soft and vulnerable.

A sharp pain hit the center of his chest. A familiar ache settled there. "Why go back now?"

"For starters, you're back in my life, and it used to be my favorite place."

"Most beautiful place in the world."

"I'm sure coming here isn't easy for you. I appreciate you doing this," she said, unable to hide her concern.

"It's fine. It's part of moving forward, right?"

"Yep."

"So Whiskey's never been here? Does he swim?" He opened her door, grabbed her pup off her lap, and set him on the ground to check things out.

She chuckled. "*Mr. Whiskers* has never been here. I don't think he swims. I've never taught him."

The big house looked the same on the outside, but the landscape was more lush and full now. Staring out at the lake, his gaze settled on the tree line where he'd first met her. Happy memories lived here, too. He'd forgotten about those for a long time. The breeze was cool and crisp, and the smell of pine filled the November air.

"I love fall in South Lake," she said. Her pup frolicked around, relieving himself several times on multiple bushes.

"Me, too."

Memories slapped him in the face when he entered the house. He'd kissed her in this entryway more times than he could count. They dropped their bags and headed for the kitchen.

"I'm starving. My dad's housekeeper stocked the fridge. Are you hungry?"

"Yes. Go sit. I'll make us something," he said, guiding her to a chair.

"You don't think I can cook?"

"We both know I'm a better cook," he said with a wink.

She chucked her empty water bottle at him, and he caught it in one hand. Pulling out some deli meat and cheese, he found some crackers and made a platter. Peyton grabbed a bottle of wine and poured them each a hefty glass. He followed her out back to sit by the lake. The view spectacular, even this late at night. He turned on the fire pit, and they sat on the comfortable couches beside the roaring fire.

"I swear this is the best view on the lake. This house is positioned so you can see all the way around," he said, taking it in.

"It's so peaceful. I forgot how relaxing it is here."

"Hard not to get lost in it." He breathed in the light breeze dancing in the trees around them. Couldn't remember the last time he enjoyed the smell of pine and the view of this magnificent body of water. After Chloe died, he'd left Peyton, and everything good in his life vanished. In the blink of an eye. Sure, he had Joseph, loved him like a father, but he'd been drowning in grief for a long time. Being with Peyton, after all this time—the beauty around him started to return.

In more ways than one.

She wore a white hooded sweatshirt and black leggings. Her dark eyes glittered in the firelight. No makeup. The bruise on her cheek grew more prominent with each passing hour, but she insisted the ibuprofen kicked in. Her dark hair swept to the side in a long braid. A few pieces fell around her pretty face, as the breeze rustled around them. He relished every moment with her. Her plump pink lips turned up in the corners when she looked out at the water. The most beautiful woman he'd ever laid eyes on. His patience worn thin—desire moved through him with a fierceness he couldn't stop. She turned to look at him with a knowing smile. The simple act almost undid him.

"Come here," he said, not meaning for it to come out as a command, but it did.

"So bossy," she teased, scooting closer.

He wrapped his arms around her. "I don't want to push you, Pea. So you need to tell me what you want."

"You know what I want."

"Tell me."

"I want you. All of you. What do you want?" She pulled her bottom lip between her teeth, staring up at him.

"I want all of you. But your face is bruised, and you've been through a lot tonight. I think we should wait and see how you feel tomorrow."

"I think nine years is a long enough wait. Yeah, my face is sore, and it's been a crappy night. But this, you, and me"—she motioned her hand between them—"this makes me happy. I don't want to wait another day. I don't want to wait another minute."

His mouth came over hers. He ached in ways he hadn't experienced in years and kissed her like his life depended on it. She gave as good as she got. His insistent mouth parted her trembling lips, and his hands slipped down the smooth curves of her sides. The sound of their breathing filled the air. Everything else went silent around them. Unquenched desire built as he pulled her onto his lap, and she straddled him. Their mouths never lost contact. His hands moved beneath her sweatshirt and trailed up her soft, heated skin. Pulling away from her mouth, he moved his lips gently down her neck, wanted to savor and worship her.

Tonight, he would take his time. Adore every inch of her. His body quaked beneath her delicate fingers. He moved up to take her mouth again, and she reached for the button on his jeans. Cutting off the kiss, she whimpered. He needed to make sure she wanted this as much as he did.

"Let me look at you, Pea," he whispered, his fingers tracing the soft lace of her bra. Her head fell back on a gasp.

"Jackson, please." The desperation in her voice challenged his restraint.

"There's no rush. I'm taking my time with you tonight," he whispered, lips grazing her ear when he spoke.

He loved the way she responded to his touch. Frantic and feverish. Loved how she lost control with him, digging her fingers into his shoulders, she pulled his mouth back down to meet hers. Her hips pressing with need against his.

He took her face in his hands. "Promise me you'll tell me if you're hurting and need to stop."

"I promise you it's not going to happen," she said with confidence.

"You're killing me. Let me take you inside."

She nodded. "You don't want to go down to our

beach?"

The first place they'd ever made love. A lot of memories took place in that very spot. But tonight—it would be the first time in a different way. They'd been through so much together, and he didn't have any idea what the future held for them.

Knew he wanted her. Needed her. It wasn't about the past, and it wasn't about the future. It was just about them. Right now. In this moment. He pushed to stand, and her legs wrapped around his waist, her arms around his neck. "No. Tonight is about a fresh start and making new memories."

"Yes," she agreed.

He shouldn't take what he didn't deserve, but in this moment—he didn't fucking care about right and wrong. All reason now overshadowed by his need for her. Desire extinguished sanity. He set her down on the bed, wanting to see her. All of her. When her beautiful dark gaze latched on to his, heat streaked through his veins.

She raised her arms. He pulled the sweatshirt over her head, leaving nothing but her white lace bra. Jesus, she was beautiful. He peeled her leggings off, then climbed over and propped himself above her. "Are you sure you want this?" he said pressing his hips against hers, and she gasped.

So fucking sweet.

"I'm more than sure."

He ran his thumb over her bottom lip. "Tell me you're mine, Pea."

"I'm yours."

"Mine," he whispered against her ear, and she arched up in response. His mouth came down over hers.

He wouldn't stop again. Every last bit of restraint fell away. He reached behind her, unclasped her bra. Needing to see her. Touch every inch of her.

Planting gentle kisses down her neck, he nipped and taunted. Her body trembled when he lingered over her perfect breasts. His tongue teased the soft peaks. Her fingers tangled in his hair, urging him closer. Goddamn, he'd never get enough of her.

"Jackson," she gasped.

His fingers hooked into the edge of her silk panties, sliding them slowly down her gorgeous legs. Standing over her, he stared in awe. Memorizing every inch of her. It had been so long. Too long.

He took in his beautiful girl. "So fucking perfect, Pea."

Her cheeks flushed pink, and she pushed up to sit, reaching for the button of his jeans and pushing them all the way down. He grabbed the fabric behind his neck and yanked the shirt over his head, dropping it to the floor.

"You're beautiful," she said, voice husky and laced with need.

Her fingers traced each muscle along his stomach, and it almost undid him when she looked up to meet his gaze. So. Fucking. Vulnerable. He leaned down and took her mouth again. His tongue explored and tangled with hers. She whimpered against his lips, and he leaned back and nipped at her sweet mouth before pulling away.

Her hands shook, slipping her fingers beneath the waistband of his boxer briefs. Gasping as she took in his desire.

"This is what you do to me," he whispered the

truth. No other woman ever left him wanting, needing like this. Only her. Only Peyton. He reached down to grab the foil packet from his pants pocket. Tore it open with his teeth and rolled it on slowly as her hungry gaze took him in.

He urged her back farther on the bed and hovered above. He settled between her legs. His hard length teased her entrance. She wrapped her legs around his waist, and it took tremendous strength not to move. To savor the moment.

"I need you, Jackson," she begged.

The simple plea set him on fire. Because the truth was—he needed her more. He kissed his way down her neck, savored every inch of her gorgeous body. The smell of orange blossoms and vanilla driving him mad. He eased forward, filling her completely, staring down at dark eyes so full of trust. Her fingers clung to his biceps. Pants and gasps filled the air around them, and they moved together as one. Nothing had ever felt so good. So perfect. So right. There was no turning back. She was his.

For as long as he could have her.

Chapter Fifteen

Present

Like awaking from a coma, she stretched and twisted in the silky sheets wrapped around her. Had she slept for days? The light coming through the windows blinding when she attempted to open her eyes. Shades of the night before played in her head. She remembered Jackson's touch, his kiss, the way he'd worshipped her in every sense of the word. After all this time, nothing changed between them. At least not physically.

It was too much. Overwhelming in every possible way, yet she wanted more. She wanted, well—she wanted everything. All of him. Panic spread through her. Where was he? Did he leave? Did their night together scare him off? Sitting up, she held the white satin sheet against her bare chest. A throb pulsed in her cheek.

She was still in shock by what had transpired less than twenty-four hours ago. Wolf's attack ran through her mind. She'd pressed charges against the lunatic and hoped he would be put away for a long time. But right now her concern was about the man who'd not only rescued her, but made her feel things she hadn't felt in years.

Jackson.

Had it been too much for him? The clicking of

little nails moved in the hallway outside the bedroom door. The sound of larger feet followed. The wood floors creaked beneath him. Her stomach dipped with both nerves and anticipation. He hadn't left. At least not yet.

Mr. Whiskers hurried to the side of the bed, barking his arrival and running in little circles. She scooped him up, and he assaulted her with kisses. Jackson stood in the doorway looking beautifully male, his jeans slung low on his hips, his chest bare, with every hard line and muscle on display for her to ogle. Her mouth watered, taking him in. Moving toward her, he carried something in his hand, and the air sparked with each step he took.

"You okay?" he asked, his voice laced with concern.

"Yeah, of course." She swiped at her face, realizing a single tear had made its way down her cheek. The fear he'd left her knocked her off-kilter.

"You look upset. Are you in pain?" He ran one knuckle in a gentle rhythm over her jawline where Wolf had struck her.

The softness of his touch soothed the ache radiating from her face. "I was disoriented when I woke up," she said. "I thought you left."

No more holding back. No more being afraid. It was time to be honest, and he was worth the risk.

He cringed at her words. "I'm right here, Pea."

He grabbed something off the side table. "I took Whiskey outside and got some ice to put on your cheek. I noticed more bruising this morning. Lie back. Let's get this on there."

This man.

Such a powerful and strong exterior, yet so gentle and thoughtful on the inside. He stretched out beside her, lying on his side to face her.

"Thank you for being so sweet. I haven't looked at it yet. Is it bad?" she asked.

He held the icepack to her face. "Nah, it's nothing Rocky Jr. can't handle," he teased but watched her with concern.

"You should see the other guy," she joked, trying to make light of the situation.

"The other guy's lucky he's walking today. If I'd had my way, he wouldn't have left the parking lot conscious."

Reality slapped her in the face at the memory of what happened.

"Today's the election. I wonder if Wolf's arrest went public. I can't imagine it would be good for Sebastian."

"He has the Boones to help him through it, doesn't he?"

She laughed. Good point. Sebastian had made his bed. Now he would have to lie in it. His publicity stunt with her mother might have done more harm than good. His campaign manager hadn't turned crazy overnight, and Sebastian had chosen to ignore his odd behavior for months. He'd hired him because he was known for being cutthroat, and when you make a deal with the devil, you just might get bit in the ass.

She stroked the stubble covering Jackson's jaw, loved the way it prickled against her fingers.

"Thank you for last night." She didn't care how corny it sounded. He awakened something inside her.

Removing the icepack from her face, he set it on

the table. His fingers traced her cold cheek. The mere touch left her tingling everywhere. "You're beautiful, Pea."

"I've missed you so much," she whispered.

"I've missed you, too. We have a lot of time to make up for." His heated gaze raked her over, stealing the air from her lungs.

He rolled her onto her back. His mouth crashed into hers, scorched her in the most blissful kind of way. Her entire body trembled with need.

"Fuck, Pea. How have I lived without you for so long?" he whispered the words against her mouth and kissed her deeper.

She tangled her hands in his hair and urged him closer, taking all she could get from him. The fear of losing him lingered. Wouldn't survive if he left her again, so she was going all in—mind, body, and soul.

She dozed off after they *made up for lost time*. Again. She'd never been so relaxed and content in her life. Her body responded as if it were made just for him. He wasn't in bed with her when she awoke, but she didn't panic this time. Reaching for her phone on the nightstand, she couldn't have prepared for the slew of texts and voicemails waiting for her. The story went public this morning, both in print and on social media. Sebastian somehow managed to spin it in his favor. Old habits died hard. He claimed he'd fired his campaign manager before Wolf went to the gym last night. Insisted the man had put a wedge between her and Sebastian over the past few months. Added in a sappy story that he didn't know where she'd gone, and he was worried sick. Lying bastard. He managed to paint himself the victim. Clearly, he was taking pointers from the Monica Boone playbook to come up with this.

She'd spoken briefly with her father, Jayden, Dani, and Elle last night, and let Camille know she would be out of town for two days but had everything under control at the restaurant. The people who cared about her knew where she was.

Responding to the sixteen text messages from Sebastian, she chose her words carefully.

Really? This is the best you can do? Way to own up to what happened. For the record, your campaign manager, who physically assaulted me, also informed me you both "picked" me to play the role of your girlfriend, for the sake of the campaign. Have you no shame? Now you're spinning a story about your long-lost love gone missing? We haven't been together in weeks, and you know it. How do you plan to do right by our city when you can't even do right by me, one small citizen? You best hope nobody reaches out to me before tonight, because I'm done lying for you. I'll give honest answers, which will not bode well for you. Stop telling lies which involve me, or I will press defamation of character charges against you.

His response came right away.

I won't speak to anyone else today. I give you my word. This will be over tonight, but you must understand I'm under a tremendous amount of stress. My campaign manager has been arrested, and you've gone MIA. You can't begin to know how sorry I am about what happened.

Had it always been all about him? She read through the multiple texts from friends and family, and paused at her mother's.

I'm so sorry about what happened to you. We're

231

catching a flight home this afternoon. Brad must get back to Nashville for a show. Someone from the press approached me this morning and inquired about the incident with Sebastian's campaign manager. I refused to comment. I know it's not much, but I am trying to think before I speak. I'm quite sure I've been a huge disappointment to you, Peyton, but I do love you. I'm just not very good at showing you.

What in the world was happening? Her mother never apologized. Not once since she'd walked out on them all those years ago. Falling back on the bed, she tried to process the craziness which was her life. Jackson's voice came from the hallway outside the bedroom, and he sounded angry. She caught the tail end of the conversation. He told the person on the other end to keep him posted before ending the call.

"Ah, she's awake," he said, before diving onto the bed. He pulled her beneath him and tickled her senseless. Their laughter filled the room, and Mr. Whiskers barked maniacally on the floor beside the bed.

She managed to wriggle away and sit up, catching her breath. "You know I hate being tickled."

"I do," his deep voice teased.

"You're showered and dressed?"

"You've been asleep for hours, Pea. I took Whiskey on a run, too."

She raised an eyebrow in surprise. "Mr. Whiskers can run?"

"Yeah, and he's a hell of a lot faster than you."

Reaching for a pillow, she swung it at his head before he wrapped his arms around her and pulled her back against his chest.

"You're killing me, woman. If you don't get out of this bed, you're going to force me to ravage you again. I need food and so do you."

"I'm starving. I can be ready in ten minutes."

He followed her into the bathroom and leaned against the wall while she got ready.

"Have you checked your phone?" His tone was more serious now.

"Yes. He's unbelievable, isn't he? Spinning this in his favor." She brushed her hair back from her face and pulled it into a bun on top of her head.

"Your dad is filing a restraining order against Kenny Wolf today. He's going to fax over some paperwork."

She whirled around to face him. "You talked to my dad?"

"Yes."

"Is everything okay? Why would I need a restraining order if he's in jail?"

"Wolf was released on bail this morning. I guess it pays to have friends in high places."

She saturated her face in moisturizer before applying mascara and lip gloss, needing a moment to wrap her head around this new information. How does one get arrested for assault and get out on bail the following morning?

"Well, Wolf has bigger fish to fry than me. The election will be over when we go home tomorrow, and everyone will move on." She closed the distance between them, pressed her face to his chest, and hugged him.

The familiarity was still there, as if no time passed when they weren't together. Their bond remained.

Unbreakable.

"I hope you're right. Until then, I'm going to be glued to your side. You'll just have to deal with it."

She laughed, and they made their way out to the car. "Oooh, like a bodyguard?"

He opened the passenger door and scowled at her. "This is not a joke, Pea."

"You know what I want to do?" she asked when he pulled out onto the road.

"What?"

"I want to enjoy our day. We haven't been here together in almost a decade. All I've heard about for the last six months is the election. I'd like just one day to enjoy something not involving Sebastian or Kenny Wolf. After today, I'll go along with whatever you want me to do. Fair?"

His features softened. "Fair."

He pulled over at a cute, new café. The sign on the front window read *Grand Opening*. Things had changed a bit in South Lake. Her eyes were bigger than her stomach per usual. She ordered way more than necessary. He polished off her leftovers. With his fight coming up, she wanted to talk about something other than what had happened last night.

"Do you get nervous before fights?"

"Nah, not really. Your adrenaline is pumping, and the crowd gets you going big-time."

"Does it hurt during the fight? Or not until after?"

"Depends who you're up against and how many times you get hit," he teased.

"Leroy Sasone should be a good match from what I've researched."

He reached over and took a bite of her salad. "Look

at you. You've become the MMA pro in a matter of weeks. You're researching fighters now?"

"Hardly. And FYI—you have a better record."

He nodded. "He's only lost twice in his career. The guy is pretty damn skilled."

"I've never seen a fight. I mean, I used to go to your wrestling matches, but it's so different. Unless you count the hours I've watched Rocky."

"Fucking ridiculous, Peanut." He planted a kiss on her lips and led her out the door.

"What do you want to do now?" she asked.

"You want to go see the old Langford's?"

They'd practically grown up at Langford's, Joseph's old restaurant. It held a ton of memories.

"Yes. Let's head over now." She climbed into the Jeep.

Surprised to find Langford's empty, they took in the old building.

"Wow. Someone had bought the place and opened a new restaurant years ago, but I didn't know it closed down. It's on a prime piece of real estate. How is this place empty?"

The exterior was shabby. Filthy windows, weather damage, loose siding, and the paint tattered and distressed.

"I can't believe no one has picked up this gem, either. It's the only other place on the lake rivaling the view from my father's house." She looked out toward the water. Langford's sat in the trees right off the lake. Large windows covered the back wall of the restaurant, allowing everyone in the dining room to share the spectacular view.

"Yeah. Let's go around back. Remember, the door

never locked. I wonder if the guy who bought it ever changed it."

She followed him and ducked under a few branches from the overgrown trees around the building. The sound of dried pine needles crunched beneath their feet with each step. Jackson jiggled the handle, and the door popped open. They both laughed.

"Some things never change," she teased and ducked under his arm, hurrying inside.

"Wow. It's musty in here," he said through a cough.

"It doesn't look like anyone's been here in years. How has this just been vacant?"

They walked into the kitchen, and the sunlight made its way through the water-stained windows, allowing just enough light to see the space. Nothing had changed, with the exception of the lack of care.

"This is where Joseph taught me everything about running a restaurant. Chloe always sat right here, do you remember? On the tall barstool so she could look out at the lake."

She walked over to him and wrapped her arms around his middle, resting her head against his back. Needing to comfort him any way she could.

"I'm sure this is hard, Jackson. But thinking about the good memories is important. And there are so many great ones here."

His hands came over hers. "Yeah. I only remember the dark times surrounding Chloe's death when I think of South Lake. It's nice to remember there were happy memories, too."

"I think it's good we came here."

He turned around to face her, took her face in his

hands, and gently soothed her bruised cheek with his thumb. "I do, too."

Her heart squeezed. Maybe they really could move forward. Put the past behind them. Jackson needed to stop punishing himself for a crime he hadn't committed. Everyone else knew it, except Jackson.

"Come on." He tugged her along to the dining room.

Standing behind her, he wrapped his arms around her waist, resting his chin on top of her head. Cobwebs stretched from the high wood beams on the ceiling down to the windows. The dust piled high on the tables and chairs, and the rustic wood floors were covered in soot.

"I forgot how much I loved this place," she said, leaning back against him.

"So did I. It feels good to be here. We grew up in this place."

"Yes, we did."

"I can't believe how run-down it is."

"It just needs a little TLC," she said. She moved up on her tiptoes and planted a kiss on his perfect lips. He responded by pulling her close, his mouth capturing hers.

My God. Things were getting a bit out of control. They hadn't been this bad when they were teenagers. She couldn't help herself, urging him closer. He lifted her off her feet, and her legs wrapped around his waist. He deepened the kiss before setting her down on the bar top.

"What am I going to do with you, Peanut?"

"You could do whatever you want if you'd drop the ridiculous nickname," she teased.

He chuckled. "Never. Let's go see if our tree is still out there. I think the fire a few years ago damaged most of the trees on this side of the lake."

They took the trail leading down to the water. The sound of broken twigs and loud crackling beneath their feet mixed with the melody of a few birds chirping high in the trees. The smell of pine, vanilla, and butterscotch lingered in the air.

She scooped up a large pinecone. "I love these before they change colors. The blue-green tint is so pretty."

"Yeah, it's hard to beat this." He raised his arms in awe of the beauty surrounding them.

Nearing the water, she ran ahead and found their old tree. "Oh, my gosh," she yelled. "It's still here."

He came up behind her, his hard body pressed against her backside, making his desire impossible to miss. He'd carved their initials into this tree on her sixteenth birthday.

JV + PK

The memory was still swoon worthy. The day he'd showed her what he'd done was the day she knew Jackson Vance owned her heart. Forever. But life was cruel sometimes. Maybe this was their second chance.

He stepped back, glancing around at the surrounding area. "Look at the other trees."

"How weird. They're all damaged from the fire except this one."

"Sort of like us," he said. His finger traced over the initials he'd carved more than a decade ago.

"What do you mean?"

"Our tree's still standing even after the fire. Resilient just like us, Pea." He turned to look out at the lake.

"We may have a few bruises, but you're right. We're still standing," she said at the thought of all they'd been through. Together. She walked beside him to sit on the dock behind the restaurant, the clear blue water lapped against the beach, and they breathed in the cool air.

"How do you really feel about being here, Jackson?" she asked, and he wrapped an arm around her and tugged her closer.

"It feels good to be back. Familiar."

Butterflies fluttered in her belly. She didn't miss the hope in his voice. He'd have to face the past if they were ever going to move forward. But they were making progress. He leaned down and kissed her neck. One hand came around her waist and pushed her back. Her breathing hitched, and he propped himself above her. The sun, reflecting off the water, shone amber and gold flecks in his gorgeous green eyes. She relished the moment. She hadn't been this happy for a long time. Life would be crazy once they returned home tomorrow, but things between her and Jackson had shifted. She wanted to stay in this moment forever.

Lifting his head, he moved to his feet. "Let's go visit our beach."

"I thought you said you wanted to make new memories?"

"And I think we've made some damn good new memories," he teased. "But I want you everywhere I can have you." He extended a hand and pulled her up. He bent down and pointed to his back. "Hop on."

"Why?" she asked on a laugh.

"Because you're slow as hell, Pea. And if I don't

get you to that beach soon, I'm going to have to take you right here on these pine needles," he said with a wicked grin.

He didn't need to ask her twice. She hopped on his back and swatted his ass. "Let's get a move on, Vance."

He hurried them back to the car, and she wondered if this really was their second chance. Because nothing ever felt more right.

Chapter Sixteen

Nine years earlier

He glanced at the basket sitting on the passenger seat and laughed. Hell, the thing would need its own seat on the flight today. He couldn't believe the summer had passed so quickly. Saying good-bye to his girl sucked. He hated leaving her. He couldn't get the sight of her standing in the driveway with tears streaking down her face out of his head. He dialed her, his Bluetooth ringing.

"Hello." Her response, a half sob, half laugh.

He smiled. "You okay?"

"Yep."

"Be strong, Pea. We're going to be fine."

"Promise?"

"Promise."

"I love you."

"Love you more," he said before disconnecting the call.

When he pulled in the driveway of his home, he noticed two police cars, a fire truck, and an ambulance parked near his mother's trailer. What the fuck? What had she done now? The woman couldn't go a week without some sort of drama. Drug busts. A DUI. Two arrests. Domestic violence claims against Ryker. Joseph was at the end of his rope, and Jackson understood. Her trailer sat on his property, so her problems became everyone's problems. However, kicking her out meant risking her going back to Reno with Chloe in tow. Their mother had shown Jackson too many times who she was. His sister might want to believe she could change, but Jackson had given up hope a long time ago.

He stepped out of the truck, heard screaming, crying, hysterics. He hurried up the driveway. A sharp pain settled in his chest. Joseph rushed out to meet him. His dark hair grayed a bit these last few years, but he kept fit and healthy and appeared much younger than a man in his sixties. Except now. His face drained of color, and his eyes bloodshot red.

A chill crept up Jackson's spine. "What's wrong?"

"Jackson, go to the house. I'll come over and talk to you in a minute." Joseph's voice trembled.

"No. What's going on? Is it Mom? Where's Chloe?"

"Not right now, son. Go to the house. Please." His voice broke on a cry, and alarm bells sounded in Jackson's head.

His instincts kicked in, and he shoved past Joseph and raced toward his mother's trailer. There were police officers, firefighters, and EMTs outside the trailer, and his heart raced so fast it threatened to burst. His mom sat on the ground outside the trailer, head buried in her hands, sobbing. Her body frail, a reminder he was looking at a full-blown junkie. She raised her head to meet his questioning gaze, and he saw the devastation.

"What happened, Mom?" he said, barely able to get the words out.

She just stared. Tears streamed down her sunken face. "I don't know. I just woke up and found her."

Her.

The word spun in his head. Everything blurred. His gaze scanned the area in slow motion. People surrounded the trailer. Muffled voices he couldn't make out from inside. Movement came from the doorway of the trailer, and two men carried out a stretcher. A sheet covered the body beneath. He tried to catch his breath; his knees buckled, and he slumped to the ground. A thick lump formed in the base of his throat, making it impossible to breathe.

"What the fuck happened, Mom?" he bit out in a rage, the ringing in his ears blocked everything around him out. The men continued to move past him with the lifeless body.

"Jackson." The desperate tone barely audible as two strong, familiar hands gripped his shoulders.

Joseph. *Always there.*

"Where's Chloe?" Fear, desperation, and terror swallowed him whole.

"Son, let me get you to the house. You don't want to see this. There's been an accident. A terrible accident," Joseph said. His voice quaked.

"No. *No.* It's not her. I told her to stay at the house. I told her not to come out here. It's not her. I'm taking her to breakfast. Chloe and I are going to breakfast," he rambled with insistence, following the men who carried the stretcher.

Two officers walked over and stood beside Joseph. "Come on, son."

"Don't fucking *touch* me," he screamed, arms flailing, warning the three men to let him go. "I'm not leaving without my sister."

"There's nothing you can do. Please listen to me."

Joseph's tone was frantic, and his arms wrapped tight around Jackson's chest.

"Let me see her," he shouted.

"Stop fighting, son. She's gone," Joseph pleaded. Jackson's heart split in two, his stomach rolled, and an ache formed in the back of his throat. Dizzy. He swore his heart stopped beating. Wanted it to. Everything went numb. So numb. Dropping to his knees, he hurled, throwing up and gasping for air at the same time. His baby sister lay beneath the sheet. Unable to comprehend what had happened, he lunged at his mother.

"What did you do? What the fuck did you do?"

He couldn't reach her. Joseph and one of the police officers dragged him away. No control. Couldn't feel his legs. Couldn't feel his arms. His mother's wailing sounded from behind, and he fell onto the dirt a few feet away. Joseph dropped down beside him and gripped his shoulders.

"You need to calm down. You don't want to make things worse than they already are." His tear-streaked face was so full of despair.

"How can it get any worse? How did this happen? I told Chloe to stay at the house. Why didn't she stay there?"

A gut-wrenching sob escaped him. It didn't sound human. He couldn't keep it in any longer. Joseph kept a tight hold of him.

"We don't have the details yet. Ryker was here last night. Your mom said some sort of fight broke out. This is all we know at the moment."

Jackson tried to swipe his blurred eyes but made it worse because his hands were covered in dirt. "Why didn't she call for help last night? Why are we just finding out this morning?"

"Your mom said Chloe came out to check on her. She and Ryker were fighting. Chloe tried to intervene, and Ryker hit her. Chloe's head struck the counter before falling to the floor. Tammy was high and said she thought Chloe would wake up and everything would be fine. It's all she remembers because she passed out."

A fury filled him. Threatened to take him under. Something inside snapped. Ryker had killed Chloe, and their mother did nothing to help her. He'd left his little sister alone. And she'd gone out to help their piece-of-shit mother.

He'd fucking left her.

Chloe had begged to go with him. Why the fuck hadn't he take her? How could he be so selfish?

"Where's Ryker?" He pushed to his feet, fists clenched at his sides. He would pound Ryker's fucking face in. Needed to hurt him the way he'd hurt his sister. His innocent baby sister. Never did anything wrong in her life. And now she was gone? Nothing made sense. Nothing made any fucking sense.

Joseph grasped his arms with force. "You're not going anywhere. Ryker left before I got here this morning, but the police already picked him up. You need to sit your ass down. Do you hear me? I'm not about to lose both of you."

The next few hours passed in a blur. Ryker didn't admit to a damn thing. First, he denied being at the house, insisting he never saw Chloe. Joseph's security cameras scanned the property, which proved Ryker a liar. The police hauled his mother in as well, interrogating the two drug-addict pieces of shit.

There were no words. Nothing he could ever do to forgive himself or make things right for her. He'd left Chloe alone, and now she was gone. Murdered. For fourteen years, he'd looked out for her. Adored her. In the end, he'd failed her just like their deadbeat mother did.

He sat on the floor of his darkened bedroom Despair threatened to choke him. The oak floors creaked with his every movement. His angry gaze took in the suitcases left beside the door. His closet now empty, drawers left with only a few sparse things, and the walls still draped with his athletic and academic achievements. None of it meant a damn thing now. Sorrow and self-loathing engulfed him whole. He looked down at his filthy hands and replayed what happened over and over. Hatred for both his mother and Ryker so real he'd do just about anything for one minute alone with either of them. The phone rang nonstop, and muffled voices came from the living room. He didn't want to see or speak to anyone. His phone was lost somewhere in the mayhem. Word spread, and people wanted to know what happened. None of them knew the role he'd played in his sister's death. How Chloe had begged to go with him, and he refused to take her. Denied her this simple request.

Such an easy fucking request.

The bedroom door opened a crack. Peyton stood in the doorway. The light from the hallway made a bright cocoon around her silhouette.

The intrusion from the quiet darkness caused him to squint. "Not now, Pea."

She dropped down beside him on the floor. Their

backs pressed against his bed now stripped of the linens.

"I'm so sorry. I came as soon as I heard. I can't believe this is happening. I thought you were on the plane. I'm so sorry, Jackson," she said. Her voice crumbled with raw emotion.

He felt—nothing. Couldn't comfort her. Didn't want her to comfort him. He wanted to wallow in his own misery. Alone.

"I need to be by myself right now." His throat was thick with despair, making it difficult to talk.

Placing both hands on the sides of his face, she looked into his eyes. Tears ran unchecked down her cheeks.

"No. You're the one who taught me not to run. I'm not leaving you."

"Fucking Christ!" he roared, startling them both, and jumped to his feet.

She scrambled to stand. Her gaze searched his in the little bit of light coming from beneath the door. She reached for his hand, and he pulled away.

"For the first time, I'm asking you to go, and now you won't run? Are you fucking kidding me?" he spewed ugliness. Wanted to push her out the door. Push her as far away from him as she could go.

"I'm not going anywhere," she said, her stare steady on his. He saw her bottom lip tremble, yet still, he remained numb.

"I'm not asking. If you won't leave, I will."

Her hand moved up to swipe the flood of tears. He couldn't fucking comfort her right now. He was so angry. Devastated. And lost. Nothing made sense anymore.

"Don't push me away. Please, don't do this. I love you. Let me help you," she pleaded, her voice just above a whisper.

"Help me? Chloe begged me to bring her with me last night. She fucking *begged* me. I told her no. I wanted to be with you. Now she's dead. And you want to help me?"

She broke on a sob. "Jackson, this was an awful accident. You couldn't know anything like this would happen."

He moved away from her. His hands gripped fistfuls of his hair. "When I look at you, it reminds me of how I betrayed my sister. I need you to fucking leave!" he shouted.

Joseph and Thomas Kroft entered his bedroom. Peyton's father had returned to Tahoe upon hearing the news. Jackson was glad, because he couldn't be there for her and needed to know someone else was.

Her father would be there.

"Everything okay in here?" Joseph looked exhausted.

"No. I can't have her here. Not right now." Sitting on the bed, he stared down at his hands. When did they get so filthy? There were small cuts and dirt smeared across his palms.

Peyton's quiet sobs and whispered conversation from Joseph and Thomas surrounded him. He didn't fucking care. Why wouldn't they just leave him alone? He didn't give a shit if they whispered in the living room, the kitchen, or the fucking hallway. He just wanted them to leave him the fuck alone. A hand clapped his shoulder, and he flinched.

"We're here for you, son," Thomas said, voice raw

with emotion.

Jackson didn't reply.

"Peyton, honey, you need to respect his wishes. Let's go." Peyton's father's tone was unwavering.

"It's okay to let people help you, son," Joseph said, his own grief wearing him down when he followed Thomas and Peyton out of the room.

****

Hours turned into days, and the darkness swallowed him whole. Memories of Chloe flooded him. The two of them against the world—that's what they'd always said when they were younger. Neither he nor Chloe ever knew who their fathers were, and their mother wasn't much of a parent. Chloe had spent her entire life trying to save a woman who didn't want to be saved.

Why hadn't he just taken her with him to Peyton's? He would never forgive himself. Never. He remembered walking her into her first day of kindergarten, teaching her how to swim, and teasing her about the crush she had on a kid in her class—he swore he felt his heart fracture right down the center when he closed his eyes and saw that little girl with blonde hair and freckles clear as day. Nothing he could do about it now. She was gone.

Joseph spoke to Jackson's coach at the Naval Academy because he never flew out the day they'd expected him, and they offered him a few days to figure out what he wanted to do. He didn't want to talk to them or anyone. Didn't know if he wanted to go to school, but he sure as fuck didn't want to stay here, either. He wanted to get as far away from home as possible. His mother was released for the time being, and Joseph requested she stay with friends down in Reno. Due to the overwhelming evidence against Ryker, bail was denied. He could rot in jail for the rest of his life for all Jackson cared. Peyton visited him every day. Sat beside him, though he never looked her way nor spoke. When tired of the silent treatment, she went out to the kitchen and helped Joseph make dinner. Jackson never joined them. Joseph brought him a plate after she left, and he ate just enough to keep himself afloat.

A knock on his bedroom door startled him. Joseph stepped in. He looked older. Tired. He sat down on the chair in Jackson's room and rested his elbows on his knees.

"I spoke to Coach Oliver."

"Yeah." He didn't meet the older man's eyes.

"Yep. You're leaving Thursday. Day after the funeral."

He bit the inside of his cheek. The salty, metallic taste of blood pooled on his tongue. "All right. What about the trial?" He wanted to leave. Too painful here. The constant reminder of what happened and the role he played in it.

"I'll attend the trial every day and give you updates. Coach and I agreed it's not in your best interest to sit through it. It may last months. This isn't healthy. You need to go."

"I want to make sure the fucker rots in hell," he spewed, scrubbing a hand over his face.

"You have no control over what happens, Jackson. There's enough evidence to put him away for a long time. You sitting in a courtroom won't make a difference. But you can go on with your life away from all this."

He nodded. Exhaustion made it challenging to argue. "I get to go on with my life, and she doesn't get to live? Does that sound fair?"

"Nothing about this is fair. But it sure as hell isn't your fault. I'm not going to stand by and watch you punish yourself." Joseph bent down, looked him in the eyes.

"Isn't it? If I let her come with me, this wouldn't have happened."

"Are you really going to do this to yourself? Come on, son. If I hadn't been at work, this wouldn't have happened. If Chloe had gone to a friend's house, this wouldn't have happened. If you'd both had a different mother, this wouldn't have happened. Christ. The truth is, your mother is a drug addict. Her boyfriend is a bad guy. He killed Chloe. No rhyme or reason. You didn't play a role in this. The best thing Chloe had in her life was her big brother, who loved and protected her. She loved you, Jackson. She would not want you blaming yourself. You're a good kid. The best I've ever known. Don't lose yourself in this." His voice broke.

"I didn't do a very good job of protecting her, though, did I?"

"You couldn't sit here twenty-four hours a day for the rest of her life. She loved her mama. It was a disaster in the making. I should've kicked your mom out a long time ago. I kept her here for Chloe, and now I have to live with my decision."

"You are the best thing to happen to Chloe and me." He was drowning in grief.

"We're going to go to the funeral tomorrow and give your sister a proper send-off. Just as she deserves.

Then you're going to get on a plane the following morning and go to school. I'll keep you posted on the trial by phone and email."

"Okay."

"You're grieving, and it's normal. Don't push everyone away. You'll regret it. Peyton loves you, son. She is trying to be here for you. You push her too far, and she may not come back. This isn't either of your faults. Don't punish her."

He ran his fingers through his hair. "Of course, it's not her fault. But I'm no good for her. Not now. Maybe not ever. I couldn't take care of Chloe, and I can't take care of Peyton, either. This could have fucking happened to her, too. I have no control over who or what my mother brings into my life. I don't want to have to worry or care about anyone. Especially Peyton. Never again." He meant it.

"The way you feel today—you won't feel forever."

He doubted it. He'd failed his sister. Failing Peyton wasn't an option. He wanted to get as far away from home as possible. His mother reached out a few times, but Joseph encouraged her to stay away for now. Thinking about Chloe—fury consumed him. Anger rippled through every bone in his body.

He didn't want to make small talk or pretend everything would be okay. The truth was, it never would be. He'd never needed much. A sister he adored, a girlfriend he loved, and a man who treated him like a son. It'd always been more than enough. Now, he didn't want anyone to depend on him. Nor did he want to depend on anyone.

All of South Lake came to the service to pay their condolences to the sweet girl who'd grown up here and lost her life in a horrible way. It didn't sit well with anyone. *A life taken too soon* was the mantra in town. White lilies spilled out of multiple arrangements lining the aisles, contrasting with the sea of black. The smell of grief loomed. The endless sound of sniffling and crying caused the hair on the back of his neck to stand on end. Everyone watched when he and Joseph made their way to the front pew.

Red, swollen eyes. Grief-stricken faces. Empathy everywhere he turned. The most devastating—the dark brown gaze of the girl he loved. Her shoulders drooped, stare lost and empty, and her chin trembled. His chest tightened at the sight of her. She grieved the loss of his sister, who she considered family, and the loss of her boyfriend, who turned his back on her. His cold expression was unfamiliar to her, and he made sure she saw it. For the first time in all the years they'd known one another, he wanted her to run. He needed her to run. To run as far away from him as she could get.

A beautiful picture of Chloe, which Joseph selected for the service, sat on an easel up front. His mother took the seat beside him. Some nerve showing her face at Chloe's funeral. The woman never deserved the unconditional love Chloe had shown her. His mother reached for his hand, but he pushed it away. Didn't speak to her, nor did he plan to before leaving in the morning. The rest of the service was a blur. Unable to push away thoughts of his last conversation with his sister. The guilt so strong, making it difficult to breathe. Regret like a steel weight he couldn't escape.

Joseph invited close family and friends to the house after, but Jackson never spoke to anyone. The exhaustion and grief were overwhelming, and the pain in his chest threatened to suffocate him. An unexplainable sense of loss. *A stab of guilt and shame lay buried deep in his soul.*

The door creaked open while he lay on his bed facing the opposite direction. He didn't turn to see who came in. He didn't need to. Her sweet, delicate body stretched out on the bed, pressing against his back.

Peanut.

Her arm came around him, and he couldn't push her away. Not this time. Wrapped in a cocoon of despair, hanging on by a thread, he lay still. Her nearness kept him above water. Closing his eyes, for the first time in days, he drifted off. The first few hours of peace since he'd lost his sister. When his eyes opened, the anguish returned. Haunting images of Chloe. The grief so acute it caused him physical pain.

Peyton's arm still around him. Still there. Willing to drown right alongside him if he let her. He didn't have anything to offer her. *Not anymore.* She touched his back, and he flinched before turning to look at her. She bit her lip and looked away. The pain in her eyes brought him to his knees on a normal day, but today wasn't a normal day. Everything remained numb.

Her face clouded with uneasiness. "I understand you're grieving. Trust me, I get it. I loved Chloe very much. But I don't understand this anger toward me. Did I do something?"

He let out a frustrated breath. "I'm angry at myself. Don't you get it? I'm angry at the fucking world. I don't have anything to offer you anymore. I'm leaving for school in a few hours. It's for the best."

Her composure was a fragile shell around her. "Why won't you let me help you? I love you. Please don't push me away."

"I don't want your help. I don't want to be reminded of what I did."

"You didn't do anything, Jackson." She reached for his hand, and he recoiled.

"I'm sorry. I don't want to talk about it. I don't want to think about it. I just want to be alone. Why can't you understand that?"

"Okay. Okay. I'll leave, Jackson. If it's what you really want," she said. Her bottom lip trembled, and she bit down on it. Eyes wet with overflowing tears, like a dam ready to burst.

"It's what I want." He would say whatever it took for her to let him go.

She nodded, studying him. "Okay. I'll go."

She walked toward the door and choked on a sob. Stopping in the doorway to look back, waiting for him to stop her.

He met her hopeless gaze. "Good-bye, Peanut."

The words hit a nerve. They were final. A closure to this chapter of his life. She turned on her heels and didn't look back. *Fucking fight or flight?* He just made sure his girl was going to take flight and get as far away from him as she could. For the first time since Chloe died, he felt something.

Relief.

He'd set the only girl he ever loved free. The first unselfish thing he'd done in a long time. A terrible pain radiated from deep within. An overpowering awareness that nothing would ever be the same.

Chapter Seventeen

Present

The days after leaving Lake Tahoe were hectic, but he didn't give a shit. He and Peyton were together. In every sense of the word. Though it might not be forever, he planned to enjoy every goddamn second until it ended. What surprised him most—he didn't want it to end. Didn't want to think about it. There was no alternate plan. He would move to Miami soon, and Peyton deserved better than what he had to offer. She should have the big wedding, a couple kids, the white picket fence, and all the fairy-tale bullshit that comes with it.

The people elected Sebastian mayor of San Francisco in the tightest race this city had seen in the last decade. The bastard sent flowers to Peyton with a note of apology, which bugged the shit out of Jackson. Peyton's father, Thomas, found out Sebastian had posted bail for Wolf. He was involved to some extent but most likely hadn't planned on his campaign manager getting physical with her. Either way, he didn't want Sebastian or Wolf near her. Keeping his eye on her proved easy so far. They spent their days and nights together.

He couldn't get enough of her. Kept waiting to feel the need to pull away, but it didn't come. Back in their routine, she went with him to the gym after work. His fight was in two days, and the soft opening of PBV the following night. Roberto, Davis, and Nelson were flying in for the fight and the opening. The timing worked out well with both events taking place on the same weekend.

He still hadn't told Peyton he was leaving. Guilt engulfed him. It never seemed like the right time to talk about it. He'd fucked up, had no one to blame but himself.

His relationship with Peyton left him off-kilter. He was in so deep he risked drowning them both.

While working on the final revisions for the menu in his office, he saw his attorney's name flash across the screen of his phone. "What's up, Pete?"

"Can you get away tomorrow for a few hours?" he said, voice hesitant. The attorney Joseph had hired nine years ago stuck with Jackson through the entire fucked-up situation.

"If I need to, yes. What's going on?"

"Ryker has his parole hearing tomorrow. I've filed every possible complaint I could, but by law, he's entitled to the hearing."

"How is this fucker entitled to anything?" Jackson punched his desk in frustration. Ryker got to live, and his sister didn't. Regardless of the shit way the bastard currently existed, he was getting a hell of lot more than Chloe.

"I know. We're going to argue it until we talk some sense into them. May not even need to. It could just be a formality, but Ryker claims he has some new information to shed light on the case."

"Any idea what it could be?"

257

"None. I'd like to get ahead of it, but I don't know what rabbit he's trying to pull out of his hat," Pete said, frustration etched in his tone.

"I'll be there. What time?"

"Eleven in the morning."

"See you then." He disconnected the call; fury struck.

Would this nightmare ever end? The fucker didn't deserve to wake up and take a breath each day, and a chance at freedom should be out of the question.

A knock on his door startled him, and he didn't hide his irritation. "It's open."

Peyton leaned in. "Everything okay?"

Shit. He couldn't explain this to her, didn't want her anywhere near Ryker Jonze, and sure as shit didn't want her involved in this. He needed to handle it on his own—the kiss of death for someone in a relationship. Exactly why they didn't work for him. And why the fuck did he deserve to be happy any more than Ryker fucking Jonze deserved to live? Chloe didn't get to do either.

"Yeah, sorry, come in." His tone was clipped.

She sat in the chair across from him, dark hair falling over her shoulders. His gaze scanned her fitted white blouse. He'd helped her put it on this morning, and the memory of what lie beneath was enough to drive him mad with desire. His need for this woman was dangerous. It wouldn't be easy to walk away. When this ended—fuck, the thought of hurting Peyton again made him sick to his stomach. His mind should be on the bastard trying to get released from prison for murdering his sister, not being consumed with the woman sitting across from him.

"You sure you're okay?"

No. Not okay. "I'm fine. Did you need something?"

Her posture stiffened in response to his harsh tone. Maybe it would be better to start ripping off the bandage now instead of all at once. She pushed to her feet, and he saw the hurt in her eyes. He was the asshole who put it there. Again.

"I stopped in to see if you were ready to head to the gym," she huffed, turning to leave.

"Yep."

She paused. "Did I do something?"

"No. I've got a lot going on. Didn't mean to be short. I'm ready."

Neither spoke on the drive to the gym. His mind consumed with Ryker Jonze, the man who starred in his nightmares. And he sure as hell didn't want to talk about it. Arriving at the gym, Peyton walked in ahead of him, and they went their separate ways.

Mick gave him a funny look. "What's with you today?"

"Why the fuck does everyone keep asking me the same goddamn question?"

Mick shook his head and told him to go warm up. His gaze landed on Peyton, couldn't help but watch her. She stood a few mats away doing burpees, and Nico pushed her for more. She'd come a long way in the last few weeks, a bit of muscle already prevalent on her slim physique. With her hair back in a high ponytail, he studied her beautiful face.

Eyes full of fire and strength. He'd watched her sleep this morning, the girl so content and peaceful. Happy the darkness which often consumed him when he slept didn't show on her angelic face. He'd kept her up late every night since they'd returned from Lake Tahoe. He couldn't get enough of her, and she seemed to feel the same way. She required more sleep than him, and he always got up long before her in the mornings. Her bruises began to fade, but what Wolf had done to her still enraged him. How the fuck would he pull away from her now, when he needed to keep her safe? His plan was fucking flawed.

His stare locked with her dark gaze. She dropped to the mat and started doing push-ups. Vulnerable yet strong. He fucking loved everything about her.

"Vance, let's go," Mick prompted from the cage.

The next few hours were spent sparring with multiple partners in the ring, anger released with every punch he landed. When one of them made contact, he egged it on, relished the pain, wanted to feel something other than the engulfing darkness threatening to take him under.

He tore off his gloves and reached for a water. Mick went over a few strategies for the fight and told him to take tomorrow off from the gym to prepare for the match. Good timing—his mind would be elsewhere tomorrow night.

Peyton returned a work call on the drive to her house, allowing him to brood even more. He thought about going to his own place, but leaving her alone wasn't an option with Wolf out on bail. She insisted on making dinner, so he sat in the living room doing busywork on his computer. Her batshit-crazy-whiskered dog pawed at him relentlessly for attention. Just like his owner, the annoying little fur ball had weaseled his way into his heart.

He cursed under his breath, settling the little mutt

on his lap. The pup calmed down and looked up at him with knowing eyes. If Whiskey could speak, he was pretty sure he'd tell him he was an asshole right now. A fair assessment. Peyton called him to come and eat. She'd whipped up baked chicken, mashed potatoes, and salad, and damn if it didn't smell amazing.

"So you want to tell me about it?" She took the seat across from him.

She knew him. Probably better than anyone. No sense denying it. Didn't mean he wanted to talk about it.

"No. Not right now." His tone was gentler.

"All right. I hope you will eventually, but I'll respect your space," she said, cutting into her chicken.

"Thank you for dinner. You can cook, Pea. This is damn good."

"I told you." Her cheeks flushed pink.

"You did."

"So I talked to my dad today, and he asked if you were going to join us for Thanksgiving at his house."

Could this fucking day get any worse? He didn't have the balls to tell her he'd be long gone by Thanksgiving.

"Yeah, sounds like fun." He'd hurt her enough for one day. He couldn't stand to see the disappointment in her eyes.

"It's the best. Dad and I cook together, and Jayden brings the pies. We always do Thanksgiving at his house, and I host Christmas Eve dinner. I'm so glad we'll be able to do it together this year. Remember all the Christmases we spent together up at the lake?"

Christ. She was the real deal. Full of holiday cheer and family traditions. He hadn't celebrated any holidays in the last decade, but seeing her excitement did something to him. It made him want things he had no right to want.

He roughed a hand through his hair. "I'm sorry I'm being a dick. There's a lot going on. My head's pounding, and I'm exhausted." He needed to say something, couldn't stand her thinking she'd done something wrong.

She moved to her feet to sit on his lap before he even finished speaking. Her arms wrapped around him, and her face nuzzled into his neck. "I get it. You're still holding back, and it's okay. Let's go to bed early tonight. We both need to catch up on sleep."

He kissed the top of her head and agreed. She snuggled up against him, his arms wrapped around her. No words spoken, they just closed their eyes and drifted off. Darkness engulfed him.

Chloe called his name. Again and again. Couldn't get to her no matter how hard he tried. He crawled toward the trailer—she was nowhere in sight. Ryker Jonze appeared. Taunting him about what he did to Chloe. The devil himself. He needed to pay for what he did. A fury so fierce took over, he charged at the man, but when he reached him, Ryker disappeared.

"Jackson." His name repeated until he realized someone shook him.

He opened his eyes. Peyton. Her worried stare filled with fear. Tears streamed down her face. What the fuck did he do?

"What happened? Did I hurt you?" he said, trying to rein in the panic coursing his veins.

Her hands gripped his shoulders. "No. Of course not. You were yelling."

Christ.

The same fucking nightmare he couldn't ever escape. Ryker never taunted him before. The dreams were more prevalent when things triggered his memories. And today, he'd been flooded by dark and grief-filled reminders.

He scrubbed a hand over his face. "I'm sorry. I shouldn't have slept here tonight. I have things on my mind, and I should've known better."

"What? No. You can't stay away from me every time you have things on your mind. It's not how this works." She placed a warm hand on his cheek.

History repeated itself. His beautiful girl always trying to rescue him—but he didn't want to be rescued.

"I told you I'm not that guy. This is how I deal with things." He moved back to put some distance between them.

"And how's that been working for you, huh?" She squared her shoulders and closed the space between them.

He wouldn't admit it, but she was fucking right. It hadn't been working for him, but he didn't know how to change it.

"Listen, I don't want to do this tonight. I don't have the energy. You need sleep. I've somehow managed to deprive you yet again," he said, both settling back on their pillows.

Peyton fell fast asleep. Her gorgeous face easy to get lost in. So peaceful. So good. He could only bring her pain. He needed to get through tomorrow and then figure out what to do.

****

Leaving a note, he told her he'd be away from the

restaurant today, but Ryan would be available for anything she needed at PBV. He couldn't look at her and lie to her, so he took the coward's way out.

He went home to shower before the Parole Suitability Hearing. He prepared to face the man who'd fueled his hate and anger over the past nine years, and met up with his attorney Pete outside. They entered the sterile white room where four men and a woman sat behind a long rectangular table. Pete informed Jackson they were the board commissioners and led him toward a row of chairs facing them. His gaze landed on the woman in the front row. His entire body tensed. Their smoking gun.

His mother. Tammy Vance.

The air left his lungs. Did she come to help the bastard who'd murdered her daughter? Bile rose in his throat. Ryker and his attorney entered the room. His mom looked over her shoulder, and her gaze locked with his. Christ, he fucking hated how much Chloe looked like her. However, the resemblance ended there. His sister had a heart of gold, strong and loyal. Tammy would sell her soul to the devil for her next hit. Ryker had probably offered her something leading in the direction of her addiction, which always came first.

Pete knew his mother's history with drug abuse. More than familiar with this case. He gave Jackson a knowing look. One of the male commissioners stood and requested each person identify themselves for the record. When Jackson spoke, Ryker's head spun in his direction before he quickly turned back to face the panel before him.

The commissioners reviewed the relevant information about the case and asked Ryker several questions in regard to his incarceration, before offering him a chance to speak on his behalf.

"Thank you for granting me this opportunity to speak today. My girlfriend, Tammy Vance, is here to collaborate the misrepresentation of my first trial," Ryker said. A gasp escaped his attorney, and it didn't go unnoticed by the board members, who traded glances.

"This bastard is going against his own council," Pete whispered to Jackson.

"Mr. Jonze, please keep in mind we are not here to revisit the outcome of your original trial. If you choose to appeal a past verdict, it would be handled in a completely different court of law. We are here to discuss whether or not you pose an unreasonable risk to public safety and if you are fit to rejoin society at this time." Her harsh tone indicated she wasn't pleased with his opening statement.

"Yes, Ms. Lopez, I am aware this is a parole hearing; however, I feel it necessary to share how unfairly I was treated in my first trial. Tammy Vance, the mother of the deceased, Chloe Vance, is also the only other witness to the crime. She wasn't in her right state of mind at the time of the first trial and is now here to revise her statement. I hope you will allow her to share how the events from that horrible night were just one big accident. Once the parole board hears her testimony, I'm quite certain you will feel I've served enough time and will consider my request to cut my time short," Ryker finished before taking his seat.

Jackson's blood boiled beneath his skin. The casual manner in which Ryker spoke of Chloe made every muscle in his body tense. The asshole believed *he'd* been treated unfairly? He couldn't be serious? He'd murdered a fourteen-year-old kid and thought he was the victim. Jackson couldn't begin to make sense of it. Where was the regret? The guilt? He never owned up to what he'd done all these years later, called it an unfortunate accident. He'd been convicted of second-degree murder and sentenced to twenty-five years in prison. His dangerous conduct as a known drug dealer and his lack of concern for human life had led to the maximum sentence.

Pete leaned close to Jackson, voice low. "Sit tight. He just buried himself."

"Mr. Jonze, I just stated this is not a trial for the crime committed. This is a parole hearing. Ms. Vance testified at the original trial, and we have read through her testimony already. We have no reason to hear from her today unless she is here to speak on behalf of her daughter. It is now time for the victim's family to have an opportunity to speak on behalf of Chloe Vance."

The veins in Ryker's neck bulged. Pete stood and introduced Jackson to read a statement on behalf of his sister. Jackson pushed to his feet. Hands trembled. Speaking about what happened so many years ago never got easier. Hated dredging it up, but he'd be damned if his discomfort would get in the way of making sure his sister's killer remained behind bars.

"Thank you for allowing me to speak today. My sister, Chloe Vance, will never be a nameless victim nor a statistic. Not to me. Chloe was fourteen years old when her life was taken. I'm sure it's easy for Ryker Jonze to call what happened an accident, but I take issue with his choice of words. An accident, by definition, is an unintentional, unfortunate incident, such as running a red light or rear-ending someone with your car. Chloe's death was neither—it was a *meaningless tragedy*. Ryker Jonze was in my mother's trailer the night my sister lost her life. He was there to get his *fix*. No one was going to get in his way. This is the life of an addict. I should know. I lived with one for most of my life. My mother, Tammy Vance, is an addict. Her addiction comes first, which is evident as she sits behind the man who took her daughter's life. I don't believe Ryker Jonze has changed, or he wouldn't be communicating with a woman who is still clearly using. My sister found herself in the middle of a violent fight that fatal night. She heard my mother screaming for help. Neighbors confirmed shouts came from the trailer, which, unfortunately, wasn't uncommon. I'm sure you've read this in the testimony from the trial. The skin found beneath my sister's fingernails matched the wounds from Ryker Jonze's face and body."

Jackson paused and reached for his bottle of water, needing a minute to gather himself before forging ahead. Reliving what Chloe went through was as difficult today as it had been nine years ago. His mouth dry and his hands trembling, he slowly allowed the cool liquid to travel down his throat.

"I only bring this up because Ryker Jonze believes he deserves early parole because he considers Chloe's death an *unfortunate accident.* Throughout the trial the prosecution proved a struggle between the accused and my sister, which conflicts with Ryker Jonze's version he swung his hand once and accidentally knocked Chloe to the floor. My sister fought this man, for whatever reason, whether to protect my mother or herself. We will never know the full story because the only two people who survived are both addicts. One of those individuals, Ryker Jonze, fled the scene, which is not typically a sign of innocence. The other person, my mother, passed out from her drug use. Neither called 911. Neither attempted CPR. Neither did a damn thing to help a young girl lying on the floor bleeding from a head wound."

Jackson paused to clear his throat before he turned to face Ryker. Nine years of anger rushed to the surface. "This man should not be granted early parole. He has never shown an ounce of remorse for the life he took, as he continues to see himself as the victim. My sister was a brave, beautiful, and kind soul—she believed everyone was worthy of being saved. There is not a day that goes by where Chloe's death does not knock the wind from me, and I will forever be missing a piece of my heart. I ask you to honor what Judge Garrett originally deemed a fair punishment when he sentenced Ryker Jonze to twenty-five years in prison. Keep in mind, he still gets to wake up each day and see the sun. He still gets to communicate with the people he loves. He still gets to breathe fresh air when he steps outside. My sister was not granted this same courtesy when he selfishly took her life. Thank you."

The room fell silent after Jackson took his seat, and Pete looked over at him with glossy eyes and gave him a nod of approval.

Ms. Lopez stood. "Thank you, Mr. Vance. I'm certain what happened to your sister is not easy to share, but we appreciate your heartfelt words, and I promise you they will be taken into consideration when we make our decision."

Everyone was asked to leave the room so the

commissioners could deliberate. Ryker and his attorney went through a separate door. Jackson and Pete settled in the chairs out in the lobby.

"You did well, Jackson." Pete clapped him on the back.

The stale décor in the waiting area matched the room they just exited. A musty odor lingered, and outdated fluorescent lights above flickered and buzzed. His mother stood steps away. He studied her. Physically no one questioned she still used. She weighed maybe ninety pounds soaking wet, her skin discolored and yellow, and her eyes bloodshot. She couldn't go more than thirty seconds without sniffing or scratching her arms.

She didn't expect to see him there; he'd never told her he'd moved back from the East Coast. They didn't talk, but she texted him with endless sob stories begging for money. He'd been a cash source to her for many years. It would be the last piece of him that she got. He justified sending her money to honor his sister, who'd truly loved their mother. The truth was, turning his back on her proved challenging. A part of him still wanted to hold out hope. The little scrap he allowed to exist, now extinguished.

"Jackson." His mother's voice sounded raspy and battered.

"Surprised to see me, I'm sure."

"Ryker and I have reconnected. He knows he made a mistake, and I've forgiven him," she said, wiping her nose with the back of her sleeve, looking like a strung-out junkie.

"You've forgiven him? You forgive the man who took your daughter's life? Chloe went there to help you.

This is how you honor her? You're a lost cause, Mom. I knew it nine years ago, but today, I wash my hands of you. Don't text for money; don't call for help. You've made your bed."

"Jackson, you're all I have left," she said on a sob.

"If I were all you had left, you wouldn't be sitting with Ryker today," he spewed.

The doors opened, and they were invited back inside. His mother returned to her seat, and he and Pete sat several rows behind.

"Is it a bad or a good sign they made their decision so quickly?" he whispered to his attorney.

"Depends. But I can't imagine they'd consider setting him free. He represented himself poorly."

Ms. Lopez didn't mince words. She simply stated they would not be granting parole and Ryker would not receive another hearing for nine years. Ryker punched the table, which didn't earn him any brownie points with the commissioners, and they requested he be removed from the room. A small weight lifted from Jackson's shoulders when he walked out beside his attorney and thanked him for his assistance. They agreed to be in touch soon.

"Jackson." He paused at the sound of his mother's voice.

"Isn't it visiting hours? You may want to go say good-bye. It's going to be a while before your boyfriend gets out."

"Aren't you tired of being angry?"

Her words startled him. They were quite possibly the most sobering thing his mother said in years. "Nah, there's still a lot of life in my anger. Hey, maybe you should try it? Your boyfriend is in prison for murdering your daughter. This doesn't trigger anything? You're not even slightly annoyed?"

"It was an accident, Jackson. And you may hate me now, but I'm still your mother. You are a part of me, whether you like it or not."

"Good-bye, Mom." He turned and walked away. But her words hung in the air around him. He was a part of her. Like it or not. She was the reason they were leaving a parole hearing for his sister's murderer. This ugly part of his life. This shit followed him, and he'd never be free of it. Couldn't escape it no matter how hard he tried.

Chapter Eighteen

Present

Peyton left work to meet the girls for lunch, thankful they chose a place within walking distance of the restaurant. Desperate for a break from PBV, time with her friends was just what she needed. Jackson continued to shut her out, and things had been off for the past two days. He'd left the morning after his horrible nightmare, and he wouldn't talk about it.

Jackson was strong. And stoic. And brave. Those were his strengths—but they were also his weaknesses. He didn't want to ask for help. However, handling things on his own would not allow him to move forward. She hadn't seen him yesterday, aside from the note left on the counter informing her he would be gone all day. No explanation or details. Later, he'd sent a text asking her to go to her father's house and spend the night. He wouldn't be able to make it over to her place and wanted to know she was safe. A restraining order against Kenny Wolf prevented him from coming anywhere near her, but Jackson didn't trust a piece of paper to stop him from crossing the line. At this point, no one believed Wolf mentally stable. She'd agreed to go to her father's, knew Jackson couldn't afford another night without sleep, but asked him what was going on. His lack of response had caused her to toss and turn all night. Having him beside her in bed these last few weeks made it impossible to sleep without him.

Spending the entire day in his office, he barely spoke a word to her in passing. It didn't stop her from the humiliation of trying multiple times to find a reason to speak to him. Hell, it wasn't by accident she chose her tightest black pencil skirt and sky-high Manolo's today, per Elle's insistence, of course. The outfit proved an epic fail. His fight was tonight, and the tension between them lingered.

"Peyt," Elle shouted and waved to get her attention.

The restaurant was one of their favorite local secrets because you could get a table and actually hear your conversation while eating lunch. Not the most common occurrence in the city. The quaint, small eatery also served the most delicious food. The smell of fresh bread and pumpkin spice filled the air around her. Her belly rumbled to life.

"Hey, thanks for getting us a table," she said, in desperate need of some girl time.

"Of course. We get double duty today. Lunch and a fight," Dani said.

They were going to join her tonight, along with Dani's boyfriend, Cam, her sister, Jayden, and Zach. Roberto, Davis, and Nelson were also flying in this afternoon. Maybe the pressure of tonight's fight combined with the restaurant's soft opening tomorrow overwhelmed him. It was a considerable amount of stress for one person.

"Okay, if your outfit didn't do the trick, then the man has come down with somethin' serious," Elle said.

"No. He barely spoke to me. I have no idea what's

Laura Pavlov

going on. It's so frustrating. He couldn't keep his hands off me just two days ago, and now he's avoiding me. I don't know what changed."

"Could it be the fight? Or the restaurant opening?" Dani pressed.

"I don't know. But if it is, why not talk to me about it?"

"Hmm—you know, there's more than one way to skin a cat. Maybe the outfit was the wrong approach for this situation. I'm thinking you force the issue. Demand to know what's going on," Elle insisted.

"Maybe it's the change coming. I mean, you've spent endless hours together every day for the past eight weeks, and now everything's about to change," Dani said.

She hoped it was something simple, something they could fix. But her gut told her this ran deeper. He'd been distant. So far away. Distracted. Closed off. It didn't add up.

"I don't know. I'll talk to him after the opening tomorrow. I don't want to stress him out before his fight tonight."

"Good plan. Tell us more about the amazing trip to Tahoe," Dani said when the waiter set down their plates.

Her stomach fluttered at the thought of their trip, everything and more than she could have asked for. They'd crossed so many barriers.

"We had the best time. He's…" She bit down on her lip, tried to hold back every thought rushing through her mind.

"As good as the dream?" Elle leaned in and whispered.

"Better," she said, filling them in on all the juicy details, and they listened with big grins. No need to analyze Jackson's sudden change any further. He held all the answers.

Elle would drive them to the fight, and Dani's boyfriend Cam would meet them there after work.

"Are either of Jackson's friends hot like him?" Elle mused.

"Roberto is handsome, older, and married. Davis and Nelson are both good-looking, charming, and athletic," Peyton said.

"Are any of them dukes or lords?" Elle wriggled her eyebrows.

"The endless quest to be a royal." Dani chuckled.

"Hey, a girl can shoot for the stars, right? We're picking you up from work early, so we can swing by my place. I want to dress cute for the fight. You never know who you'll meet at these things." Elle's southern drawl was a bit more pronounced now.

"You're dressing up for the fight?" Dani rolled her eyes in disgust.

Elle changed multiple times a day. The fashion pulse of their group, she gave input about what they wore, whether they wanted it or not. Dani would never consider changing outfits for an after-work event, and Peyton landed somewhere in between her two besties. She didn't take it to the extent Elle did, but enjoyed indulging in fashion and shopping as much as the next girl.

Elle feigned offense. "You don't become Miss Savannah by using only one oar in the water. It's all about utilizing your resources."

"Well, since you brought it up, shall we discuss

why you didn't go beyond being Miss Savannah?" Dani chuckled.

Peyton fell back in her seat laughing because of the theatrics about to be on full display. Her friends sure knew how to cheer her up, especially now.

Elle's hands came down on the table. "You did not just go there, did you? Did she, Peyt?"

"I believe she did," Peyton's said, her muffled laughter impossible to hide.

"You both know what a sore subject it is for me. The title was mine to lose. I was a legacy, for goodness' sake," Elle hissed before she took a bite of her sandwich.

"Well, there was the whole *setup*." Peyton sat back and waited for the usual fabulous, over-the-top, dramatic response from her friend.

"It was a setup, all right. Suri Sandemeyer is nothing more than a minnow in a fishing pond. She may be pretty as a peach, but the little heathen is pure evil. She put some sort of mystery oil on those batons. Have I mentioned no one ever twirled flaming batons before me?"

"Hmm, has she ever mentioned it?" Dani asked with a smirk.

"I think you may have." Sarcasm rolled off Peyton's tongue.

"I'm sure *Little Miss Sunshine Sandemeyer* messed with those batons at the pageant, but didn't you have your own mishap a few weeks before then? One involving burning down someone's barn?" Dani raised her eyebrows, unable to hide her smile.

Elle pushed her tongue in her cheek. "Your memory sure is workin' well today, huh? Well, let me tell you, James Ratcliffe the Second believed in my talent. We'd sneak out behind his barn so I could practice without fear of the annoying busybody, Suri, finding out what I was doing. But one slip of the wrist and the whole barn went up in flames so fast my head spun. It was hotter than a goat's butt in a pepper patch."

Every time Peyton heard the story, she laughed so hard her stomach hurt. James Ratcliffe the Second, a.k.a. Elle's first love, had encouraged her to try the cutting-edge talent. Their relationship had not survived, nor did his barn, but the animals all made it out safely, and Elle's reputation as a flame-throwing, fire-starting pageant queen was born.

Dabbing her eyes, she fought a bad case of the giggles. The timing couldn't be better. Doom loomed, and she desperately wanted to push the feeling away. Spending time with her besties always proved the best distraction. Her phone vibrated. A text from Jackson.

I'm leaving to pick everyone up from the airport. Going to head straight to the fight after to change and warm up.

He didn't ask her to join him.

Okay. Tell everyone I said hello, and I'll see you at the fight. Good luck.

She sent the text—and then sent another. Didn't allow herself to think about it.

I love you.

Her stomach twisted. He hadn't said it to her in two days, but she needed to hear it now more than ever.

Love you, Pea.

Relief flooded her. Everything would be fine. Her friends were right. Jackson was just anxious over his upcoming fight and opening the restaurant. She was being silly. A new project waited for her, and he'd be busy running PBV. They'd have their time at the gym and spend evenings together, like any other normal couple. The future was theirs. And though he didn't know what he had to offer—all she needed was Jackson. He made her happy and she loved him. What else mattered?

****

Elle's wardrobe change turned into a time-consuming ordeal. Outfit changes led to hair and makeup adjustments. Who knew? But now, Peyton was anxious to leave. She wanted to get good seats. Elle's fitted skinny jeans, long-sleeve vintage concert T-shirt, and ankle boots contrasted Dani's black wool pants, white blouse, and stilettos. Elle insisted Peyton change and chose black leggings, booties, and a cream, hooded fleece sweatshirt. It did feel good to get out of her work clothes and heels, allowing her to focus on the fight.

Adrenaline surged once they arrived at the event. People were packed into the warehouse, chairs tightly pressed together. Along the back wall, spectators stood shoulder to shoulder. The place was huge and smelled of stale beer and sweat. Exposed ductwork hung overhead. The lighting dim and the growing excitement contagious. They bumped into Roberto, Davis, and Nelson at the entrance. Cam arrived, and Peyton introduced everyone before they hurried inside.

"How's he doing?" Roberto asked, walking with her ahead of the group. She didn't know how to answer. He'd completely shut her out.

"I think he's good," she replied, securing a row of seats up front.

Roberto studied her for a moment. "Don't let him

pull away, Peyton. I've never seen him so happy."

Surprised, she met his gaze. "I don't know how to reach him right now."

"Just keep getting in his face. It's the only way you'll get through to him. He's stubborn, so you need to be *more* stubborn."

"I can do that," she said with confidence.

"I believe you're the one person who can."

His words sank in. She wanted to be the one person who could get through to him. She knew him better than anyone and loved him even more. No more running. She wanted to fight for him. For them. She waved over her sister and Zach when they entered. Everyone spent the next few minutes buzzing about the fight..

Her heart raced. She wished there was a way to talk to Jackson before the fight. An aching need to see him, to know he was okay. Everyone sat except for her. She paced the aisle. Leroy Sasone came out first, and the crowd cheered. Jackson followed, and the spectators went wild. He turned to speak to Mick and tugged his shirt off. Elle let out a loud, embarrassing howl.

Everyone focused on the octagon, the cage in the center of the room. The bell dinged, and the two men touched gloves. Jackson leaner than Leroy, a bit taller and broader in the shoulders. His opponent built more like a tank. Stockier. Thicker. Tattoos ran down his arms, and he appeared several years older than Jackson. Did this make him more experienced?

Leroy exerted more energy with his quick movements. Jackson turned on his feet in a calm, cautious manner. Leroy attacked first. Jackson blocked the powerful low kick, grabbed Leroy's leg, and dropped him to the mat. The older man recovered, scrambled to his feet in record speed. Leroy threw several jabs. Jackson landed a monster left kick, leaving the other man stumbling to his corner. Round one ended.

Mick and Nico spoke to him and applied ointment to the small cut beneath his eye. Her heart pounded in her chest so fast, threatening to burst. Dropping to her seat, she buried her in her hands.

"He's fine. I've seen him fight many times." Roberto's calm voice relaxed her.

"I know. I just want it to be over." Her legs bounced up and down at Mach speed.

Roberto chuckled, and the bell sounded once again. Within seconds, she was on her feet screaming with everyone else. Jackson's strong and powerful body moved around the octagon. A born a fighter. Leroy used a cross move. Nico had taught her that same move last week. The blow connected with Jackson's jaw. Leroy attempted a double leg takedown with no success.

Her hands were clammy. Elle and Dani howled and cheered. Zach pulled Jayden close, and they yelled for Jackson. The two men continued to grapple until the bell sounded, ending round two.

"Well, slap my head and call me silly. This is the best thing I've seen in a long while, and I don't usually care much for sports," Elle shouted.

Adrenaline surged through the warehouse. The bell sounded for the final round. Jackson charged in full attack, and landed a monster left hook to Leroy's face. The man dropped to his knees. Jackson pounced. His Brazilian jiujitsu training played to his strength. The spectators screamed for more. He used a leg lock around Leroy's neck, applied pressure, and forced him into submission.

Jackson won.

He spoke to Mick, and the crowd continued to cheer. His gaze moved around the room until it locked with hers. The playful grin on his face left her weak in the knees. She scanned his body for injuries. His hair sweaty, cheek swollen, and hands bruised and bleeding. He never looked sexier than in this moment.

After saying good-bye to their friends, she went to find Mick, Nico, and Jackson. How did this man manage to make her stomach dip every time she saw him?

"What'd you think of your first fight, Rocky?" Nico asked.

"I liked it. Very exciting. Congratulations." Her stare met Jackson's.

"Okay, we're heading out. You beat a tough contender tonight, my friend. You've got mad skills. Take the next few days off. See you both next week," Mick said, and he and Nico hugged her before exiting the back door of the warehouse.

"How do you feel?" she asked, walking beside him toward the parking lot.

"A little sore, but not too bad."

"Do you have your car?" A bit hesitant, she didn't know if he wanted to stay with her tonight, but it didn't stop her from pushing for it.

"Yes. Did you drive here?"

"No. I came with Dani and Elle."

He turned to face her. "Something on your mind, Pea?"

"There's always something on my mind. But right now, I'd like you to come home with me so I can clean you up." She lifted on her tiptoes and ran her finger along the cut beneath his eye. He didn't so much as flinch, just watched her with his intense green stare.

"Let's grab some food and head to your place," he said.

Maybe she could get him to open up tonight. Tomorrow was another big day.

She didn't press for answers during dinner. They talked about the fight and headed upstairs to get ready for bed. His posture notably stiff when she trailed behind him. Stepping into the bathroom, she filled the tub, lit a few candles, and called for him.

"What's up? Are you taking a bath?" he asked leaning against the doorframe.

"Nope. You are."

He chuckled. "I don't do baths, Pea."

"Well, then, it's a good time to start. I poured in a ton of Epsom salt. You'll feel a lot better. Trust me."

He didn't respond. Didn't argue. Exhaustion evident in his gaze. Pushing her hands beneath his hoodie, she pulled it over his head. His big body tensed. A large bruise colored his ribs. Reaching for the string of his joggers, she pushed them down. He wore nothing beneath. A large bruise also covered his thigh, and one of his knees swelled to twice the size of the other. She bent down to inspect it, and desired stirred; his knee wasn't the only thing that had swelled.

"You must be in pain," she said, trying to hide her smirk, leading him to the tub.

He stepped into the hot water. "Does it embarrass you? My reaction to you?"

"What? No. I hardly noticed," she teased.

He sank down slowly, flinching before settling into the hot bath. Her little pink boxer shorts made it easy to sit on the edge of the tub behind him, while her feet sank into the water, one on each side of his shoulders.

Leaning back, he settled his head between her thighs. Her body tingled at his nearness. Using her loofah to wash his chest, she avoided the large bruise darkening before her eyes.

"This is nice." His voice was gruff, eyes closed. It made her happy to see him relax after being tense and distant for the past couple days.

"There isn't much a hot bath can't fix," she whispered against his ear, washing his upper arms. Bathing him proved an intimate act, and her body responded in every way. His hard muscles rippled beneath her fingertips. The hot water rolled down his arms and chest.

"I'm sorry for being an asshole." His eyes remained closed.

Trying to mask her surprise, she wanted him to share more. Needed him to share more.

"Go on."

A grin spread clear across his handsome face. "Guess you're not going to argue with me."

She stayed silent, lifted his arm, and used the sponge to clean the dried blood off a cut on his hand. Holding his hand in hers, she took in its massive size and strength compared to her own.

"Ryker had his appeal two days ago, which is why I was gone from PBV all day." His voice was just above a whisper, body tense like it caused him pain to speak about Ryker aloud.

Laura Pavlov

She froze for a moment but tried her best to keep judgment and hurt from her voice. "Why didn't you tell me?"

He opened his eyes and looked at her. "Because I figured you'd want to go with me. I don't want you anywhere near that piece of shit. And seeing him takes me back to a dark place, you know? Probably doesn't make any sense after all these years. But it's like reliving it all over again."

His words cut her so deep her heart physically ached. She pushed him forward just a bit and dropped into the water behind him, wrapped her arms around his chest, and rested her cheek on his back. They didn't speak. She hugged him with everything she had. She needed to comfort him. It frustrated her he hadn't shared this until now. Yes, she would have wanted to go with him but would have respected his wishes to do it on his own.

"I'm sorry, Jackson," she whispered.

He didn't move, stayed perfectly still for a moment before bringing his hands over hers, resting on his chest.

"I'm sorry I didn't tell you, Pea."

"What did they decide to do? Are they letting him out?"

"No. They denied his request."

"Thank God. Did you say anything to him?"

"Yes. I read my statement, and it felt pretty damn good to get it off my chest."

"I'm glad you were able to have your say and stand up for Chloe."

"Yeah, me, too. My mom was there."

She lifted her chin to rest on his shoulder. "Did you

speak to her?"

"Not much. She was there to support Ryker."

A gasp escaped her, and she pressed her lips to his cheek. "I'm so sorry. What did you say to her?"

"I said good-bye."

Her arms wrapped around his chest again, hugging him tighter. "I'm proud of you."

He shifted, lifted them both out of the water, and set her on the floor in front of him. He peeled her soaked tank top and shorts from her body. With hunger in his eyes, he wrapped her in a towel, sending shivers down her spine. He dried himself off in record time, scooped her up into his arms, and carried her to the bedroom. Her head fell back in laughter. He set her down on the bed as if she were made of porcelain, though he was the one with bruises all over his body.

"Aren't you sore? You need to take it easy tonight." She smiled up at his beautiful face.

He was all man. In every sense of the word. Body and soul.

"Nothing hurts more than being away from you, Pea."

He reached for the nightstand drawer for protection. She watched his every move with awe. His mouth came over hers. Possessive and needy. God, she'd missed him. She pulled him down to sit on the bed, climbed onto his lap, and straddled him. He broke their kiss, tangled his fingers into her long hair, his green gaze locked with hers.

"What are you doing to me, Pea? I missed you so damn much, and we were only apart one night."

"I couldn't sleep without you next to me," she admitted, grinding against him, his moans urged her on.

"You know I love you, right?" He lifted her hips and shifted beneath her.

"I do." She gasped when he pulled her down slowly over his desire, filling every inch of her. They moved together, stares locked on one another. His mouth crashed into hers, and pleasure built.

And she gave herself to him. In every sense of the word.

Chapter Nineteen

Present

He watched Peyton sleep, and a heavy weight rested on his chest. He was fucking leaving. Moving to Miami in less than a week. The thought of hurting her proved a hell of a lot more painful than the bruises and cuts covering his body. The betrayal would devastate her. Her instinct would be to retreat. Be angry. And most importantly never speak to him again. And he deserved it.

She snuggled against him. Her white fur ball lay on the other side, just beneath her chin. So peaceful and content. Her world was so different from his. Traditions were important to her. Hell, her life resembled a goddamn Hallmark movie during the holidays. Always excited to pick out Christmas trees and put up decorations, while he dreaded the nightmares which always worsened during the festive time of year. She deserved better than—him.

He was the dark to her light.

She stirred, stretched her arms above her head, and gave him a peek at the beautiful body beneath the sheet. He ran his hand down her soft curves, she arched into his touch, and her eyes fluttered open. That stunning brown gaze he swore could see through to his soul.

"Morning, beautiful." He leaned down and took her

mouth. He pulled back to look at her, and she smiled.

Tell her now, dickhead.

"Good morning. I'm so glad you didn't leave," she said. Her fingers traced the cut beneath his eye.

"I must be relaxed from the girly bath you made me take, because I haven't been able to get out of bed this morning," he teased.

Her sexy, raspy laugh made him want to climb on top of her and take her again.

"I told you, there's nothing better than a hot bath. How do you feel this morning?"

"Not too bad."

"I'm glad."

Do it. It's time. He owed it to her.

"Why don't I go grab us some coffee?" he offered.

She reached for his arm. "Don't leave. I'm so glad you told me about Ryker, and you stayed with me last night. I haven't been myself these past two days, and today I feel—lighter. The soft opening tonight is going to be great. I just want us to enjoy it, Jackson."

Fuck. Her night to shine. She'd pulled off a near impossible deadline, worked her ass off to get PBV open, and created a design which far exceeded his expectations. Her talent impressed the shit out of him. How could he take today from her? Her family, her boss at Shine, and her friends were all attending tonight. A well-deserved celebration. Hell, he'd waited this long. One more day wasn't going to make a difference.

"I'm glad you're happy, Pea. No one deserves it more than you." He ran his fingers through her silky hair.

"Not true, you deserve to be happy, too." She

tugged him down to lie beside her.

"I'm happy right now. Always happy when I'm with you."

She pulled back to look at the bruise on his ribs. "Oh, my gosh. You need some ice on this."

Before he could stop her, her feet hit the floor, and she hurried down the stairs. Her mutt didn't follow. He moved to lie beside Jackson and rested his furry head on his chest. Maybe the stress was getting to him, but he swore her pup looked at him with disappointed eyes.

"I know, buddy." Jackson stood.

"What are you doing? Lie back down so we can put this on your ribs," she insisted when she entered the room.

He had other plans in mind. He took the icepack from her and tossed it on the bed. "I'll ice later. Right now, all I want is you. In the shower."

She yelped when he threw her over his shoulder and carried her to the bathroom. He turned on the hot water and set her on her feet. The water ran down her gorgeous body, and he made a mental note to memorize every perfect curve. Savor every minute left with her.

And that's exactly what he did.

****

"You ready for tonight?" Roberto stood at the bar in Jackson's apartment and handed him a glass of wine while they waited for Nelson and Davis to get ready.

"Yep. I think we're all set."

Roberto studied him before speaking. "What does Peyton think about you moving to Miami?"

Shifting on his feet, he felt like the world's biggest douchebag. "I haven't told her yet."

His friend's eyebrows rose in surprise. "Really?

Well, the woman was ready to jump in the cage last night and attack your opponent. I got the feeling you two were very close?"

He didn't meet Roberto's gaze, stared out at the view of the city from his floor-to-ceiling windows instead. "I'll tell her tomorrow."

"Priorities, Jackson. We've talked about this on many occasions. Family first. It's how I've lived my life. It's the reason I've been married for thirty-one years to Marta and have a close relationship with my daughter." Roberto's tone remained calm and steady while the look in his eyes appeared more severe. Angry. Disappointed. Hell, he couldn't blame him. He was annoyed and frustrated in himself.

"You have a family. Not everyone can say the same."

"It's a choice. Yes, you've had to deal with some horrific things in your life. There's no argument there. But the future is what you choose to make it. You've talked about this woman for nine years. You have a second chance at happiness with her, and you aren't going to take it?"

"Christ, not everyone gets to be happy. You don't see me whining about it, so why are you?" he snapped. Irritation engulfed him. He didn't want to answer for the mistakes already made.

"I see. I'm curious. Does Peyton make you happy?"

He rubbed a hand on the back of his neck. "Jesus, you really want to do this now? I'm opening the doors to the restaurant for the first time in less than an hour. And come on, you've met her. She's amazing. Who wouldn't be happy with her?"

"You're not answering the question. I asked you if she makes *you* happy." Roberto's voice was steady, while Jackson was anything but. Irritated and uncomfortable. Agitated and annoyed.

"Why does it matter?" he hissed just as the other two men joined them in the living room.

"I think the bigger question is, why does my asking get under your skin so much?" Roberto clapped him on the shoulder.

Well, the hell if he knew why any of this shit got under his skin.

Roberto let things go when they left the apartment. Jackson made it clear there wasn't anything else to discuss. And he was more than aware he'd fucked up and would have to deal with the consequences. But not tonight. He'd explain everything to her tomorrow.

Ed Sheeran's voice rang through the restaurant, his manager, Ryan, fiddled with the volume on the speakers, and staff bustled getting ready for the soft opening. It was just close friends and family, and Camille had invited a few important Shine clients.

Garlic and basil flooded his senses, and the light from the industrial candelabras above danced against the distressed brick walls. PBV was everything and more than he ever anticipated. His gaze landed on Peyton, walking into the dining room from the kitchen. A fitted black cocktail dress hugged her feminine curves. Gorgeous dark hair cascaded down her back. Black ribbons laced around her ankles on her higher-than-normal heels. Sexy as hell.

He mingled with friends, took several people on tours of the facility, and enjoyed the delicious food and drink. Time to let loose a bit. He was wound tight since

Wolf attacked Peyton. Not to mention Ryker's hearing, his fight, and PBV opening. But most of all, the lie he kept from her loomed like a dark cloud.

"Mick, Nico, thanks for coming. Ladies, it's nice to finally meet you. I've heard a lot about you both, when these two aren't kicking my ass," Jackson teased his trainers and their dates.

"The place looks amazing. You're going to do well here, buddy." Mick's gaze traveled around the room.

"Doesn't hurt having the best designer doing all the hard work." Nico winked at Peyton.

Peyton's cheeks pinked before Camille pulled her out of his arms to introduce her to a future client. He made small talk with his friends before excusing himself when Peyton's father arrived.

"Thomas, Lael, glad you made it. This is all the doing of your daughter, pretty amazing, right?"

"Yes. This place is incredible," her father and his girlfriend said in unison. They'd grown close over the last few weeks.

Though Peyton had filed a restraining order against Wolf, they were both still concerned about him. Peyton came over to stand beside him. He nuzzled her neck, the smell of orange blossoms and vanilla doing crazy things to him. Thomas smiled and told Peyton about a security system he wanted installed in her home.

"I have the best security system around." She patted Jackson on the shoulder and winked. A sharp pain settled in his chest. His presence provided a sense of security. A false sense of security. Abandoning her when she needed him most. Just like he had before.

"Well, I'd feel better if you let me send someone over to have this put in for you," her father said.

Jayden and Zach joined them, and they visited and laughed some more. The once-packed restaurant started to thin out, and Peyton's family said their congratulations and good-byes. Camille pulled her coat on and gave Peyton a hug.

"I'm proud of you, kiddo. You did an amazing job. Get ready to be really busy," her boss teased.

"Thank you, Camille. I appreciate you being here tonight," Peyton said, settling back against his chest. His arms came around her almost on instinct.

Like she belonged there.

When the door closed behind her boss, Nelson shouted from the bar, "Okay, we're down to just the eight of us. Who's ready for some celebratory shots?"

Dani laughed, and she, Cam, and Elle walked toward the bar. "It looks like we'll be Ubering home tonight. Thankfully, we don't have to get up for work tomorrow."

"I'm fixin' to have me some fun," Elle shouted.

"Let's all raise our glasses to Peyton and Jackson. You did an amazing job getting this place open. Here's to many years of success." Roberto toasted, and Jackson held his glass up to meet his friends'.

Ryan and the rest of the staff cleaned up and agreed to return in the morning to finish. Another full but good day. One of the best in a long time. Surrounded by everyone he cared about, celebrating something a long time coming. Inspired by a man who'd practically raised him and left him the resources to go after his dreams. And it all came together because of this woman beside him. Her vision and her faith in him were just what he needed to pull it off. He and Peyton sat at a table beside the bar while the rest of the group played some sort of drinking game and taunted poor Roberto into joining them.

"I'm happy for you. You're going to do big things here, Jackson," she said.

"Couldn't have done it without you, Peanut." He reached into his pocket and pulled out his wallet.

He stared at the napkin Joseph had left for him. With her drawing on it. He'd visualized this moment so many times. Believed in it. Sometimes it seemed like that day was a hundred years ago, other times it seemed like just yesterday.

She ran a finger along the drawing on the napkin. "I still can't believe Joseph saved this."

"Yeah, he was a sentimental bastard deep down," he chuckled.

She leaned over and reached for his wallet, taking a picture from the side pocket behind his credit cards. A puzzled look spread across her gorgeous face when she unfolded it. One of the last photographs taken of them. Gifted to him their last night together before everything went to shit.

"I can't believe you have this. Where'd you find it?"

"I've had it with me since the day you gave it to me."

Studying the picture, she smiled. "I guess Joseph isn't the only sentimental bastard then, is he?"

"Only with you, Pea."

Elle and Dani slammed their glasses on the bar in triumph. The ruckus startled him from his conversation with Peyton.

"Cheaters," Davis shouted. A shit-eating grin spread across his face.

"You're barking up the wrong tree, Davis," Elle shot back with a smile.

"You just lost a beer-drinking game to a bunch of girls. You best sleep it off." Dani patted Davis on the shoulder and laughed. Nelson and Roberto both threw up their hands in defeat.

Cam, Dani, and Elle called it a night, and Peyton walked them to the door to their waiting Uber. Jackson put the bottles away behind the bar. They'd all had more than enough to drink.

Nelson stood. "I need to get some sleep tonight. The goddamn moving company woke us up at seven this morning to drop off boxes."

"The guy pounded on the door like it was some sort of emergency," Davis slurred.

"You better get packing, brother. You're in Miami this time next week," Nelson said. Jackson turned to see Peyton standing beside the bar, taking in the conversation.

Fuck.

Not the way he'd planned to tell her, and no one to blame but himself.

"Moving boxes? Who's moving?" Her face hardened in a matter of seconds. The room grew so quiet you could hear a pin drop. Nelson winced and excused himself to use the restroom. The guy was probably aware he'd just let the cat out of the bag. But this was all on Jackson. Roberto and Davis sat at the bar in silence. Jackson moved toward her, but her hand went up to stop him.

"Who's moving this time next week, Jackson?" Her voice trembled, and she backed away from him each time he stepped in her direction.

"Listen, Pea. I was going to talk to you about it tomorrow."

Her eyes widened. "You were going to talk to me *tomorrow*? What were you going to tell me?"

He stammered, "Peanut, come on. Let's get out of here, and we can talk in private."

"It appears everyone else already knows what's going on. There's no need to talk in private, is there?"

Anger radiated from her, and he knew right then and there, he'd blown it. Fucked up the best thing in his life. For the second time. "I'm moving to Miami to open the next PBV. I'll move to each city we open and get things up and running. It's my role in our partnership."

He might as well have stabbed her in the heart given her expression. "You've known you were leaving the whole time, haven't you?"

Instinct told him touching her would be a bad idea, so he slipped his hands into his pockets. "Yes. I was going to tell you. It just—it was never the right time." His explanation was weak, but it was the truth.

"Never the right time? Not when you kissed me? Or when you told me you loved me? Or when you spent *every night* in my bed? It still didn't seem like the right time?"

Out of the corner of his eye, he saw Roberto and Davis quietly leave the room. Nelson returned from the restroom and followed them into the kitchen. No one wanted to watch this train wreck. He took a step forward. "Pea, I told you I wasn't that guy. Not the forever kind. You said you understood."

She gasped. "How dare you throw this back at me. I thought you meant you were afraid of *allowing yourself* to go there with me. I didn't know you meant you weren't a forever guy because you were leaving. Why didn't you tell me?"

He didn't have a defense. He hadn't told her because she would have pulled away. He was a selfish prick. Did this with his eyes wide open.

"You're a coward. You had no intention of staying, and you let me think we had something." Her voice cracked, and tears sprang from her eyes. His heart ripped from his chest. She was right.

"Pea. *This* is something. It always will be."

"Don't call me that," she shouted. "Not ever again, Jackson. *This—is nothing.* Nothing worth fighting for, right? You can't stay in one place? It's your choice." With a hand on her chest, her glossy gaze locked with his. "What kind of a fool do you think I am? Who's running now? I thought you were all about the *fight*, but you're the one running." She dug around in her purse and pulled out her phone.

"Please don't leave, not like this," he said. Desperation slammed him. He moved fast to grasp her arm and try to keep her there so he could explain. But what more could he say? The truth was out, and she wanted nothing to do with him.

"Don't leave? Really? Could you be more of a hypocrite?" She stormed toward the front door.

"I'll be back every couple of months to check on the restaurant." It was a frantic plea. Panic set in.

She stopped in her tracks. "You'll be back every *couple of months*? This is what you're offering me? You want to stroll into town a couple times a year, spend the night in my bed, and then leave?"

"No, of course not." He ran a frustrated hand

through his hair.

"So then, tell me, Jackson—what is it you're offering?" Tears streamed down her beautiful face. He'd managed to hurt her as badly as he did nine years ago. Maybe even worse because he went in knowing the outcome this time.

"I don't fucking know, Pea. I don't know what the hell I'm doing. I love you. I do. I want to remain friends." The words left his mouth, and he regretted them immediately. Not what he meant to say.

Her cheeks reddened. "Here's a little tip for you, *buddy*. Friends don't lie to one another. I don't have sex with my friends, either. You don't get to do this and then ask me to be your friend."

"I'm sorry, Pea. You deserve better." He reached for her. Wanted to pull her close. Have one more night with her. One more anything with her.

Her hand came up fast, slapping his face hard. "You're damn right I do."

And she was gone.

****

The next few days were the worst Jackson lived in a very long time. Peyton completed her work at the restaurant. He hadn't seen nor heard from her since the night she learned he was leaving. He left voicemails and sent her several texts asking if they could talk. No response. He'd gone by her house the day before he left for Miami, but she didn't answer the door. Hell, it was for the best. He needed to move forward. So did she.

Four miserable days in Miami, and he couldn't get Peyton out of his head. He'd seen sixteen commercial properties and found a problem with every single one of them. Dominic, his realtor, continued searching. They were to meet up again today. It didn't matter. Nothing had been right since leaving San Francisco.

"So there's a new space available, just came on the market last night. It's down near the water in South Beach, and it meets your needs as far as square footage and location," Dominic said, merging onto the freeway.

The guy jumped through hoops to accommodate Jackson. Picked him up at his hotel and carted him around the greater Miami area day after day. His white BMW suited him. Trendy like the man behind the wheel. Dominic looked to be in his early thirties. Impeccably dressed each time they met and very personable. He knew people everywhere they went, and Jackson got the sense the man was an expert in his field. They spent several hours a day together and formed a fast friendship. He liked him.

"I'm looking forward to seeing it."

"It's a prime location. My wife and I love to go to South Beach for a night out on the town."

"Yes, I've heard the night life goes off there. Do you guys have any kids?" Assuming him a family man, although he didn't know how well little kids would fit in his immaculate Beemer. Dominic's posture stiffened.

"Sorry. It's none of my business." Hell, he was just making small talk. He didn't want to make the guy uncomfortable.

"No problem. My wife has stage-four breast cancer. No kids in our future."

He ran a hand over his face, unsure what to say. "Christ, I'm sorry."

"It's okay. It's not new. We've been together for several years and been dealing with it for a long time. But we had a kick-ass wedding six months ago. Best day of my life. She's a strong woman. Puts on a brave face every day when there's not a goddamn thing she can do about it."

Dominic's sorrow filled the space around them. "Shit. There's nothing they can do? Is she going through chemo?"

"No. She did it for a long time, and I sat with her at every appointment. She handled chemo like a boss, but unfortunately it's a wicked disease, and it spread before they could get it under control."

The words were out of his mouth before he could stop them. "You got married *after* you knew there was nothing she could do to fight it?"

"Hell, yeah. A lot of people wonder why we did it. It was a no-brainer for me."

"What do you mean?"

"I love her. If I'm able to call her my wife for a day, a week, or six months, I'm the luckiest man alive. No one knows how long they have, but if you get the chance to be happy for even a short time, wouldn't you take it?"

He admired his honesty and his loyalty. Dominic knew he was going to lose the person he loved and jumped in with both feet anyway—it spoke volumes. A sharp pain hit the center of Jackson's chest. For the first time in his life, he realized just how weak he was. Might put on a good show in the cage, but his strength ended there.

"I'm guessing most people are just afraid. You've got an incredible attitude."

Dominic pulled in front of the location and put the car in park, then clapped a hand over Jackson's shoulder. "It's not incredible. It's love, man. You can run from it, or you can fight for it. It's not perfect, and it's messy, but I wouldn't trade one minute with her."

Entering the space, Jackson continued to process Dominic's words. It reminded him of something Joseph used to say. *Fight or flight.* Some people ran, and some people fought. He'd always been a fighter for everything he wanted. Been proud of it. But since the day Chloe died, he'd lost his fight in some aspects of his life. Not in the cage when he fought his opponents, and not in his professional life. Intimate relationships were a different story. Sex was fine. Love was different. Until he'd found her again.

Peanut.

And he'd run. Hell, he didn't know anymore—was he punishing himself for not protecting Chloe and not thinking he deserved to be happy? Or was it something deeper? Was he afraid of how much he loved Peyton? Afraid of losing her, too?

"You okay, buddy?" Dominic asked.

He nodded. "Yeah, sorry."

"Looked like you were a million miles away."

Not quite. He'd run about three thousand miles away from the woman he loved, all because he was afraid. Afraid of being happy. Afraid of losing her. But he lost her anyway.

"Nope, I'm good. This place is great." He changed the subject quickly. Time to pull his shit together. Focus on what he'd come here for.

The interior wouldn't need nearly as much work as the first PBV Bistro he opened. It was already a restaurant but would just require a bit of a makeover. Distressed white brick covered the walls, dark wood floors ran throughout, and it had a cool vibe. He

301

thought about how much Peyton would like it. Wanted to call her and share it with her. But it didn't work that way. He couldn't have it both ways. Dominic took him on a tour, and for the first time in days, the location checked every box.

"So what do you think?"

He rubbed the back of his neck. "It's pretty perfect."

"But?" Dominic didn't hide his confusion.

"But—nothing. Let me just run the numbers and talk to my partners. It looks like you may have found it."

He made an effort to cover his apprehension. He didn't know what was going on, but something wasn't right. Being here—it wasn't right. He needed time or a sign, something to tell him he'd done the right thing moving to Miami. Dominic dropped him off at his hotel. He wanted to clear his head and blow off some steam. A workout usually did the trick. He took the elevator to the gym on the third floor. A lady and a little boy joined him. The kid looked to be about seven or eight years old, holding on to the leash of a small, tan dog. The pup sat next to Jackson's foot and scratched him with his paw numerous times, leaving him no choice but to bend down and pet the little mutt on the head.

"Sorry, he's very friendly." The lady tried to pull him back.

"It's no problem. Cute pup." He'd grown close to Peyton's dog, ridiculous name and all, and it surprised him how much he missed him, too.

"Yeah, he gets under your skin, and you can't help but love him," the woman stated. He understood those words better than anyone. The elevator dinged, and the doors opened.

"Come on, Peanut," the boy called, leading him away.

Are you fucking kidding me?

Of course, the dog was named Peanut. He couldn't escape her. She was everywhere.

Everything.

****

After tossing and turning until well past midnight, he finally gave in to the exhaustion of the last few days since leaving San Francisco. Sleep came.

"Why can't I go with you, Jackson?" Chloe called out again and again.

Jackson hurried down the driveway, feeling the gravel move beneath his feet. The trailer grew closer, and he heard his sister call out to him. Distress in her voice. Panic set in and his legs lost feeling when he dropped to the ground and crawled toward the trailer.

"Jackson." Someone shouted his name, but it wasn't his sister's voice, wasn't coming from the trailer but the opposite direction. He ignored it and continued to move toward Chloe.

His heart raced. Bile rose in his throat when he looked down to see the ground beneath him covered in blood. He lifted his hand to move across the liquid, and someone reached for his arm and stopped him.

"Don't go there, Jackson." Peyton's voice was desperate.

Peanut. His girl, dressed in a white dress, looking like a vision.

"I have to go help her," he insisted, pulling away.

"You can't help her anymore. It's time for you to

303

help yourself," she pleaded, bending down to offer her hand again.

"How, Pea?" A lump formed in his throat. Her gorgeous brown gaze held so much hope.

"Fight, Jackson."

"For what?" he asked when she pushed to stand, and his hand slipped from hers.

"For us."

His world spun, and he grabbed hold of the ground to keep still. Gravel flew underneath his hands.

Peyton vanished. Red no longer covered the ground. The trailer disappeared. The graveled driveway was all that sat beneath him. The voices calling his name quieted. Just him. His panic was no longer about finding his way to the trailer—but finding his way back to the girl who'd tried to save him. The one he'd left behind.

His girl.

He pushed to a sit position. Sweat covered his body and face. He gasped for air, threw the sheet off to the side, and reached for the water bottle on the nightstand. It might have been the same fucking nightmare haunting him for the last decade—but for the first time, there was a different ending. Maybe this was the sign he needed. Maybe it was time to change the ending he'd written for himself.

Chapter Twenty

The M Hotel project completed and checked off on her calendar. One month since she finished PBV. One month since she saw Jackson. A dull ache permanently settled in her chest. He'd contacted her before he left for Miami, but she didn't respond. Soon his efforts ceased. It wasn't like he wanted to reconcile, just wanted to preserve a friendship. She didn't need any more friends. And she didn't want Jackson Vance as just a friend.

She continued her workout with Nico three days a week. No one asked her about Jackson at the gym anymore after her inconsolable tears at the mention of his name. Thanksgiving came and went. Her family tried their best to be supportive but didn't hide their disappointment at the way things had ended with Jackson. Her father told her Jackson had stopped by before leaving San Francisco. He'd expressed concern about Kenny Wolf and hoped her dad would keep tabs on him until he was prosecuted. Jayden made a big deal of Jackson going out of his way to speak to their father. Peyton was unimpressed. He'd passed the buck on his way out of town, once again leaving her to pick up the pieces.

After a whole lot of soul searching these past few weeks, she reached a few conclusions. Abandonment came in many forms. Her mother leaving when she was young had less to do with Peyton and more to do with her mom. She wasn't happy with her life. Nothing Peyton did would have changed the outcome. So many years spent trying to force something that really never existed.

She and Jackson were different. From the first day they met as kids—they'd fit. When they were older, he'd become the other half of her soul. It'd just always felt right. When he came back after all those years of separation, it had still been there. Stronger than ever. Like a blazing fire forever burning in her soul. Like it or not, he was her person. And she was his. Not being with him for reasons out of her control proved difficult to accept. She didn't fault him for leaving anymore. He loved her the same way she loved him, but wouldn't allow himself to be happy. He wasn't out there chasing a better life. Jackson hadn't abandoned her the way her mother had—but her heart ached because they weren't together. A soul-deep, gut-wrenching sadness settled inside her and took up permanent residence.

Camille shared her new project to start in two days. The large lobby of a swanky building in the city. She welcomed the distraction. Anything to keep her from thinking about him. A brief knock on her office door startled her from her thoughts. Elle rushed in, eyes wide as saucers.

"The *mayor* is in the waiting room. He wants to see you," she whisper-shouted, hands flailing around in frantic motions.

"Sebastian is here?"

Elle put one hand on her hip and tilted her head. "Yes, ma'am. He looks as nervous as a long-tailed cat in a room full of rocking chairs. Serves him right. Shall

I send him packing?"

"No. Don't be ridiculous. Send him back."

"Okay but remember—I can go from southern belle to ghetto thug faster than you can say *bless your heart*."

Dani and Elle had kept her from sinking into a puddle of heartbreak these last few weeks. Bringing enough Ben and Jerry's chocolate chip cookie dough ice cream to feed a small village, and finally agreeing to watch a marathon of *Outlander* with her. It had managed to leave her even more depressed, a reminder of a love lost. They'd forced her to go to dinner with them often and spent the night at her house on the days when the reality of him being gone hit her even harder than normal. They'd both been a lifeline to her this past month.

"Trust me, I know about your questionable ways," Peyton teased.

"Fine. The door stays open."

Why in the world would Sebastian even be here? She hadn't heard anything from him since he sent flowers after the attack. Elle brought him in, made a point to prop the door open, and glared at him for good measure.

"I'll be in my office if you need me," Elle said before leaving.

He turned to face Peyton. "She's terrifying."

Peyton forced a small smile. "What are you doing here?"

"Okay, here we go. May I sit?"

She motioned to the chair across from her desk.

"I wanted you to know Kenny Wolf has been charged with assault by three other women who came forward because of what happened to you. He's going to serve some time behind bars, and I wanted you to hear it from me."

Surprise flooded her at the news. "Oh, wow. I wouldn't wish this on anyone else, but I'm glad he's being held accountable."

"I'm sure your father and your *guard dog*, Jackson, told you I bailed him out. I did. I couldn't come to you until this was all over because I was working with the police. I got Wolf out on bail to gain his trust so I could gather information to make sure he paid for what he did to you." Sebastian slumped in his seat.

"Did you know he was coming to see me that night? What he planned to do to me?"

"No. God no, Peyton. He said he was going to try to convince you to attend my gathering on election night. I never in a million years thought Wolf capable of putting his hands on you. But another woman confided in me after he attacked you. He also got physical with her. I started questioning other people. The security guards told me Wolf cornered you by the elevators a few days before being arrested. Peyton, you should have come to me. I knew Wolf wasn't a Boy Scout, but I never thought he'd be aggressive toward a woman. The police questioned me about your attack, and I shared what I'd learned. Two other women came forward. There were surveillance cameras in the building lobby, which the police viewed. The incident of Wolf cornering you by the elevators, as well as him harassing another woman near the restrooms, were captured on film. They asked me to bail him out and play along, pretend to be on his side, which I did. The bastard was proud of what he did to you, and he had no problem saying so while being recorded."

She didn't have any idea what to say. "Well, I'm glad he won't be able to do this to anyone else. Thank you for your part in it."

"I get it. You hate me. I made a lot of mistakes, and I got a little lost along the way. But I am trying to do the right thing, and I am sorry about what happened." Guilt was evident in his gaze.

"I appreciate your honesty. There is something I'd like to ask you."

"Anything."

"Wolf made a comment about how you'd both *chosen me*. What was he talking about?"

He shook his head. "Christ, Peyton. I made so many mistakes. The way we met, it was more planned than I'd shared. When I decided to run for office, Wolf thought having a girlfriend would help my image. I went along with it. He made several suggestions, and your name came up. I was open to it, but I swear to you, after the first week we met, my feelings for you were genuine. It may have started out phony, but it changed for me. I wasn't the perfect boyfriend, Peyton, but I did love you. The feelings were real."

It didn't matter if Sebastian were telling the truth. Choosing to date her to help his image made sense in a way, because their relationship was superficial at best. These revelations didn't even hurt. Her heart was in a shambles, and it had nothing to do with Sebastian Worthington.

"Thank you for being honest, and thank you for helping to put Wolf away."

"I hope someday you'll be able to forgive me."

"I do forgive you, Sebastian. And congratulations

on becoming mayor. I'm happy for you."

His lips turned up in the corners. Probably the first sincere smile from him. "Maybe someday you'll give me a second chance?"

Tempted to tell him there wasn't a shot in hell, instead she smiled and said her good-byes. The truth—she hadn't been honest with him, either. Her heart had belonged to someone else the entire time they were together. Always had. Always would.

****

The lobby project downtown proved more challenging than expected. Exactly what she needed. Late nights spent on Pinterest pinning ideas for her holiday dinner kept her mind busy. The tree was up. Mr. Whiskers danced around her feet the entire time she strung lights and hung ornaments. Christmas music blasted through the house, an effort to keep her from giving in to the sadness growing with each passing day. Baking eight different types of holiday cookies, she took on the most challenging recipes and tried everything possible to get lost in the excitement of the holidays. Every night spent sobbing until she grew tired enough to give in to sleep. How long would this last? It only worsened with each passing day. Wasn't it supposed to get easier?

Christmas Eve morning she woke to the sound of rain pelting her windows. Mr. Whiskers curled close to her, with no intention of trekking out into a rainstorm.

"Merry Christmas Eve." She kissed the top of his head.

Climbing out of bed, she wore her favorite Santa pajamas and carried her pup downstairs. She turned on the fireplace and stared out the window before making the coffee. Flames reflected off the walls while she watched a holiday movie and sipped her coffee, with Mr. Whiskers curled up beside her on the couch. Memories of her pup preferring Jackson's lap to hers those last few weeks they'd spent together returned. How many times had they been on this couch snuggled up together? Closing her eyes, she attempted to push the memories away, and sorrow took up residence inside her. She missed Jackson. There was no way around it. No avoiding it.

Elle or Dani would be there in a minute if she reached out, but what more was left to say? How much could you talk about something with no solution? Giving herself until noon to wallow, she resolved to get up, start cooking, and set up for the party. And that's exactly what she did.

Well, sort of.

She cried herself to sleep and didn't wake up until closer to one o'clock, made a sandwich, and fed her pup before putting on her apron. Holiday music rang through the house, cinnamon and pine candles burned, and within a few hours, everything in the kitchen was prepped. Adding the extenders to her dining room table, she set out her formal dishes. With tons of decorations for each place setting, she played around to see what looked best.

The red and white square plates, white linen napkins with jingle bell napkin rings, and the cute name tags scrapbooked in coordinating colors tied the theme together like something from a magazine. She placed the gorgeous red water goblets and matching wineglasses on the table before adding the silverware, finishing off each setting. She loved the little touches.

Her living room mimicked its own winter wonderland, with a snowman-themed Christmas tree and cute decorations.

She walked over to the tree and pulled out the gifts for her father, Lael, Jayden, Zach, Elle, Dani, Cam, and an entire pile of presents for little Harrison. Teasing Mr. Whiskers with his stocking full of treats, she gave him one of the bones early. There were a few wrapped packages behind the tree for Camille, Nico, and Mick.

One present in particular nagged at her. The one wrapped for Jackson, chosen while they'd still been together. The frame held the picture her father had taken of her and Jackson the very first day they met so many years ago, sitting on a log. The start of an amazing friendship. He'd told her he loved her first. But—she loved him last, and it hurt a hell of a lot more loving someone who couldn't love you back. She empathized with his guilt over what had happened to Chloe, but still didn't understand why he couldn't forgive himself. It wasn't his fault. Not in any way, shape, or form. If only he saw himself through her eyes. Strong and brave. Loyal and protective. He fought like a warrior in the cage, but on the inside, Jackson was a teddy bear. Had she told him often enough how amazing he was? Had it been wrong to refuse his calls before he left for Miami? He'd hurt her, lied to her. She also hadn't expected him to give up so quickly.

She lifted the package. Inside lay a beautiful frame with three large cutouts. Their childhood photo in the first space. The middle held the last picture they'd taken together before he left nine years ago. Turns out they'd both held on to that photograph. It was one of her favorites. In the final opening, a picture Dani had taken of her and Jackson at the PBV opening. They were near the kitchen, and he stood behind her with his arms wrapped around her middle, looking down at her while she laughed at something. The way he looked at her—it would drop her to her knees if it weren't covered with gift wrap right now. His gaze so full of adoration and love. She placed it back under the tree, and a lump formed in her throat.

After a quick bath, she slipped into a black velvet jumpsuit, pulled her hair into a low chignon at the nape of her neck. She fiddled through her jewelry, settled on some pretty, dangly earrings, and took a quick check of her makeup before heading downstairs. Mr. Whiskers strutted around in his Santa hat, carrying his red and white bone in his mouth.

One by one, everyone arrived, shaking out umbrellas and admiring the décor. She poured wine and cocktails and handed Harrison his special mug of warm cocoa. The house smelled like Christmas. The laughter and conversation flowed. She sneaked off to the kitchen to check on the beef tenderloin. Her father walked in after her.

"Do you need a refill, Dad?"

"Nope, sweetie. I'm good. Just wanted to see how you were doing." He leaned against the kitchen counter.

"I'm fine. Excited everyone's here." As excited as she could be with her heart ripped from her body and fighting the urge to curl up in a ball and cry. Every moment of the day.

"Okay, I'm here for you if you need me."

"I know." She blinked several times to stop the flood of tears threatening to unleash. Thankfully, the world's cutest human rushed in.

"Auntie P, can I have more chocwate?" The adorable munchkin with big blue eyes identical to her sister's looked up at her. Her dad chuckled, and she scooped him up in her arms. Little Harrison might just be the temporary cure to a broken heart.

She nuzzled his neck. "You smell like candy canes, Harrison."

His head fell back in laughter. The most adorable sound trickled around the room. "I'm not a candy cane, Auntie P. I'm a wittle boy."

"Are you sure you're not a candy cane?"

"I'm a wittle boy." He giggled again. His two chubby little hands rested on her cheeks.

"Okay, well, little boys can't have too much chocolate, or they'll get a tummy ache."

He tilted his head. A mischievous smile spread across his face. "What if I am a candy cane? Then I can have more chocwate?"

Her watery gaze was full of adoration for the amazing little person in her arms. "I love you, my little candy cane."

"I wuv you more, Auntie P."

Her dad shook his head with a chuckle when the doorbell rang. "Are you expecting more guests?"

"No. Probably a package. You know me and my online shopping addiction," she joked.

Harrison clapped while she carried him in her arms toward the door. "Maybe it's Santa Cwaus."

She froze seeing who stood on the other side of the door.

"It's yo fwend, Auntie P."

She set Harrison down, and the room went silent. Her hand trembled. She turned the knob. Her heart raced with anticipation and fear mixed together. His hair was damp, from standing in the rain with no umbrella. His gaze locked on hers with an intensity that nearly took the air from her lungs.

"Jackson, what are you doing here?"

"I wanted to bring you your Christmas present. I didn't have time to ship it." He stepped inside and waved to her family.

"You didn't have time to ship me a gift, so you flew here from Miami to give it to me?"

"I did, Peanut." He dangled the small black gift bag in front of her.

Her stomach dipped with excitement, but she raised her chin and crossed her arms. "I told you not to call me that anymore."

"Well, you've told me to stop calling you *Peanut* for the last eighteen some years. I'd think you'd figure out that I'm not going to listen to you by now."

"You don't listen to me about anything," she hissed. Emotions stirred inside her, joy, pain, terror he'd be gone tomorrow and the hurt would start all over again. She wasn't sure what to feel. Happy or mad. Overjoyed or furious. She looked around the room. No one said a word. No one appeared surprised by his appearance either, which left her puzzled.

"I do listen to you from time to time." He jiggled the bag in his hand again.

"Why don't we go into the kitchen, where we can talk in private?" Everyone sat in silence, gazes ping-ponging back and forth between her and Jackson.

"I don't want to go in the kitchen."

"Excuse me? Are you drunk?" she spewed. The man was acting crazy.

"Not drunk, Pea." He laughed and shook his head.

"Well, it's Christmas Eve, and I'd rather not get my heart stomped on in front of my family, if you don't mind."

She stormed toward the kitchen, and he chuckled from behind her. Was he serious? He wanted to hash this out in front of everyone? When she turned around, a grin spread across his handsome face.

"Come here, Pea."

"Don't tell me what to do." She held her ground.

His stare locked on hers. "I love you, Peanut. Always have. Always will."

"You've told me this before. And you left anyway. Twice."

"I'm not leaving."

She licked her lips, unsure what was going on. "Of course, you're leaving. You live in Miami if memory serves."

"Not anymore. I live here. I'm actually homeless at the moment. Hoped I could stay here with you if you'll still have me?"

"Live here? What are you talking about?" she whispered.

Before she could process her thoughts, he dropped down on one knee.

"You are my first love. My only love. My forever love. It's always been you. Life tore us apart once, but this time—this time, I was an idiot. I was afraid, Pea. Afraid of being happy, afraid of allowing myself to live again. I found the perfect location in Miami. Right on the ocean. Had the pen in my hand ready to sign, but all I could think of was you. You were everywhere. Everything reminded me of you. Because you're a part of me. Nothing else matters," he finished, and she stared down at him with complete and utter disbelief.

Tears streamed down her face, but she couldn't speak. He reached for her hand and held it in his.

"No more running, Pea. You belong with me. I've waited a lifetime for you. I'm done waiting. Marry me." Pulling out a small black velvet box from the bag, he opened it to reveal a gorgeous, sparkling princess-cut diamond. It took her breath away. Gasps and cheers came from behind her. Harrison walked up next to her. She was still unable to speak.

"Auntie P, yo fwend wanna mawee you?"

She swiped at her cheeks to stop the stream of tears running down her face. "I think so, sweetie."

"What you gonna do?"

"What do you think I should do?" she asked, and everyone laughed, including Jackson.

"You like him, Auntie P?"

"I like him a lot," she chuckled.

"I fink you should say yes."

"I do, too."

"Not to break up this adorable conversation, but I'm kind of dying here," Jackson said with one raised brow.

"You knew the answer before you asked. The happiest times I've ever known begin and end with you, Jackson. Yes—it's always been yes," she said, and he pulled her to him. His mouth crashed down over hers.

Right there, in the middle of her winter wonderland of a living room, the man she loved said he loved her, too. It wouldn't have mattered if they were standing in the middle of the street, as long as Jackson was standing beside her. He pushed them both to their feet, and Harrison jumped up and down, clapping his chubby little hands. Her dad wrapped his arms around her first, before he pulled Jackson in for a hug.

"It hasn't been easy keeping this quiet," her dad admitted.

"You knew?" she shrieked.

"Everyone knew." Jackson smiled and stared down at the beautiful ring on her finger.

"I didna know," Harrison's little voice shouted, and Jackson scooped him up.

"Sorry, buddy. I should have told you."

"You gonna marry my Auntie P?"

"I sure am."

****

After dinner they opened gifts. Jackson loved the framed photos. He lingered over them one by one and told everyone what had happened just before each was taken. After dessert her friends and family said their good-byes. Finally. She loved them but wanted to know how he made his way back to her. They sat on the couch in front of the roaring fire, Mr. Whiskers curled up on Jackson's lap, when he reached over to grab a bag under the coffee table.

"I have a little something for ol' Whiskey here." He handed her the package to open.

Unwrapping the gift, she asked, "So what you change your mind?"

"Everything. From the minute you walked out of PBV, I was more than aware I'd fucked up. I made the biggest mistake of my life a decade ago, too lost in grief to grasp it at the time. But when I got to Miami, everything reminded me of you. I even met a dog named Peanut." He chuckled and squeezed her hand. "I had another nightmare, but this time you were in it."

She fell back against the couch in laughter. "You met a dog named Peanut and had a nightmare about me, and that's why you came back?"

"You were there to pull me out of the darkness. It's what you do, Pea. The next morning, I'm sitting in my hotel room, and it hit me like a bolt of lightning. I wasn't sleeping more than three or four hours a night, my head throbbed—I realized it was because I missed you so fucking much. I called Roberto, Nelson, and Davis and asked what to do."

She studied his face. He seemed lighter, more at ease. "What did they say?"

"Hell, they were happy. They love you and thought I was making the biggest mistake of my life. We agreed to expand someday down the road if we want, and we can hire someone else to run the new locations. As long as we're together, we'll figure it out. This first location is packed every day, and I want to be involved in the momentum we have here. And focus on my girl, if you'll let me. I'm sorry, Pea. It took me a hell of a lot longer than it should have to find my way back to you, but I swear to you—I'm never leaving again."

"Of course, *I'll let you.* I'm so glad you came back. It's been a rough couple weeks."

"Yeah, your dad kept me posted on how you were doing."

"I can't believe he knew," she said when he pushed Mr. Whiskers' gift toward her again, and she reached inside the bag.

A loud laugh escaped her. She held up the blue dog tag, which read *WHISKEY...one badass mutt.*

"You're ridiculous." She intertwined her fingers

319

with his.

"I got you something, too, Pea."

So full of surprises tonight.

"An engagement ring wasn't enough?" she teased.

"Well, I would have proposed to you any day of the week. It just happened to fall on Christmas Eve. And marrying you is more of a gift for me. This is your actual Christmas gift."

He handed her another package. She lifted the top off a white square box and took out a beautiful sparkly gold frame. Inside was the napkin with the drawing of the restaurant on it. It was a symbol of what led him back to her. Holding it against her chest, she smiled. "I love it."

"I think there's something else buried in the tissue paper."

Digging around, she pulled out a little velvet pouch. "What do we have here?"

She tipped the small bag over, and a key landed on her lap. She held it up and studied it with confusion.

"What does this open?"

"Langford's. I bought it for us."

Her mouth fell open. "What? You want to open a restaurant in Lake Tahoe?"

"Nope. I want to build a cabin of our own. Start new traditions in the place where we met. I want our kids to spend their summers there. It's the second-best lot on the lake," he teased. Her eyes welled with tears, making it difficult to see.

"Our own place in Tahoe. I love it," she said, overcome with emotion.

"I want our kids to know about Chloe and Joseph. A piece of them will forever live on there."

"Okay, you've mentioned these kids of ours a couple times now. How many are you thinking, because right now, Mr. Whiskers is plenty," she chuckled.

He pulled her onto his lap. "I want as many little Peanuts as we can have. With your big brown eyes and gorgeous hair." He nuzzled her neck.

"Let's get you down the aisle first, Vance."

"I'm ready. For all of it. I've been running for so long, Pea. I found a letter from Joseph right before we went to Tahoe. I didn't understand it at the time, but he said I was living in a prison of my own, punishing myself for something I couldn't control. He said his wish for me was that someone would help me find my way back to the life I deserved to live. I think in a way, Joseph was leading me back to you this whole time. First with the napkin, and then through his words. You're the person who makes me want more out of life. Only you."

She was ready, too. Had been since the day he'd walked back into her life. "I want those things with you, too."

He tipped her back on the couch and nipped at her ear. "That's all I need to hear. I don't know what I ever did to deserve you, Peanut. But I plan to spend the rest of my life finding out."

She placed a hand on his face, looked into his green eyes. Flecks of amber sparkled in the firelight. "It's always been you."

There had never been a truer statement. His mouth crashed into hers, and his soft lips took control. Her hands tangled in his hair, pulling him closer. She'd never get enough of this man. The other half of her soul, and she was never letting go.

Laura Pavlov

Epilogue

He arrived home just in time to pick up Peyton. "Pea, you upstairs?"

"Yep. Almost ready," she called from their bedroom.

He'd moved in with her over eight months ago on Christmas Eve. These last few months a whirlwind. They'd been married for three months, and he'd never been happier. He wanted to get a new home together with a bit more space, but he agreed to live in her house for the next year. She'd spent two years renovating the place and wasn't ready to leave. He didn't care, just wanted her to be happy.

They'd been working with an architect to design their home in Lake Tahoe. Build a new home on the property but salvage Langford's and make it a guest house. *Hold on to what's good from the past—and embrace the fresh start in front of you.*

He hurried up the stairs as she came out of the master bath. Her cutoff jean shorts showed off her tan, sexy legs. Gorgeous dark waves trailed down her back, over a loose-fitting white linen top.

"*Mrs. Vance*, didn't I warn you about wearing these sexy jean shorts again?" He pulled her into his arms.

It didn't take much these days to drive him mad with desire. There was a lot of lost time to make up for.

"We're going to be late," she said with a giggle, and he propped himself above her. Her breathing came fast, and he nuzzled her neck. Orange blossoms and vanilla flooded his senses. He'd never get enough of her. Always wanted more. She lay there on the white bedding, her concession when he moved in. She insisted on removing the frilly, lacey crap and claimed white the neutral color for the sexes. A crystal chandelier surrounded by a dark wood orbit hung above their bed. He didn't have the heart to tell her it wasn't remotely masculine. Hell, he didn't give a shit. He'd let her paint the walls pink if it made her happy. She wanted this to be *their* home, and decorating was her thing. What she didn't know, none of it mattered to him. He only needed her.

"They can wait. I missed you." His mouth covered hers hungrily.

He raised his head when their four-legged bastard barked in a high enough pitch to shatter a window and yelped for his attention at the foot of the bed. "Damn you, Whiskey. What have I told you about interrupting time with my girl?"

Peyton laughed, and he pulled her to her feet.

"We need to get going, anyway." She adjusted her top and ran her fingers through her hair.

"Are you excited?"

"Yes. How about you?"

"I'm ready." He winked, leading her out of the room.

Walking down the stairs, he smiled at their wedding pictures hanging on the wall. He paused to take in his favorite photo—their wedding party surrounded them. Everyone laughed in an un-posed picture. They'd said their vows in front of their friends and family at her dad's home in Lake Tahoe on the very beach that held a lifetime of memories. Peyton looked stunning in an elegant spaghetti-strap satin gown. A floral crown rested above her loose waves trailing down her back. Jayden, Dani, and Elle stood beside her as bridesmaids. His traditional black tuxedo mimicked by his groomsmen, Davis, Nelson, and Maverick, his best friend from high school. Roberto officiated the ceremony, and little Harrison carried the rings down the aisle. Peyton described their reception as *romantic and intimate*—but he'd call it a kick-ass party. It managed to be everything they wanted.

"Can you grab those bags?" The woman took every possible occasion and turned it into a party. Favors and decorations were par for the course.

"Do I even want to know what this is?" he teased, loading the bags in the car.

"Just a little something."

Ryan greeted them when they arrived at PBV Bistro. "Everyone is in the back room. They're taking drink orders now, and we'll bring out some appetizers in a little bit."

"Thanks. I appreciate it," Jackson said, clapping the man on the shoulder.

Nelson and Davis were in town for final meetings to go over the details of the next PBV, which would open in Miami. Roberto attended remotely from New York. They'd made some changes to their business plan. Davis and Nelson would both move to Miami and oversee the opening of the new location. An exciting time for the four men with large visions for PBV's future.

Elle and Dani hurried over to greet their girlfriend when they walked in. Cam was deep in conversation with Nelson and Davis. Jayden and Zach were visiting with Maverick, who was recently drafted as San Francisco's new quarterback. Already quite the local celebrity, preparing for his first season on the team. The last three years being the backup quarterback in Tennessee hadn't granted much playing time. Jackson was thrilled to have his buddy living nearby and playing for their home team.

Elle hated Maverick with a passion. They'd hit it off when they met at his and Peyton's wedding three months ago, but that had since gone to hell. Jackson had warned Maverick not to mess around with Elle as she was his wife's best friend. But Maverick had talked her into a date, which Elle later called a *complete waste of her time*. Maverick had since become enemy number one, and Elle couldn't stand the sight of him, something about leopards not changing their spots. Hopefully the whole mess was long forgotten. They took their seats. Peyton passed out the gifts and placed a rolled-up T-shirt, tied with a frilly white bow, on each place setting.

"Oooh, gifts for us? I thought this was just a wedding reunion dinner?" Elle clapped her hands together.

"Just a little something we wanted to do, but you have to open them together," Peyton insisted. Jackson came up behind her, wrapped his arms around her waist, and rested his chin on her shoulder.

"I told you this one was a keeper years ago, Vance," Maverick teased, pointing to the gifts.

A loud, dramatic moan of sheer disgust came from Elle. Her theatrical eyeroll caused Peyton to put a hand over her mouth to keep from laughing.

"Ah, you're finally acknowledging my presence, huh, Peaches?" Maverick said. A wide grin spread across his face.

Did he call her Peaches? What the hell? Jackson wouldn't bring any more attention to it by asking. Obviously, things hadn't blown over yet.

"You know, *Maverick*, I actually have a name, which I'm sure is difficult for your tiny brain to comprehend. Just because I'm from Georgia doesn't mean you get to call me Peaches. What happens when you meet multiple people from the same state? Do you call them all the same thing?" she hissed.

"I reserve Peaches just for you," Maverick said with a wink. Everyone, except for Elle, chuckled at the charming bastard. He leaned back in his chair like he didn't have a care in the world.

"Go sell some crazy somewhere else, Maverick. We're all stocked up here," Elle snarled, and everyone tried to hold back their laughter, but it proved impossible. Maverick laughed the loudest, which only made her face redden with anger.

"What the hell is going on with them?" Jackson whispered in his wife's ear.

Peyton shrugged before chuckling, "She thinks he's the devil."

"Ah, good to know."

His wife kissed his cheek before she spoke. "Okay, let's open our gifts first, and then we can eat."

Elle insisted on counting down from ten, and when she got to one, they all began untying the ribbon. One by one, he watched them scan the writing on the front of the T-shirts, which read: GUESS WHO'S KNOCKED UP?

The backs of each shirt were customized with AUNTIE or UNCLE and each of their names.

"Is this what I think it is?" Jayden's voice cracked.

"Hush your mouth, is this for real?" Elle screamed, jumped to her feet, and threw herself into both Jackson and Peyton's arms. One by one, each congratulated them and fired off endless questions.

"I'm so happy for you guys. When are you due?" Dani beamed.

"She's three months along." Yep, his girl was pregnant, and everyone toasted to the new little peanut due to arrive on Valentine's day. They were starting a family. The craziest part—he couldn't wait. He'd urged her to get off birth control. Now that he'd found his way back to her, he wanted everything. He hadn't had a nightmare in almost six months. Peyton had read everything she could find about nightmares and was prepared if he had one. He loved the way she embraced every part of him. The good, the bad, and the ugly. There were no secrets between them.

"You wasted no time, my friend," Maverick laughed before Elle chucked a dinner roll across the table at him. He caught it, ate it, and winked at her. Elle feigned disgust.

"I guess it's a good thing we're moving to Miami. Looks like you're going to be pretty busy here, huh?" Davis smirked.

"I've got six months to help you get this next one up and running. I promised Pea I won't travel for the first few months after the baby is born."

"How is he handling you being pregnant? Is he treating you like a porcelain doll?" Dani asked with a laugh.

Laura Pavlov

They'd be correct. He worried about her. Wanted to make things easier for her. "I think she works too much. She's carrying a human in there. She should rest for the next six months." He patted her still-flat belly.

Jayden choked on her water and covered her mouth with her napkin before she spoke through her laughter. "You do realize women have been carrying *humans* for a long time, right? Good luck making Peyton rest for six months. Not happening."

"That's what I told him," Peyton insisted.

Jackson had suggested she take a leave from work, but getting her to agree proved impossible. They also disagreed about how much a woman should eat when carrying said human. Why not double up on her portions? She insisted *eating for two* was more of a metaphor than a reality, and told him the baby was currently the size of a small carrot, not a full-grown adult. Hey, he'd never claimed to be an expert, but he would damn well make sure she didn't overdo it.

He spent the next hour talking with the guys and wanted to hear about Maverick's time so far on the team. Everyone was curious how he was adjusting. Well, everyone but Elle, who scrolled through her phone when he spoke, making her disinterest known.

The food at PBV never disappointed, but he wanted to get his girl home. The warm breeze surrounded them when they walked to the car. Intertwining his fingers with hers, he pulled the car away from the curb.

"Did you have fun?" she asked.

"It was great."

"You look like you're deep in thought."

"Just thinking how lucky I am." He stopped at a

red light a few blocks from home and looked over at his girl.

"I'm the lucky one."

"I'm so happy our kids get to have you for their mom. You're going to be the best mom, Pea."

Her gaze grew glossy. A wide grin spread across her face. "Well, I have to keep up with you. The world's best dad."

"You think so?"

She squeezed his hand. "I know so."

He chuckled and pulled in front of their house, putting the car in park. He looked over at his beautiful wife and realized right then and there, he wasn't afraid anymore. Fight or flight. He didn't want to run, and he didn't need to fight. He'd found his way back, and for the first time in a long time, it's where he belonged. With her. She repaired all the damaged pieces and put him back together. She deserved the fairy tale, and he would do everything in his power to give it to her. Walking toward the door, he paused to look at the front yard.

"What's wrong?" she asked. Whiskey barked from the other side of the door. Hell, they were the real deal, since the day they'd met. There was only one thing left to do.

"How do you feel about a white picket fence around the yard?"

She shook her head and smiled. "You know it's harder to run away if there's a fence keeping you in."

"The only way I'm running is if I'm chasing after you, Pea."

She looked over her shoulder and pulled her lip between her teeth. "Is that so?"

"It sure is," he teased.

"No time like the present," she said and took off running up the steps to their home.

And he chased her. Just like he planned to do for the rest of his life.

A word about the author…

Laura Pavlov writes sweet and sexy contemporary romance that will make you both laugh and cry. She is happily married to her college sweetheart, mom to two awesome almost-grown kids, and dog-whisperer to a couple crazy Yorkies. Laura resides in Las Vegas, where she is living her own happily ever after.

Visit her at:

laurapavlov.com
Instagram ~ @laurapavlovauthor
facebook ~ LauraPavlovAuthor
Pinterest ~ laura pavlov
Twitter ~ laura pavlov author
Goodreads ~ Laura Pavlov

Thank you for purchasing
this publication of The Wild Rose Press, Inc.

For questions or more information
contact us at
info@thewildrosepress.com.

The Wild Rose Press, Inc.
www.thewildrosepress.com

To visit with authors of
The Wild Rose Press, Inc.
join our yahoo loop at
http://groups.yahoo.com/group/thewildrosepress/